THE GATHERERS

Mike Wall

the Peppertree Press

Sarasota, Florida

ISBN: 0-9778525-8-x
Printed in the U.S.A.
Printed July, 2006

DEDICATION

Dedicated to my wife, Chanda Wall.
She is my love, my life, my ever lifting light.

THE AWAKENING

"We can easily forgive a child who is afraid of the dark; the real tragedy of life is when men are afraid of the light."
~Plato~

John was awakened by the sound of laughter coming from the pool area. It seemed so high-pitched as it came through the half-open sliding glass door of his bedroom. The light was brightly shining through the thin white curtains, which were gently swaying in the warm summer breeze. He remembered for a second that he had argued with his wife, Emily, in the department store that the curtains should be darker and thicker so the morning sun wouldn't wake them. It was logical reasoning, he thought, but just as she always did, Emily got her way. He rolled over and looked at the clock. Well, at least he got to sleep in until ten today. On most weekend mornings when his son Nathan had sleepovers, he was awakened much earlier than this.

It seems that eleven-year-old boys have a built-in alarm clock that gets them up before eight on every weekend morning. John wondered for a second why that alarm clock never worked on weekdays when it wasn't summer vacation. It was so hard to get Nathan up for school, but when it came to days off, he never missed a minute.

John was thankful for the extra whiskey and coke he had had the night before. It was probably what allowed him to get such a peaceful night of sleep. It also seemed to be the cause of the pounding in his head.

He rolled over and got up out of his bed. As he walked over to the glass door and slid it shut, he caught a glimpse of

1

Nathan doing a cannonball into the pool. He turned back around and walked to his bathroom. His throbbing head needed some medicine. As he fumbled through the medicine cabinet for aspirin with one hand, he reached for the faucet and turned on the cold water with his other. John splashed some water on his face and took two pills. Hopefully this would get rid of the pounding in his head.

After drying his face with a hand towel, John hung it back on the chrome towel holder. He remembered how he had wanted wooden towel holders, but, once again, Emily had gotten her way. Why did she even ask his opinion on things around the house? She always got her way with everything when it came to their home.

John hadn't even wanted to get this house. He had wanted to buy one on a lake or a river. The only reason he agreed was because of something his father once told him. His dad had said, "Always let your wife do whatever she wants when it comes to your home, or else you'll hear about it for the rest of your life." He tried to live by this rule, and it seemed to work out just fine. He was happy, and Emily was happy, so what more could he wish for? As for Nathan, he was an eleven-year-old boy, and happiness always seemed to effortlessly exist in his life.

The carpet in the hallway felt extra soft today as he walked towards the wooden banister staircase that went down to their living room. He slid his hand down the smooth railing as he walked following the smell of coffee that was drifting up, pulling him towards the kitchen. John passed through the living room and then entered the kitchen. He stopped in the doorway for a second and watched Emily. She faced away from him working diligently at cutting something on the counter in preparation for breakfast.

Even after seventeen years of marriage, he was taken at how beautiful she was with her blonde, straight hair hanging just below her shoulders. She was proud of her hair and how she was still a natural blonde. She had told him several times how she had never had to have it lightened like so many of her friends. He didn't get this; it must have just been a girl thing.

Today she was wearing a white blouse with some little designs on it, but John couldn't make out what they were from where

2

he was. It hung slightly over the top of her white capris pants which snuggly covered her tight, perfectly rounded bottom. Emily had a great body due to her daily running routine. He could see the lines of her white silky panties through the thin material of her pants.

"Good morning, sweet pea," he said with a slight southern drawl added for effect.

"Oh, hi, honey. I see the boys finally woke you up," she responded in her usual but always beautiful voice.

Turning the southern charm off, he said, "Yeah, I slept in quite a while, though, for a Saturday, considering Nathan has two friends over."

"Well, you should have with all the whiskey you and Brad drank last night," she said with a bit of sarcasm in her voice. She then added, "How late were you two up, anyway?"

"I don't know, but you were sound asleep when I came to bed," he responded.

"Well, sit down, and I'll get you a cup of coffee."

"Okay."

Emily then poured him some coffee, walked over to the table, and gave it to him. She gave him a good morning kiss and said, "John I'm going to leave around two o'clock today to go stay with my mother tonight. Billy and Tim's moms are coming to get them at noon. You and Nathan can have another one of your father-and-son Saturday evenings."

"Okay," John replied and took a sip of coffee.

Emily had been staying with her mom on Saturday nights since the death of her father three months earlier. John never said anything because he knew how grief-stricken his mother-in-law, Mary, had been. Plus, he kind of enjoyed spending the night alone with Nathan watching movies and eating popcorn. It was becoming a weekly event that he looked forward to during his long work week.

He had been putting in sixty to seventy hours a week at the office lately. Since his company, American Molded Products, had just bought two smaller manufacturing companies, he had to get all their books in line. Although his accounting department had kept meticulous records on American Molded Products, the companies they bought had lacked good record-keeping skills.

This was probably why they couldn't keep going anymore.

John sat at the table, finishing his coffee and staring out at the beautiful summer day. It was amazing to think that it could be so warm and nice out now, but in two months, the harsh, cold reality of a Michigan winter would settle in. The summer seemed to go so fast while the winter lasted an eternity.

"Well, I'm going to go upstairs and take a shower," John said.

"You don't want any breakfast?" Emily asked and added, "I made potatoes and French toast."

"No, I don't think my stomach could handle that right now."

"Okay, but after I call the boys in, there won't be any left. So are you sure you don't want any?"

John answered, "No, I'm fine, honey. All I want is a shower."

He got up from the table and walked up behind Emily, who was facing away from him cooking on the stove. He reached his arm around her slim waist. John gently pulled her back into him and hugged her. He kissed her cheek just in front of her ear and said softly, "I'm fine, Em. I love you, and thanks for cooking breakfast."

"I love you, too," Emily responded.

"I'll be upstairs showering."

John then proceeded upstairs and went into the bathroom. He turned on the shower, undressed, and got in. The hot water gently massaged his head. He thought, "Now this is just what I needed, a nice, warm shower."

After getting out of the shower and drying off, he put on a pair of shorts. He felt a little tired, so he lay back down in bed. Through the closed sliding door, he heard the muffled sounds of the boys in the pool. John then heard the back door open and the sound of Emily yelling, "Boys, come in and get breakfast."

The shower had relaxed John, and his headache seemed to be going away. He was imagining the boys downstairs eating French toast and talking about their antics in the pool. Then he slipped away into a dreamy sleep.

John was wakened some time later by the sound of Emily's voice, "John, wake up."

He woke up and looked at Emily who was standing next

4

to the bed with her duffle bag over her shoulder. John asked in a half awake voice, "What is it, Emily?"

She responded, "You don't have to get up. I'm leaving now to go to my mom's. Billy rode his bike home, and Tim's mom came to got him. Nathan is in his room taking a nap. He was pretty tired; I think they stayed up most of the night last night. Well, anyway, I'll call you when I get to my mom's house." She leaned over the bed and gave him a kiss, then added, "I love you."

John replied, "I love you, too." He rolled back over and curled up in the bed. The bed felt soft and comfortable today as he fell back to sleep.

It must have been several hours later when John awoke. He was facing the sliding glass door. There were no longer any bright lights coming through it, and his room seemed much darker than it was earlier. He stretched a little and stared at the curtains hanging over the door.

A strange feeling started to come over him. His hair was standing up on the back of his neck, and there was a slight tingling sensation all through his head and his upper body. Whatever the feeling was, he didn't like it. It was the same feeling that John got when somebody was staring at him. Only there was something else that he couldn't figure out, like whatever was causing the feeling wasn't just staring, but was all around him, almost as if it was making its presence known to him.

John rolled over in bed to see what time it was. Out of the corner of his eye, he noticed a strange shadow in his room. His eyes darted to the doorway, and standing there was a shadowy dark figure.

"Nathan, is that you?" he said with a slight crackle of fear in his voice.

The figure stood there with no response. John began to panic now because he knew this figure wasn't his son. A streak of terror ran through him and he began to say, "Who are..." but the words didn't come out fast enough.

The shadowy figure streaked across the room so fast that John couldn't finish his sentence. He didn't even have time to react before the figure leapt onto him in his bed. It pinned his shoulders to the mattress and put its face and mouth right in front of his. The figure then began to suck with such a velocity that John was unable catch his breath. It made a quiet hissing noise that seemed to be sucking all the air that John needed to breathe.

John used all of his strength to try to get the figure off of him, but it seemed to weigh hundreds of pounds. It held his arms stretched out and pinned above John's head by his wrists. Its legs were straddling each side of his rib cage and squeezing together tightly. Its head was pushing against John's forehead, holding John deep in the pillow. It's mouth was less then an inch from John's but not touching. John wanted to scream but the figure robbed him of his precious air.

He was beginning to get light-headed and felt like he was going to pass out. He squirmed and tried to break free from the figure, but it was so heavy and its grip on his wrists were so tight that no matter how hard he tried he could not escape.

As he began to loose consciousness, the image of Nathan sleeping in his bed ran through his thoughts. The thought occurred to John that after the figure was through with him, it would probably move down to Nathan's room if it hadn't already. The image of the figure doing what it was doing to him to Nathan infuriated him. He thought of how scared Nathan would be and the terror that would run through him.

The thought of this sent him into a rage. The rage coming out of him was like an uncontrollable explosion of energy erupting out of John's body. With the newfound energy shooting through him, he arched his back and legs up and rolled over in a quick flipping motion. The figure was thrown from John, and as quickly as it had pounced on him, it ran out of his room disappearing down the hallway.

John jumped up and ran across his room towards the hallway after the dark figure. He was now infuriated and angry at the realization that it could, at this second, be attacking Nathan. John took off in a full sprint down the hallway towards Nathan's open bedroom door. As he ran John began to shout, "Nathan, are you okay? Nathan!"

He burst into Nathan's doorway only to find Nathan half-awake sitting up in his bed asking, "Dad, what is it? I'm okay."

John ran over to Nathan's bed and hugged him. He then said, "Come on, there's somebody in the house. We have to get out of here."

Nathan, sensing his father's fear and hearing the panic in his voice, began to cry and said, "Where? Where are they, Dad? Are they going to get us?"

Seeing the fear he was creating in Nathan, John realized he needed to calm down in order to get through the situation. He scooped Nathan into his arms and ran out of the room into the hallway. He then went down the stairs and toward the doorway leading into the garage.

Nathan was crying and said, "Dad, what is it? You're scaring me!"

Trying to have confidence in his voice to calm Nathan, he replied, "It's alright, son, we just need to get out of here."

John grabbed the keys to his car, which were hanging on the key ring holder on the wall next to the door that lead into the garage. He flung the door open and hit the button to the garage door as he hurried to his car.

The noise of the door opener engaging startled him for a second until he realized what it was. Holding Nathan in his left arm, he opened the driver's door and set him across into the passenger seat. As John opened the door, he accidentally bumped into his golf clubs, sending them loudly to the ground. John then got into the driver's seat and started the vehicle. Quickly throwing the car in reverse, he backed out of the garage and swung the car around. He put the car in drive and drove out the driveway onto the paved country road that headed toward town.

John knew he had to call the police and tell them that he had an intruder. In his panicked race to get out of the house, he had forgotten his cell phone. It was about three miles into town. As he drove from his house, he looked in the rearview mirror. It looked the same as it always did, but the thought of his attacker being in it sent a chill up his spine.

John looked over at Nathan who was sitting with his knees pulled up to his chest and sobbing. He reached his right hand over and gently stroked Nathan's head and in his calmest voice, said, "It's alright buddy, calm down."

Nathan looked over at him. His eyes and some streaky tear marks running down his cheek glistened from the sun that was lying so low on the horizon. He said in a scared jerky voice, "Dad, who was in our house, and what did they want?"

"I don't know, Nathan, but we'll go into town and call the police, and they'll find out for us. Just calm down. Everything is going to be alright."

"But what if they're still there when we go back?"

"Don't worry Nathan, the police will go to our house and catch the bad guy and put him in jail." John paused and added, "So just relax. They'll take care of everything."

"I'm so scared."

"Don't be scared, Nathan. I said everything will be okay." John ran his fingers through Nathan's hair and gently rubbed his head.

He said again, "Just sit there and relax. It'll be alright."

Nathan then put his forehead on his knees and sighed deeply, "Okay, Dad."

John felt as if Nathan was calming down. He pushed down on the accelerator and brought the speedometer up to eighty miles an hour. He was anxious to get to a phone so he could get his house checked out. There were always cops on this road. Why couldn't one be around now to stop him for speeding?

As he came around the bend in the road before town, he saw the Shell station up on his right approaching. He pulled into the gas station and drove through the parking lot up to the payphones. Opening his door to get out, Nathan grabbed his hand and said, "Don't leave me in the car, Dad. I'm scared."

He replied, "Okay, come on. Let's call the police." Nathan hadn't acted this dependent on him in years. It was as if he was five years old again.

They both got out of the car and quickly walked over to the phone. John then picked up the receiver and dialed 911. The phone rang once on the other end, and then a lady answered, "Sanilac County Emergency line. Can I get your name and address, please?"

John answered, "Yes, hi. My name is John Watley, and my address is 1844 Black River Road, Croswell, Michigan 48422."

The voice on the other end asked, "What is the problem, Mr. Watley?"

John reported, "I'm at a payphone in Croswell now, but I just left my house because there was an intruder in it."

She asked, "At the address you just told me, Mr. Watley?"

"Yes, ma'am. We had an intruder and he attacked me so I got my son and we left."

"Is anyone injured, sir?"

"No."

"Was it just you and your son in the house at the time of the attack?"

"Yes."

"Is there anyone still at your house?"

"No. Well, I mean there might be, but not anybody that's supposed to be there. My wife is at her mother's house, and just my son and I were there when the intruder came in. The intruder may still be there."

"Okay, sir, we have a unit in route to your house to check it out." She paused and then asked, "So, nobody who lives there is there now?"

"No, if there's somebody there now, it's the intruder. So tell them they better arrest him."

"Mr. Watley, can you give me a description of the intruder?"

John thought about it for a minute and then responded, "No, it happened so fast, but he seemed to be wearing some type of dark mask over his face and dark clothing on his whole body."

John could now hear a police siren echoing in the distance. It sounded as though it was coming from the direction of his house. He then said, "I can hear sirens by my house. Is that where they're going?"

"Yes, sir."

"Well, I'm going back to my house to talk to the police."

"That is fine, Mr. Watley. They will want to talk to you. But if you could please wait in your car while they are looking for the intruder, that would be helpful."

"Okay, well I'm heading out there now. Bye."

John looked at Nathan and said, "Nathan, I don't want you to be scared, but we have to go to the house and meet the police to help them catch the intruder. I want you to be brave and remember I'll be there and the police, too, so nothing will happen. Okay?"

Nathan's eyes slowly rose and stared into his dad's. John could see in his eyes that he was starting to calm down now. Nathan said, "Okay, Dad."

John put his arm around Nathan's shoulder and started turning from the payphone to the car. As they approached the brown Buick, John noticed their reflection coming off the side of the car. He thought that Nathan was getting so big, and yet, as he reflected back, it had seemed so easy to carry him down the stairs and out to the car.

Nathan walked over to the passenger door, opened it, and got in as John got into the driver's side. The car was still running due to the panicked state John had been in to get to the phone. He put the car in drive and took a deep breath. He could feel himself calming down from the earlier excitement. John was still anxious to get to his house and catch whomever had broken in, but the panic that he had felt earlier was slowly leaving him.

As John turned the car around and pulled up to the road, he looked right and noticed a police car coming out of town in his direction. He paused as the police car zipped in front of him and down the road in the direction of his house. He looked over at Nathan and said, trying to ease some tension, "See our hard-earned tax dollars at work, son."

Nathan looked at him and grinned. This relaxed John more as he turned left onto the road and headed towards home. The shadows from the now low sun seemed to be long and dark over the road. As they passed in between them, the sun seemed to flicker on and off. He wished for a moment that he had his sunglasses, but then remembered he had left everything at home in the rushed moments to get out of the house. He looked down at his feet and realized he wasn't even wearing any shoes. It seemed odd to him that he could have been so worked up that he didn't even notice this. He was always so particular with all the details in his life that it was amazing to him that something could send his life into such chaos in a split second.

Thinking about this made him think back to the incident earlier back at his house. It all seemed like a horrible dream. Everything happened so fast that it was like a big blur to him. He had been sleeping in his bed, and when he awoke, there was an intruder in his house who attacked him. Right, yes, this is what happened, but it just didn't seem right to him. He felt violated by the intruder, but what didn't seem right and what he couldn't get out of his head was the intruder itself.

10

John thought back about the incident, trying to remember every little detail. He knew the police were going to want to know everything he could remember. This would probably help them get the intruder, and he definitely wanted whomever attacked him to be caught immediately. What would he do if they didn't get him? What if he came back? He didn't know, but he did think that the intruder was a man. Judging at how fast the intruder moved and how powerful he was, John was convinced that he was a man and a very strong one at this.

John had always been in good shape and was a pretty powerful person. He was six foot three and weighed two hundred forty pounds. He wasn't considered to be overweight by any means. He was slim but muscular with broad shoulders and a pretty thick chest.

The way his attacker manhandled him reminded John of himself wrestling around with Nathan. He could effortlessly toss Nathan around when they horse played, and this is what his attacker had done to him. It was as though the intruder was a man confronting a little kid. Only John was definitely no little kid. His attacker seemed to just give up and leave. It wasn't like John had fought him off; it was just like the intruder had just quit attacking. This is what really scared John about the whole incident. He liked to be in control of situations, and he felt like he had absolutely no control of this one. He felt like the only reason he was alive was because the intruder had given up for some reason.

This made him wonder what the intruder's purpose in his house was, anyway. John's attacker didn't seem to attack him in a way that would really harm him, but the intruder had almost suffocated John to death. If he had really wanted to hurt John, why didn't he attack him in his sleep? It was as if the intruder had been standing in the doorway waiting for John to awaken before he attacked. The whole thing just didn't make sense to him. Well, hopefully the police could make more sense out of the situation then he could.

John's house was now approaching on the right. As he slowed down to turn into the driveway, he observed the policeman who had passed him in town getting out of the car. There was another police car in front of him.

Turning into his driveway, his house looked eerie to him.

The low sun from across the road shined brightly on half of his house. The other half was covered by a dark shadow cast by the huge oak tree in his front yard. The shadow seemed so huge and dark, as shadows often do in the later parts of the day, as though a huge darkness was in the process of swallowing his beautiful, two-story Cape Cod home. It was such a dark contrast to the left side of this house, which seemed so bright and welcoming.

The officer who had just gotten out of the car turned and looked at John as he pulled into the driveway. As John pulled up behind the officer's car the policeman approached him.

John rolled down his window as the officer walked up to his car.

"Are you the owner of the house, sir?" the officer asked.

"Yes. I'm John Watley, the owner, and this is my son, Nathan."

"It's nice to meet you, Mr. Watley. I'm Officer Lampton with the Croswell police. We have a couple of officers inside looking for the intruder, but they haven't found anybody yet. Why don't you and Nathan sit tight here by the car? I'm going to get my clipboard so I can get a statement from you, okay?"

"Okay."

The officer walked to his car as John and Nathan got out. He reached inside, grabbed a clipboard, and walked back to them saying. "By the time we finish with this paperwork, they should be done in the house."

"Well, if it helps you out at all, I was attacked upstairs in the master bedroom. After I got the attacker off of me, he ran down the hall. I don't think he ran down the stairs, though, because I never heard him. The more I think about it, I don't think the intruder made any noise at all."

"You mean he never said anything to you?" Officer Lampton asked.

"No, I mean when he moved, there were no footsteps or noise of any sort. It was almost as if he..." John paused for a minute and thought.

"Oh, nothing. It was so chaotic and everything happened so fast that my memory seems to be playing tricks on me."

"That happens to a lot of people during traumatic experiences, Mr. Watley. Don't feel bad. We're going to have a detective come by tomorrow to get a full description of what happened, and we'll have a patrol car come by your house every hour tonight just in case the intruder tries to come back."

John thought about this for a minute and then decided, "That's good, but I think we're going to go stay at my mother-in-law's house over in Sandusky tonight anyway. Nathan is pretty shaken up, and so am I, to tell you the truth."

"I don't blame you a bit for that Mr. Watley. You've had a rough night."

Just then, a short, blonde-haired, slender female police officer and an overweight, older officer came walking out of the front door. The overweight officer yelled out, "Hey, Lampton, the house is all clear. You hear anything from the unit circling the block?"

"Yeah. They haven't found anybody."

"What about the K-9 unit?"

"Yeah, there was a state boy over in Yale. He should be here in the next ten minutes or so. Why don't you guys recheck the upstairs. Mr. Watley says the attacker ran out of his room, but he never heard him go down the stairs."

"Alright. We'll check it out," the overweight officer replied as he turned around and headed back into the house with his partner.

Nathan interrupted, "Dad, let's go stay at Grandma's."

John looked down at Nathan and patted him on the head. "We're going to. We just have to help the police first so they'll be able to catch the bad guy, okay?"

"Okay, Dad."

John looked at officer Lampton and asked, "How much longer before we can go in and get some stuff for the night?"

"Let's just let them go through the house one more time just to be safe, and then you'll be able to go in and get your things. It should only be another five or ten minutes. We also have a K-9 unit in route that will cover the area around the outside of the house to see if maybe our intruder is hiding somewhere."

"That sounds good. I want to catch this guy."

"Oh, trust me, Mr. Watley, we want to get him, too. You live around here, so you know there isn't much crime. When something like this happens, we put all of our resources on it. Croswell is a safe town, and we intend to keep it that way. Well, let's finish up this report so you can get to your mother-in-law's for the night."

Nathan stood next to his dad and watched as the officer asked what seemed to be a million questions. He was still scared from everything that had occurred during the evening. He just wanted to get in their car and go to his Grandma's. It seemed very silly to him to have to sit here and wait for all of the police to do their work.

What really had scared Nathan more than anything was how scared his dad had been. He had never seen him scared of anything before. If there was somebody in their house, why didn't his dad just beat him up? He knew that his dad was very strong and tough, so why would he even need for the police to come help him?

He really didn't even know what had happened earlier. Nathan hadn't seen an intruder in the house. The only thing he remembered was being awakened by his dad and then being carried through the house. The whole time, he hadn't seen anybody.

The bad guy was lucky he didn't see it, too. If he would have been there when his dad got attacked, he would have taken his little league bat and hit the bad guy so hard that it would have knocked him right out.

Then, when the cops got there, he would have told them what he did and probably been in the paper. If it would have only happened like this, he could have been a huge hero.

Nathan remembered how a while back a boy who was one year older than him had saved a girl out of the Black River when they were swimming down at the park. From then on around town, that boy was a hero. They even had an assembly at school, and the police department gave him a badge for being so brave.

He would have definitely gotten a police badge if he would have knocked the bad guy out with his baseball bat. Everyone in his school would have been jealous of him if he had only gotten the chance to do that. Oh well, sometimes things just didn't work out the way they should.

At least they were going to Grandma's for the night. He was much too scared to stay here. What if the bad guy came back? He knew he would be safe at Grandma's, and she always had cookies and ice cream. His favorite, too: chocolate chip mint ice cream. Gosh, what was taking so long? This was just so stupid that they had to stay here and wait for the police.

If he were a cop, he knew he would have already have caught the bad guy and would already had him in jail. He didn't see what the big deal was with catching bad guys anyway. Why did it take so many cops? He wouldn't ask a million stupid questions like these cops. He'd just go catch the bad guy, no questions asked. Then he'd bring him to jail and lock him up.

As John was finishing the report that officer Lampton was filling out, he looked down at Nathan. Nathan was staring with a blank look upon his face at the side of the house. John couldn't help but wonder what was going through his head right now.

The officers were out of the house now, so they could go in and get their stuff for the evening.

John looked at Nathan and said, "Nathan?" No response, so he said it again, "Nathan!" This time, Nathan turned and looked towards him, startled as he left his daydream and returned to reality. "Let's go inside and get some stuff together for Grandma's, okay?"

"Yeah, Dad."

Seeing Nathan's hesitant response, Officer Lampton said, "I'll go in with you, even though there doesn't seem to be any sign that the attacker is still around."

"Thank you, officer. I appreciate that. It should only take a couple of minutes to get our stuff together."

"That will be fine, Mr. Watley. You can take your time. I don't have anywhere else to be for the time being, so don't feel rushed. You've already been through enough tonight."

John took Nathan's hand and began to walk up the stairs onto the front porch of their house. Nathan hesitated for a moment. Seeing Nathan's reluctance, John looked over at him and smiled. In his most confident and reassuring father voice, he said, "Come on, Nathan. Let's go get our things."

Nathan made eye contact with his dad for a moment and,

feeling his father's confidence, walked up the stairs and into the house. Officer Lampton walked closely behind.

As John stepped into the vestibule of his house, he paused for a moment and looked up the stairs. His eyes slowly moved down the stairs and looked all around. He was relieved that it still felt like his home and that he had a safe and confident inner feeling. He was aware that Nathan was still shaken up, though, so for his sake they would get their things for the night and go to Emily's mother's house.

John walked up the oak staircase and onto the white carpet of the hallway leading to his room. Then they walked into his and Emily's room. As he entered the room, he glanced over at his bed where he had been attacked. One pillow was thrown off of the bed and was now lying on the floor.

The once snug white sheet was pulled off on the top-right corner of the mattress. These physical signs of a struggle brought the reality of what had happened back fresh in John's head. The thought had occurred to him that maybe he had just had a bad dream and the attacker was all in his imagination. By the looks of his bed, he knew that he had really been in a fight. Although it felt odd to John, he was reassured that he had been attacked and wasn't just going crazy. He thought that this was very strange. It seems as if his family would be better off if it was just a dream, but as for his own mind's sake, he was oddly pleased that these were signs that his attack had been real.

He walked into his closet and grabbed a bag that would be big enough to accommodate both his and Nathan's clothes and bathroom items for the night. The reality that he had been attacked in his own home was slowly settling in. This made him quickly gather his clothes. He walked into the bathroom and grabbed his toothbrush and some deodorant. Walking back out of the bathroom and over to his nightstand, he grabbed his cell phone and wallet. He then put on some shoes and said to Nathan, "That's all for my things. Let's go to your room and get your stuff."

"Okay, Dad."

On the way out of his room, he switched off all of the lights and continued to Nathan's room. Nathan ran ahead of John. Officer Lampton was standing in the hallway looking at a picture on the wall.

He looked at John and asked, "Where was this picture taken?"

"That's from out in Lake Tahoe. We go there every year on vacation."

"It's beautiful."

"Oh yeah, it is. If you ever get the chance, you should go there. The picture doesn't do it justice. It's one of the most beautiful places I've ever been."

Officer Lampton looked at the picture of Emily and John with the mountains in the background again and then looked back at John and said, "I've always wanted to go out West on vacation, but my wife doesn't like to travel much."

"Well if you want to see some of the most serene countryside in the U.S., you should talk her into going."

The officer nodded his head and replied, "Yeah, I'm gonna have to work on that."

John walked past Officer Lampton and into Nathan's bedroom. Nathan had already gone in and was now opening his dresser drawer.

John set the brown duffle bag on top of Nathan's white dresser and began grabbing some clothes for him for the night. Seeing that his dad was getting his stuff, Nathan walked over to his bed and sat on the edge of it.

After John had put Nathan's clothes in the bag, he turned and looked at him. Nathan was sitting on his bed holding his stuffed bear, Bobo, and dreamingly staring out his window at the now dimly lit outside world. Seeing Nathan with Bobo surprised John for a minute. Even though Bobo was still in Nathan's bed every night, he had not seen Nathan hold him in several years. Looking at him sitting there with Bobo made John remember back when Nathan was much younger and had to take Bobo everywhere they went. John briefly thought of the time they had forgotten Bobo in a hotel room in the Upper Peninsula of Michigan. They were already two hours away from the hotel heading back home when Nathan had realized Bobo was missing. Nathan had been so hysterical about leaving his bear that they had to turn around and drive back to the hotel to get Bobo. Luckily, when they had gotten there, Bobo was in the lost and found and everything was all right. Instead of getting back to their home at six in the afternoon, though, as they had planned, they ended up getting home at 10:30 at night.

Breaking the silence, John said, "Alright, buddy, I got your clothes. Let's get your toothbrush from the bathroom and then we should be ready to go."

Nathan stood up from the bed and, holding Bobo by the arm, said, "Okay, Dad."

John then asked Nathan, "Are you bringing Bobo with you?"

In a shy, almost embarrassed voice, Nathan quietly said, "Yes."

"Okay, let's go then."

They then walked into the hallway bathroom. John opened the top drawer and grabbed Nathan's toothbrush. He tossed it into the duffle bag and zipped the bag shut. Walking back into the hallway where Officer Lampton was standing, John said, "Alright, we've got our things. Are you all finished in here?"

"Yes, sir. We have a K-9 unit that should be here any minute, but as for the house, you can go ahead and shut all your lights off and lock it up like normal. We are just going to check out the little woods behind your house, but we don't need you to be here to do that."

John was now starting to go down the staircase with Nathan directly behind him. On his way down, he shut off the hallway light and then replied to the officer, who was walking ahead of him, "Sounds good then. I'll lock up on our way out."

They walked the rest of the way down the creaky oak staircase and out the front door. Standing on the wrap-around front porch, John looked at Nathan and said, "Wait here with the officer. I'm going to go shut off the rest of the downstairs lights and make sure the back door is locked, okay?"

Nathan looked back at his dad and hesitantly agreed by nodding his head.

Seeing that Nathan was still shaken up and realizing that a little distraction might help, Officer Lampton looked at Nathan and said, "Hey Nathan, do you want to look inside my police car while your dad is finishing up?"

Nathan's eyes lit up, and he said excitedly, "Yeah, that would be neat!"

"Okay, let's go."

Nathan and Officer Lampton walked down the stairs and over to the police car as John went back inside his house to lock up. Once John made sure the back door was locked and had shut all the lights off, he walked out the front door and locked it. He then walked down the porch steps and over to the police car. Nathan was sitting in the driver's seat wearing Officer Lampton's hat, pretending he was driving. Officer Lampton was standing next to the driver's door with it open and looked over at John. "You all set Mr. Watley?"

"Yes, I think I got everything." Then, to Nathan, he said, "Come on, let's go to Grandma's."

Nathan jumped out of the police car and walked back to their car. He then hopped into the back seat where he always rode. John opened the driver's door and tossed the duffle bag in to the passenger seat.

"Mr. Watley, Dectective Flannigan will be in touch with you tomorrow. Try not to worry too much tonight. We'll catch this guy and figure out what's going on, okay?"

John, looking back at the officer, said, "Good. Hey... thanks for all of your help."

"No problem, Mr. Watley. It's my pleasure and my duty. Have a good evening."

"Okay, you too." John climbed into the car and closed the door. He put the keys in the ignition and started the vehicle. He backed up and turned around, put the car in drive, and headed out the driveway.

As John took a left onto the road, a blue State Police SUV pulled into his driveway. Through his rearview mirror, he noticed the writing on the side of the SUV in big white letters: "CAUTION: K-9 WORKING DOG." John thought that it was about time that the K-9 got to his home. If his attacker was walking, he could be miles away by now. A typical stereotype popped into his head as he pictured the K-9 officer eating some donuts back at the station. He figured, in a sleepy town like Croswell, what else could be more important than to get to somebody almost being killed. John knew for a fact that there weren't very many murders in this area, so he would think that if there was a chance for a cop in this town to find a potential murderer, he would have dropped everything, turned his lights and sirens on, and hauled butt to get to the location of the attack.

It was about 30 miles to Mary's house. John usually took the back roads there, but since he was ready to end this long day, he decided to take the main route. As John brought his Buick up to the speed limit, he reached up with his right hand and tilted the rearview mirror down so he could see Nathan in the back seat. Nathan had his seat belt on and was slouched over with his head leaning against the back door window. His eyes were closed, and it appeared to John that he was sleeping. John thought for a second that there was no way that Nathan could have fallen asleep that fast, but then he remembered what Emily had told him earlier in the day. She said that Nathan and his friends stayed up all last night, so even with his nap, he only had a few of hours of sleep in the last twenty-four hours.

Being in an over-protective mode, John said, "Nathan, are you feeling alright?"

Nathan groggily moved his head as if he was beginning to wake. This was all John needed to see to feel relieved. It made him relaxed that Nathan's mind was at ease enough that he could get some rest.

As an oncoming car passed John on the two-lane rural road, his automatic headlights turned on. Dusk was now turning slowly to dark, and the once long shadows of dusk were now blending together and forcing the light to go away. He glanced back at Nathan once again to make sure he was alright. It was still light enough to just make out his blonde, moppy hair. Looking at Nathan's hair reminded him of Emily so he decided he would give her a call and let her know about the night's events.

He had to think for a minute about how to tell Emily what had happened without making her freak out too much. He and Nathan had had a very traumatic experience, but they were both safe now, which was all that really mattered. The question was how he could explain this to Emily so that she would remain calm. Emily was a very nurturing person, and to her, just the thought of somebody trying to harm John and Nathan would surely send her into hysterics. He could downplay the whole incident and tell her that the house was gotten broken into and that everything was fine, but he knew this wouldn't work either because Nathan couldn't hold a secret from his mom even if he wanted to. Nathan was still

20

at the age where he told his mom everything, and he would surely talk to her about this. He was still a couple of years away from understanding that sometimes in certain incidents it is better that you don't mention every little detail of your life to your mom.

John remembered when he was fifteen, his father had explained this to him and he was old enough that it had made sense. His childhood friend, Mark, at the time was sixteen and had just gotten his driver's license. One day, when they were coming home from school, Mark had been getting a little crazy on a gravel road doing fishtails when all of a sudden they lost control and spun a complete 180 degrees in the road. When they came to a stop, they were facing the way they had been coming. Luckily, they didn't spin off of the road and hit one of the large trees that were in the ditch.

When John had gotten home, he had told his mother what had happened. Much to his surprise, she hadn't thought that it was quite as amusing as he had. His mother had said that he couldn't get a ride to school with Mark anymore and that he was going back to riding the school bus. This had upset John, so he had gone up to his room to get away from her. When his dad had gotten home and was filled in on the story by his mother, he had gone up to John's room to talk to him. He had told John that he was old enough now to be told a little secret about women. John's dad had then said that sometimes what a woman didn't know wouldn't hurt her a bit. His father had then explained to him how women are worriers, and to keep them from worrying, it is a man's job to leave out any details in a story that would make them worry more. When his mom had asked him how his ride home from school had been, he should have simply said that it was fine. John had then told his dad that he understood, he just didn't think that his mother would have been so upset about his story that he would have to go back to riding the bus again. His dad told him from then on, John should live by this and everything would be much smoother in his life. And he had said that as for riding the bus again, he would make sure that he didn't have to. But this would be the only time he took care of a problem for him in this nature.

It had ended up all right, and John had continued riding home with Mark for the rest of school. They had many more crazy things happen to them in Mark's car, but John had remembered what his dad had told him and never told his mom about any of them. As far as she knew, they never went over the speed limit, always used their turn signals, and never did anything crazy like fishtails again. She was happy and John was happy, so it had all worked out just as his father had told him it would.

He wished Nathan was old enough to understand this, but John knew it would be a few years before he would be able to give Nathan this speech. He figured he would just have to grab the bull by the horns on this one and tell Emily the truth. If she found out later that he hadn't told the whole truth, it would be much worse then just laying everything on the table and having to deal with her getting upset. There was no way that John could protect Emily's feelings on this one; he would just have to tell her.

John felt around the leather passenger seat until he found his cell phone. He flipped it open and scrolled to Mary's phone number. After pushing the Send button, he held the phone up to his ear with his right hand and guided the Buick down the road with his left.

Ring... pause... Ring. "Hello?" his mother-in-law, Mary, answered the phone.

"Hi, Mary. This is John. Is Emily around?"

"Oh, hi, John. Yes, Em is right here. Hang on one second."

There was a slight pause, and John could hear Mary walking over to Emily. He could then hear in a low tone, "Em, it's John."

"Thanks, Mom," Emily said, and by the increase in volume, John could tell she had been handed the phone. "Hi."

"Hi, Emily. How're you doing?"

"Good. How's movie night with Nathan going?"

John paused for a second and thought, "We're not watching any movies, but it seems that we just got thrown into the middle of one." He responded, "Not too good."

Emily, thinking that maybe Nathan was still tired from the night before responded, "What, is Nathan being grumpy?"

"No, Nathan's fine, and so am I. We are coming to Mary's house for the night, though."

"What? Why? What happened, John?"

"Somebody broke into the house."

Emily's voice switched from calm to very excited. "What

happened? Did you leave and go somewhere?"

"No, we were napping, and I woke up and saw somebody in the house. I think I must have startled the intruder because he jumped on me."

Emily was silent for a second as if she was in disbelief. She then asked, "Did you get hurt?"

"No, Em. Nathan and I are fine. I fought the intruder off, and he took off running. I didn't know if he was still in the house or not, so I just grabbed Nathan, got in the car, and drove into town. I called the police from the Shell station, and we went back to the house."

"Did they catch him, John?"

"No, not yet, but they searched the house, and when we were leaving, a K-9 unit showed up to look for him outside."

"Oh John, this is terrible. Is Nathan upset?"

"He was a little shaken at first, but he's calmed down now. He's sleeping in the back seat."

Emily said, "Well, I guess all that matters is you two are both alright."

"That's right, Em, and I bet you they will catch this guy and everything will be just fine. The police don't have much of anything else to work on in a small town. They seemed to really be putting some man power into it."

"That's good, John. I really hope they get him."

John, sensing that Emily wasn't too upset over the whole incident, wanted to get off of the phone and try to relax a little, so he said, "Well, Em, we're about thirty minutes away, so I'm gonna let you go. I'll tell you every little detail when I get to your mom's, okay?"

Knowing that John wasn't big on talking on the phone, Emily replied, "Okay, John, I love you, and I'll see you shortly."

"I love you too, Em, and I'll see you soon."

John heard the click of Emily hanging up and took his cell phone down from his ear. He pushed the red End button and set the phone down on the passenger seat.

Steering with his left hand, John reached over to the radio and switched it on. The familiar voice of Robert Plant came alive through the speakers. Not wanting to wake Nathan, John adjusted the fade so only the front speakers were playing. Robert was singing about his friend who was going to be hanged and how he couldn't get no silver and couldn't get no gold to save him. John tapped the steering wheel to the beat of the familiar song.

It had turned into a very dark night. The moon was nowhere to be found, and the absence of streetlights on the two-lane country road made the darkness intensify. As he passed a two-story farmhouse on his right, John glanced in the large front window. There were two people sitting on a couch, staring at what was probably a TV on the wall opposite them. The light shining from the window was a stark contrast to the pitch blackness that engulfed the outside world.

Whenever John saw another person's house, it seemed that it was so cozy and comfortable. He imagined that the two people on the couch were the parents and, off to the side of the room where he couldn't see, there was probably another couch with their children on it. They were probably eating some popcorn and watching a movie. They were all relaxed because it was Saturday night and there wasn't any work the next day. The only thing they had on their minds was the suspense of how the movie they were watching was going to end.

They would probably finish the movie and talk about it for awhile. Then they would all retire to their bedrooms for the night. The children would awaken on Sunday morning to their mother making a big Sunday breakfast. After breakfast, they might take a nice Sunday drive and visit some relatives or just hang around the house all day and be lazy. What they did wasn't really relative as long as they relaxed and spent a nice day together. John switched from thinking about the family at the farmhouse to how amusing it was that, just from one little glance into somebody else's world, so many assumptions could be made.

He figured he must have been focused in on such a nice, relaxing family evening because his and Nathan's family movie night had been ruined by a very unwanted individual. Oh well, what could he do about it now? The important thing was that everybody was okay so they would have many opportunities in the future to have evenings like the people in the farmhouse might have been having.

A car was approaching John in the oncoming lane. The other car switched its high beams to low, and

John reached with his right hand and did the same. A few seconds later, they passed each other and John switched his lights back to high. It was so dark out that the low beams seemed useless.

John had the Buick's cruise control set at fifty-nine miles an hour. Figuring that cops wouldn't give out a ticket unless someone was going more than five miles per hour over the fifty-five-mile-an-hour posted speed limit, he steadily made his way through the darkness towards Mary's house. The high beams cut a hole through the darkness, and the car glided down the pot-holed cement road.

The thumb area of Michigan was scattered with farms. His headlights lit up the tall green corn of a farmer's field as he drove parallel to the straight rows that had been planted in the spring. It would still be a couple of months until the corn turned brown and the farmers would then rush to get their crop off and sell it. When harvest time came, the fields would be lit up by combines at all hours of the night. It would be a huge contrast to the darkness of the fields now.

A few hundred yards up the road, John could see the eyes of a couple of animals on the side of the road. From driving these country roads for his entire life, he figured it was probably some deer so he tapped the brake to take the cruise control off. With hunting becoming less and less popular with the younger generation, the deer population had been getting out of control. When John grew up, he and all his friends had hunted, but today's kids seemed to be more into playing video games or other activities that were far less strenuous than walking around woods. He let the car coast down to forty miles an hour. Due to the lack of oncoming traffic, he guided the vehicle into the other lane to give the deer room in case they made any sudden movements. For the most part, John had found that deer that were grazing in the ditches on the sides of roads would usually just stand there and stare at the headlights as a vehicle passes, but it was always good to slow down and leave some room to maneuver in case they got scared and made a run for it.

He could now make out the bodies of one large deer and two smaller ones. It was probably a doe with her two fawns from the spring birthing period. As he got a little closer, he could see them all staring at the headlights, turning their heads slowly,

25

keeping up with his vehicle. This was a typical scene when driving at night on country roads in Michigan.

The relaxed mood of the night country drive changed as the hair on his neck stood up and the same tingling sensation he had gotten earlier before he was attacked rushed through his upper body. He felt as if he was being watched again, and his eyes darted to just behind the deer to the edge of the corn. There, standing half in the corn, was a dark, silhouetted figure. The headlights of the car made it possible to see the brown on the deer and even the white spots on the small fawns. For some reason, though, John couldn't make out any features of the individual standing in the corn. It was as if a shadow was being cast over it. It stood there, motionless, looking at John's passing vehicle with the green corn behind it. John couldn't see its eyes, only indentations of deep darkness where they should be.

Startled and wanting to get out of the area, he pushed his foot down on the accelerator, and the Buick leapt forward, picking up speed. He held the gas pedal to the floor until he reached seventy miles an hour and he felt he was a good distance away from whatever was standing in the corn. As he brought the car back down to fifty-nine miles per hour, a sudden urge to find out what was standing in the corn made him slow down even more.

He must have just been spooked from earlier in the night, and that was probably just a scarecrow or a tree stump. His mind was playing tricks on him, and he brought the car to a stop, deciding he would go back and prove to himself that it was nothing. He was a full-grown man after all and couldn't be going around getting scared like a little kid. John was going to put an end to this nonsense.

Being that there was no traffic coming from either direction, he swung a U-turn and slowly headed back to where the deer were. As he gradually approached the area, he could see the deer's eyes as they hypnotically stared at the oncoming headlights. He pushed down on the gas pedal and darted up to where the deer were. John swung the car to the left and angled the car across the oncoming lane to shine his headlights directly onto the deer and the area behind them. All three deer were frozen for a second as John's car came to a stop about one hundred feet from them. The doe then stamped her right front hoof on the ground several times and, with her white tail high in the air, darted across the road into the small woods across from the cornfield. Both fawns stood staring at the vehicle for a second and then simultaneously took off following their mother.

John's headlights were now shining on some tall weeds in the ditch before the rows of corn layered behind them. He quickly looked up and down the ditch and was unable to find anything but weeds and corn in the broad area his headlights were covering. He knew his mind was just playing tricks on him. All of the events that had happened earlier tonight had made him start seeing things. John thought he really needed to get to Mary's and get some rest. John spun his car back around to the direction he was once heading and sped up back to his cruising speed.

As he drove down the road, he shook his head and laughed a little at what had just happened. It reminded him of when he was in high school and a guy named Tom had been in a car accident and was killed. He hadn't known Tom very well because at the time he was only a sophomore and Tom was a senior. He had a class with Tom's girlfriend, Linda, and for weeks after Tom's death, they would be sitting in class doing school work when all of a sudden, she would say "Tom" loudly as if she had just seen him. Then she would run over to the door into the hallway and open it. Stepping into the hallway, she would look one way and then back down the other way and call out his name again. He could still hear her voice echoing off the lockers of the empty hall: "Tom!" Then, realizing that Tom was nowhere to be found, she would silently walk back into the classroom and sit down. She would put her head down on her desk and sit there quietly weeping.

He and his friends would often talk about this awkward situation after witnessing it. It was as if her mind would actually see him walk by in the hallway, but once she investigated more, she would realize that she hadn't seen anything at all. They all knew Linda hadn't seen Tom, but she didn't. This happened a couple of more times, and then all of a sudden, Linda quit going to school. The rumor around school was that she had been committed to a psych ward, but his mom had told him the truth. Linda had moved across the state with her grandparents so she could try to get over the traumatic event.

He had always looked down on Linda and thought that she

27

was feeble and weak-minded to be seeing such things. He was now laughing at himself for hallucinating that some type of dark man was standing in the corn. He jokingly thought maybe he should have gotten out of the car when he was stopped and yelled "Tom" into the empty cornfield. The deer would have thought he was really crazy.

John had always been amazed at how powerful one's mind could be, but he was more amazed at the good side of this life when people accomplished great things with mind over matter. He had never seen things before, and he felt like his mind was playing some type of game with him. Whenever he saw crazy people, he felt bad for them and wondered why they couldn't get a grasp on reality. Now, here he was, seeing things and it really scared him. He decided it was just due to the stress of being attacked earlier. He was upset that such an incident could shake him up this badly.

As he steadily drove down the road, he focused more on driving in order to distract himself. He kept his eyes on the road as if this would not give his mind another chance to play tricks on him. He just really needed to get some rest.

Off in the distance, John could see the lit sky of Sandusky. He was relieved that his drive would soon be over. John decided to give Emily a call again to keep himself distracted until he could get into town. He picked up his cell phone from the passenger seat but then put it back down. He'd just keep driving; he was pretty sure his mind was done playing tricks on him for the night. The next few miles went quickly, and John was happy as he came out of the dark road and into the well-lit town. He relaxed a little and glanced back at Nathan who, to his surprise, was awake and staring out the window.

Seeing Nathan was awake, John said, "Hey buddy, how long have you been up?"

Nathan's eyes switched from looking outside to looking at his father and replied, "Not very long. The lights just woke me up. Are we almost to Grandma's, Dad?"

"Just about, Nathan, only a few more minutes."

Nathan stared at the passing houses one by one as they

slowly went by. He squinted slightly and thought that it seemed very bright out. As he slowly turned his head watching a dog in somebody's front yard, he rubbed his eyes with his left hand. His neck felt very stiff from sleeping with his head leaning over so much. Nathan was very confused at a dream he'd had while sleeping.

He'd seen a man standing on the side of the road not just looking but staring directly at him. Nathan couldn't tell who the man was because it was too dark to see him completely. Even though he couldn't make out any features of the dark figure, he had known that it was a man. As the man stared at him, a scary feeling ran through his body, but at the same time he felt calm. The dark man seemed to be reaching out to Nathan, trying to tell him something, but Nathan couldn't understand it. It wasn't talking to him with its mouth like normal people did.

It was as if he could feel the dark man's thought all around him, but Nathan was a little scared of the man so he pushed them away. Nathan felt that he could have talked to the dark man if he had wanted to, but he didn't. He refused to talk with the dark man because he had a feeling about him, like the feeling of calmness that the dark man had stirred within him was just a cover up for something that was bad.

Nathan was very confused from the dream he had. Most of his dreams were about fun stuff that he did with his friends and his mom and dad. This was the first time he'd ever had a dream that felt so real and that he remembered so well. Usually after waking up, he'd remember a dream but would forget them when he started doing whatever activity he was doing on that day. He had never put much thought into his dreams before this one. For some reason, the image of the dark man standing on the side of the road staring at him kept coming up over and over again. He wanted to get the dark man out of his head, so he asked his dad, "Are we almost there yet?"

"We're on Grandma's street, buddy. What's wrong? Do you have to go to the bathroom?" John asked, wondering why Nathan was asking the same question he'd asked only a couple of minutes earlier.

Nathan, realizing he did have to go to the bathroom, said, "Yes."

"Well, hang on. We'll be there in less than a minute."

Mary lived on a well-lit street in Sandusky that was lined with one- and two-story houses on both sides. It was a wide, cement street, and some cars were parked on the road. As John slowed the car and turned into Mary's driveway, he grabbed his cell phone and put it into his pocket. He then eased the Buick to a stop next to Emily's blue Suburban.

In the back seat, John could here the click of Nathan taking his seat belt off. As John opened the car door and stepped out, he heard Nathan's door slam shut. Nathan had Bobo and was walking up the sidewalk to the front door. The one-story white home looked very welcoming with its front light on. John opened the driver's side back door and grabbed their overnight bag. As he shut the door of the car, he looked over to see Emily opening the front door of the house. Nathan walked up to his mother, and she leaned over and hugged him. Nathan then slipped inside as Emily stepped out and closed the screen door behind her.

As John walked up the sidewalk towards Emily, she said, "Hi, sweetie. How are you?"

"I've been better, Em. I'm tired and kind of in shock."

Emily stepped down to the slightly lower sidewalk towards John and opened her arms wide. John, holding the duffle bag in his left hand, reached his right around Emily's waist and hugged her. Emily's arms were on his shoulders, and she had her hands on the back of his head. She gave him a quick peck on the lips and, moving in closer with her cheek next to his, whispered in his ear, "I love you."

John kissed Emily lightly just below her ear. Inhaling with his nose, he took in her familiar sweet smell and responded, "I love you too, Em."

Emily let go of John, and as she turned back towards the front door, she grabbed his right hand with her left. She took a couple of steps towards the door and opened it with her right hand. As she held the door open, John walked inside. Passing by her, their eyes met, and they both exchanged smiles.

Walking into Mary's familiar house with Emily sent a sense of relaxation through John. Mary was at the kitchen counter, and

Nathan was sitting at the kitchen table. Looking at Nathan sitting at the table waiting for some type of snack that his Grandma had made for him made a smile come over John's face.

Mary turned from the counter with what appeared to be some cookies on a plate and a glass of milk, looked at John and said, "Hi John, glad to see you and Nathan are alright."

"Thanks Mary. We're fine." Then, switching his conversation to Nathan, he said, "Nathan, did you go to the bathroom?"

"No, Dad, I'm alright."

"Okay, I just thought you had to go."

Nathan, now grabbing a cookie from the plate Mary had brought out, said, "Nope, I'm good."

Emily looked at John, rolled her eyes slightly, and lifted her brow a little as if to say 'Kids, you know how they are.' John agreed and smiled back at her.

Still holding John's hand, Emily walked over to the blue couch and sat down. John sat next to her and set the duffle bag down by his feet. Sinking deeply into the soft couch, he leaned his head back and let out a big yawn.

Seeing this, Emily asked, "Do you want to go to bed?"

Turning his head to the right and facing Emily he replied, "Not just yet. I just want to sit here and relax a bit."

"Okay, John." She turned on the television and leaned into him.

John was watching TV but wasn't really into it. He could hear Mary and Nathan talking in the kitchen but couldn't make out what they were saying. Emily was sitting next to him watching television. She was not saying anything at the moment, and John realized she was letting him wind down a bit. John knew that she was sitting there just waiting to ask him a million questions about earlier this evening. This was why he cared for her so deeply. Even though it was eating her alive not to just start asking questions, she sat calmly to let him rest for a bit. "God, Emily is great," he thought. With this thought, he leaned over and kissed Emily on the cheek.

Picking her feet off the floor and curling them under her, Emily turned and faced John. Their eyes met, and she said, "I sure am glad my two men are safe."

"Me too, Emily. I tell you, I've never had anything like this

31

happen to me before."

Taking this as a cue, Emily asked, "What exactly happened tonight, John?"

John started with telling Emily about how he woke up, and there was somebody in the house standing in their bedroom doorway. He then went on to tell her about the attack and that he and Nathan left and called the cops then went back home. He was in the middle of telling her about what the police were doing when Nathan and Mary walked into the living room.

Mary said, "Nathan says he wants to go to bed."

Parental instinct kicking in, both Emily and John went to stand to put Nathan to bed but were interrupted by Mary saying, "That's alright. You two can stay here. I'll help Nathan out." Then, moving her eyes from Emily and John, she looked at the bag and asked, "Is this where his pajamas are?"

John replied, "Yep, his pajamas and toothbrush are in there." Then, looking at Nathan he said, "You make sure you brush, alright?"

"Alright, Dad." Nathan replied as he turned and headed for the bathroom. Mary grabbed the duffle bag and was close behind Nathan, who was just turning the light on in the bathroom.

As Mary walked down the hall, Emily and John could hear her say, "Hang on Nathan. You're just too fast for your old Grandma."

Getting back to the subject, Emily said, "It doesn't seem to have any effect on Nathan at all."

"He was a little rattled at first but seemed to settle down pretty quickly."

"I noticed he did bring Bobo."

Remembering the bear, John said, "Yeah, he is pretty calm, but it seems to have made him act a little younger."

"Well I'm sure some sleep will help him, John."

"I think I could use some shuteye myself, Em." As John finished saying this, he lifted his arms in the air above his head and stretched. He yawned while stretching and then said, "Yeah I'm exhausted."

Why don't you go get ready, and I'll go tuck in Nathan?"

"Okay," John replied and stood up. He then headed down the hallway towards the bathroom. Nathan walked out of the bathroom and looked at John. In a proud voice he said, "I brushed my teeth."

"Good job, buddy. I'll come tuck you in when I'm done getting ready for bed."

"Okay, Dad," Nathan replied, turning his back and walking down the hall towards his bedroom.

Mary walked out right after Nathan and said, "Your duffle bag is in here, John."

"Thanks, Mary."

Mary then turned and went down the hall to Nathan's bedroom.

As John went into the bathroom, Emily walked by, going to Nathan's room to tuck him in. John smiled at her for a second and then closed the door of the bathroom so he could get ready for bed. After going to the bathroom and brushing his teeth, John put on the shorts and T-shirt that he'd brought. He then left the bathroom and walked down the hall to Nathan's room. As he was almost to the door, Mary walked out and said, "Goodnight, John. I'll see you in the morning."

John smiled and said, "Goodnight, Mary."

Mary then opened the door across the hall from Nathan's room and went in. John stepped into the doorway of Nathan's room and paused for a moment. Emily was sitting on the edge of the bed next to Nathan quietly talking to him. She was wearing blue pajama shorts and a top with white polka dots on them. Nathan was lying in the bed on his back, looking up at his mom. Bobo the bear was next to him on the black pillow.

The walls of Nathan's room at Mary's were a light blue. Around the top of the wall was a four-inch strip of wallpaper that wrapped around the entire room. Different numbered and colored racecars were evenly spaced on the wallpaper. Nathan's bed was a red and blue racecar. Mary and her late husband, Steve, had gotten it for him and decorated the room in a racecar theme for his ninth birthday two-and-a-half years ago. Mary and Steve had painted the room and put up the wallpaper. Even though Nathan wasn't really into racecars anymore, he still loved his special bedroom at Grandma's.

Nathan had spent a lot of time at his grandparents, and John knew that he felt very comfortable here. This was a big reason as to why he had decided to come here for the night. He figured if they would have stayed at their house, Nathan would have been scared, but he knew he would calm down at Mary's. John thought that if Nathan could be distracted, he would easily put this night behind him.

Emily looked over at John, who was now leaning on the doorway and said, "John, are you just gonna stand there all night, or are you gonna come say goodnight to Nathan?"

"I'm coming. I was just thinking."

As John walked over to Nathan's bed, Emily kissed Nathan on the forehead and said, "Goodnight, Nathan. I love you."

"Goodnight, Mom."

As Emily walked past John, she said, "I'm gonna go wash my face and brush my teeth. Then I'll be in to bed."

"Okay, Em. I'll see you in a minute."

John then sat on the bed next to Nathan and said, "Good-night, Nathan."

"Goodnight, Dad."

John had thought Nathan might be a little more upset about the night's events than he was, but Nathan appeared to be fine, so he kissed him on the forehead and walked towards the door.

John was almost to the doorway when Nathan said, "Dad?"

John stopped in the doorway and turned around.

"Yes, buddy?"

"Will you leave the night-light on for me?"

"I sure will, buddy."

This took John by surprise, as he thought Nathan was okay. Nathan hadn't used a night-light in years, but since there was one still plugged into the socket by the door, John reached down and switched it on. John then turned off the light switch to the room.

As he stepped through the doorway into the hall, he looked back into the room for good measure. The small night-light was lighting the room up pretty well. John looked towards Nathan and asked, "How's that, buddy?"

Nathan replied, "Good."

"Okay, bud. I love you, and I'll see you in the morning."

"Love you, too, Dad."

John walked down the hall and into the bedroom. He could hear the water running in the bathroom, which was directly across from their room. He went over to the bed and climbed in. The bed felt so good. His only wish was that it wasn't such a hot night. As John's head settled into the feathered pillow, he closed his eyes and listened to Emily, who was still getting ready for bed. He was very tired and didn't feel like going over the night's events again with Emily. He figured that when she came to bed, she would have more questions for him. John wouldn't have to worry about any questions for tonight, because as he lay there with his eyes shut, the noises around him slowly got quieter and quieter as he drifted off to sleep.

THE CALMING

Nathan had somehow managed to end up on his school playground. It was dark, and this scared him. He was all alone as he walked across the wood-chip covered ground in the direction of the swing set. He loved to swing, and this is where he spent the majority of his recess time. Nathan was wondering where everybody was and why it was so dark when he was startled by some leaves that blew by him from the gusty wind. The wind made strange noises as it blew through the trees. It howled as if it was trying to talk but couldn't figure out how.

It seemed to be taking longer than usual getting to the swings, so Nathan began to run. As he ran past the empty tetherball court where the older kids played, he thought he could make out the wind howling his name. "Naaathhaan."

He stopped for a minute and looked up at the low-lying, fast-moving, dark clouds over the playground which seemed to be howling his name. His upward gaze ended quickly as he looked at the tetherball, which had been hit by something hard and was now wrapping around the pole. A shriek of child's laughter suddenly echoed in the air, but there was nobody else to be found.

This sent Nathan running again towards the swing sets, which he could now see in the distance. Running past the teeter-totters, Nathan glanced over to see his bear Bobo sitting atop one of the empty, motionless teeter-totters. He normally would have run and gotten Bobo, but for some reason, Nathan felt he had to get to

36

the swings as fast as possible.

As the swing set neared, Nathan could see that all eight swings were taken by other children. As he approached the children on the swings, Nathan stopped and looked closer. The children were all wearing blue jeans and red hooded sweatshirts with the hoods up. They were all sitting there, motionless, with their heads looking down so he couldn't see their faces. Nathan looked down at his clothing and was surprised to see that he, too, was wearing blue jeans and a red hooded sweatshirt.

Nathan hadn't noticed the hood of the sweatshirt over his head earlier but it bothered him now, so he reached up and pulled it off. At the same time, the hood on Nathan's sweater went down so did those of all the kids on the swings. Nathan was frozen in place at the horrible sight before his eyes. The kids on the swing set were him, except they were ghostly pale and where his normal blue eyes should have been, there were no eyes at all, only gaping, dark, black holes.

All of the children's mouths were wide open as if they were trying to scream but no noise would come out. As the children sat on the swings, the darkness from their eyes slowly expanded out and engulfed their heads. It then moved down their necks and over their chests. Even their clothing turned to dark until there were just eight small shadowy children figures sitting on the swings.

Nathan's shock turned into fear, so he turned away from the shadows and began running in the opposite direction. As Nathan ran, he glanced over his shoulder and saw the eight small figures jump off the swings. They floated past him and lined up from the top of the slide to bottom. The bottom figure leaned back into the one above him, and like dominos, they all fell backwards and merged into one larger dark figure. The darkness quickly went up the slide until it had formed into one dark figure glaring down.

The wind picked up and howled for Nathan again: "Naaathaaan."

Nathan stopped in his tracks, standing about twenty feet in front of the slide. He was now standing face to face with the shadowy creature atop the slide. The dark man stared down at Nathan. The hair on the back of Nathan's neck stood up, and a tingling sensation ran throughout his upper body. This was the same feeling he had gotten earlier when he'd seen the figure on the side of the road.

Nathan felt that if he could run into the school, he could get away from the dark man. The only problem was that the dark man was in between him and the door that led to safety. As he quickly took a step to run around the left side of slide, the dark man instantaneously jumped up onto the railing on the same side and crouched down as if it was going to leap. Nathan stopped and switched directions to run around the slide's right side, but the dark man turned and jumped onto the right hand rail and crouched down as if it would pounce on him.

Deciding he would not make it to the school before the dark man would get him, Nathan turned away from the dark figure and began to run. As he ran, the haunting wind slowly cried out his name again: "Naaathaaan."

To Nathan's surprise, his big blue house was now sitting on the other side of the playground. It had a brightly lit area around it. He sprinted as hard as he could towards his seemingly welcoming house. As he approached it, he could see his mom through the large window of their living room. She was facing the window but looking down to the floor as she pushed a vacuum back and forth. Nathan tried to open his mouth and scream for her, but when he did, nothing would come out.

Scared of what the dark man might be doing behind him, Nathan glanced back over his shoulder. The dark man was still sitting crouched on the top hand rail of the slide, only it now turned to face him. Not looking where he was going, Nathan hit a large rock with his right foot, stumbled, and fell. He rolled once, and then, looking back at the dark figure, he got back up and began to run.

The dark man jumped from the handrail to the top platform of the slide and slid on its feet with its arms out, as if it were surfing down to the ground. He started running towards Nathan. Nathan turned back again to his house, where his mother was still vacuuming in the front window, and tried to scream. Still nothing would come out. He looked back over his shoulder and saw the dark man gaining on him.

With a sense of urgency coming upon Nathan to make it to his house, he ran faster than he had ever before. It still wasn't fast enough to escape his dark pursuer, and as he turned and looked back behind him again, the dark man was only a few feet away.

In one sudden motion, it leapt into the air, and Nathan collapsed as it tackled him to the ground. Struggling to get up, Nathan was thrown to his back and pinned to the ground. The dark man was straddling him with its knees, and it held his outstretched arms by his wrists above his head.

Nathan squirmed to get away, but the dark man was too strong and held him easily. It paused for a second and stared down at Nathan. Nathan glimpsed into the dark, deep black eyes with fear paralyzing him. The dark man slowly leaned down upon Nathan as if it were going to kiss him. Nathan let out a blood-curdling scream. "Mommmmmm!"

Nathan woke to the sound of a jingling bell and when he glanced over he discovered that it was only Henry, his grandmother's cat. With a watchful eye, he scanned the dimly lit room for any sign of the dark man whose vision stayed imprinted in his mind. He didn't see it but was scared that it could be creeping around the bed preparing to pounce. Horrified he screamed again.

Nathan was relieved to see his grandmother step into his room and switch on his light. "What's wrong, Nathan? Did you have a bad dream?" Nathan, looking up with streaks from the tears that were now flowing from his eyes, replied, "Yes."

Nathan was now sitting up, cross-legged, in bed, looking down with his arms folded. His grandmother sat next to him and patted his back gently. Turning towards her, Nathan could see the feet of his parents as they entered the room. Nathan's mother came over to him and comforted him. "I'm sorry, honey, but it was just a dream and you're alright now." Then, switching her attention to John, who was standing in the doorway, Emily said, "John, could you get Nathan a glass of water, please?"

John, in his half-awake daze, was relieved that it was just a nightmare. For a split second, he had thought that maybe the figure who had attacked him earlier was attacking Nathan. As he walked towards the kitchen to get Nathan some water, he felt foolish for thinking such a childish thought. Of course it was just a nightmare. He was just thinking this way because he had woken up so abruptly.

John walked into the kitchen, grabbed a glass from the cup-board, filled it from the faucet, and walked back down the hall to Nathan's bedroom. Emily was now standing in front of Nathan with Mary still sitting next to his side. Nathan must have dried his tears because there was no longer any evidence of him crying. He looked calm and was saying something to Emily that John couldn't hear. John held out the water to Nathan and said, "Here you go, Nathan. Have a drink."

Making eye contact with his dad, Nathan replied, "Thanks, Dad."

Nathan took the glass of water from his dad and, tipping it high in the air, took a large drink and, after he took it away from his mouth, said, "Ahhh."

"Pretty thirsty, huh, Nathan?" John commented.

Nathan looked back at him and, smiling, said, "Yep."

Emily looked down at Nathan and asked, "Are you sure you're alright, Nathan?"

"Yes, Mom. I'm fine. It was just a dream."

John was proud of Nathan for being tough even though he may have still been scared. John had noticed that Nathan had been doing this more and more lately. He figured that his little boy was becoming a man. With a sense of pride running through him, John patted Nathan on his head and roughed his hair up a little.

"Nothing but a little dream, huh, buddy?"

"Yeah, Dad. I'm not scared anymore."

"That's good, buddy. You're too tough of a little man to be scared by any stupid little dream, right?"

Looking back up at his dad, Nathan said, "Yep, Dad, I'm not scared at all."

Emily was also happy that Nathan was getting old enough to not be scared from nightmares anymore. She remembered that when he had one when he was younger, he would end up in their bed for the rest of the night. For such a little person, Nathan had a way of turning sideways in his sleep that made sleep almost im-possible for anyone else in the same bed. Emily figured that John's talks with Nathan about becoming a man were working because, besides the initial shock of waking, Nathan regained control of himself quickly once he figured out his scare had only been caused by a bad dream. Emily was sad to see her little guy growing up, but at the same time, she was happy to see him gaining such a strong side to his personality. Emily asked Nathan, "Are you sure you'll be fine sleeping in here by yourself?"

"Yes, Mom. I'm fine. It was just a stupid nightmare."

"Okay, Nathan. Give Mom a kiss. I'm going back to bed."

With this, Emily bent over and gave Nathan a kiss and then left the room. John said, "Alright, buddy. I'm going back to bed, too, so good night."

"Good night, Dad."

Mary was still sitting on the side of Nathan's bed. She looked at John and said, "Go on back to bed. I'll get the lights."

John left Nathan's bedroom and headed back down the hall to his and Emily's room. Emily was already lying in bed when John walked into the bedroom and closed the door behind him. He switched the lamp on the nightstand off and got back into bed.

Lying on his back, he felt Emily snuggle up to his right side and lay her head high on his arm close to his shoulder. She said, "Well, I guess Nathan was a little more shaken up than we thought."

Pulling Emily's head close to his chest, John leaned in, kissed her on the forehead, and replied, "Yeah, but he's a tough little guy. He'll be fine."

"Yeah, I know, John. I'm just so upset about everything that has happened."

"Me, too, Em, but this, too, shall pass."

Emily just said, "Yep," but she hated it when John said this. Whenever there was any type of tragedy or event in their lives that was serious, John always fell back on this saying.

Emily figured that, in this case, he was probably right. Nathan only had that nightmare because of everything that had taken place earlier in the evening. A sense of peace came over her and they slipped away into sleep.

John was lying in bed on his back with his arms folded and his hands behind his head. It was early, and he was wide awake, staring up at the thousands of little shadows that were being cast after every little bump on the white popcorn ceiling. The shadows were long and dark due to the light coming in from the rising early morning sun. It really shined through the cracks of the mini-blinds in the bedroom window.

John wasn't able to sleep well after Nathan had woken the house up with his nightmare. After John had gone back to bed, he had gotten a horrible night of sleep filled with bad dreams and tossing and turning from the humid summer's heat. Mary, like many older people in Michigan, refused to get air conditioning because, as she would say, why should you get something so expensive when you can only use it two months out of the year? So, when the warm, muggy Michigan nights came, as they did every year, a fleet of different types of fans were used around Mary's house.

John couldn't see much use for the oscillating fan on the dresser, which was slowly moving back and forth, pushing the heavy warm air around the room. For a moment, John thought about the irony of how hot Midwestern living could be in the dog days of summer and how, in only a couple of months, the heat would be gone and it would be so frigidly cold. Then Mary would have her furnace turned up so high her house would be like the Sahara desert. He found it strange that as humans age, they seem to gain things like wisdom and patience but lose physical abilities such as producing heat.

John would have easily traded the ability to produce heat in order to shed some wisdom on yesterday's events. Now that he had gotten what little sleep he did, John's mind was somewhat rested and yesterday all seemed to blur together like one big dream.

John could hear Mary in the kitchen performing some type of early morning ritual. This made him curious as to what time it was, so he quickly scanned the room for his cell phone. It was sitting on the nightstand on the other side of the bed. As his eyes moved from the nightstand, they came to Emily, who was lying on her side facing away from John. The red-and-black quilt rose up and down as she softly breathed in her deep sleep. John didn't know how Emily could stand using that big quilt on such a hot night.

Nonetheless, she looked like an absolute angel so peacefully sleeping next to him. He leaned over her with his chest pushing against her back and grabbed his cell phone from the nightstand next to her. Pulling his arm back, he tilted his head down towards Emily and gently smelled her hair. The smell of her hair and the feeling of being in her old room in the same bed that she had grown up in pushed John's thoughts back to high school, twenty years before, in the same bed.

John was a seventeen-year-old senior, and Emily was a fifteen-year-old sophomore. They had met at a high school football game and had been dating for a couple of months when he had brought up the idea of sneaking into Emily's room one night. Emily had been reluctant at first but then had finally agreed. So, one Friday night at one in the morning when Emily knew her parents were sleeping, John came over. He parked his car a few hundred yards down the road at a nearby park and walked from there. When he had arrived, Emily had already had the window open and was waiting for him.

Emily informed John she couldn't get the screen out, and John had quietly shown her how. She was wearing forest green silky shorts and a matching top. Once John had gotten through the window, they started to kiss. John slowly eased Emily onto the bed, but in the silence it seemed to be too loud, so they laid down on the floor instead.

They had been on the floor making out for a few minutes when the hallway light turned on. The light came under Emily's door and seemed to light up the entire room. Emily and John froze in horror at the fear of being caught. Footsteps slowly came down the hall and then went into the bathroom which was directly across the hall from her room. Emily and John could hear the sound of somebody peeing, and then the toilet flushed. John was holding his breath as the person walked out of the bathroom back down the hall. He had been greatly relieved when the light switched back off. It had freaked John out so badly that he left Emily's house a few minutes later and never snuck back again. Now, laying in the same room, John laughed inside thinking back at how silly the whole thing seemed now and leaned over and kissed Emily on the side of her forehead.

He looked at his cell phone and was surprised that he was so awake at six forty-five in the morning. During the work week, he got up at seven, but he wasn't as awake as he was now until after his morning shower and coffee.

What kept popping up over and over again in his alert mind was the attack and the events which had followed. He thought about seeing the dark figure on the ride to Mary's and questioned whether or not the event really happened. The feeling he got when he had seen the dark figure both in his house and on the side of the road was such a strange one. John was not convinced of what he saw on the ride to Mary's, but he was sure that he had been attacked in his house. The whole day and evening confused John, so he decided to push these thoughts out of his head. Everything was all right now, so what more should he worry about. Nathan did have a nightmare, but children have nightmares and, for that matter, so do adults. John was proud of how well Nathan got over the scare from his bad dream. Nathan was growing up to be a strong-minded man, and this made John gleam with joy.

"Enough about yesterday," John thought as he focused back on his surroundings. He could now hear the brewing noise of the old-fashioned coffee pot that Mary used. He pictured it sitting on the stove, gurgling as the brown coffee water splashed up into the clear glass viewing top so you could tell when it was done.

Mary's house was much smaller than John and Emily's. The walls seemed to be much thinner, too. By the quickening of the time between each gurgle of the pot, John could tell that there would soon be some fresh coffee served in Mary's kitchen. The thought of some good coffee with a little bit of creamer and sugar made John sit up and hang his feet off of the side of the bed. He gently rubbed the soles of his feet on the soft brown carpet of the room. Slowly raising his hands above his head, he arched his back slightly and stretched his arms high into the air. Bending over, he reached out with his left hand and grabbed his T-shirt that he had taken off and tossed on the floor in the middle of his restless night. He stood up, slipped his arms and head through the appropriate holes of the shirt, and pulled the bottom into place.

John walked towards the closed bedroom door and opened it. Directly across the hall was the house's only bathroom. He quietly pulled the bedroom door shut behind him and slipped

44

across the hallway into the bathroom. After taking care of his morning functions, John washed his hands and opened the door. Turning towards the kitchen, he looked down the hallway and scanned the walls, which were covered with family photos that had been taken over the years.

One particular large, wooden frame caught his eye, so he took a couple of steps down the hall and turned to face the photo. His eyes focused on the dimly lit picture of Mary and Steve when they had been much younger on some beach. The picture was cast in black and white, and in small white print on the bottom right-hand corner, it said, "Saint Pete Beach 1954." He had seen the picture before; it always seemed to catch his eye. Every time he saw this picture, he was amazed at how beautiful Mary had been when she was younger. The way her hair was so beautifully styled and her makeup was so perfect set off the snugly fit, white, old-fashioned full-piece bathing suit she wore. Her bosom stretched the top of the suit tightly, and it sharply curved inward to her thin waist.

As John dreamingly looked at the old photo, one of the perverted thoughts that pop up into all men's heads started playing out. He turned back towards the kitchen and pushed the thought back out of his head. Inside, he felt ashamed for the emotion he had just felt from looking at the picture, so he focused his thoughts on the smell of the coffee that was coming from the kitchen.

As he stepped into the kitchen, Mary, who was sitting at the kitchen table drinking coffee and reading the newspaper, looked up at him and said, "Good morning, John. There's coffee on the stove, and the cream and sugar are right next to it on the counter."

"Good morning, Mary. I think I'll have some of that coffee." John walked towards the stove as Mary focused her attention back down to the crossword in the paper. Her once-blonde hair was now, as she liked to call it, silver. She wore a small set of gold reading glasses about halfway down her nose. Time had been good to her, though, and she still possessed a twinkle of beauty. Seeing Mary sitting there looking like a grandmother out of some catalogue made John extra shameful for his earlier thoughts in the hallway.

Mary had a couple of mugs sitting out on the counter for him and Emily. He poured his coffee and mixed in some creamer and sugar. Turning to walk over to the kitchen table, he took a sip and said, "Mmm, mmm, mmm, that is some good coffee."

Mary looked up from the paper and humbly said, "Don't be silly, John. It's the same old stuff I make every day."

"Well, you have to let me in on your secret, Mary."

"It's Folgers from a can. Anyway, how did you sleep last night?" Mary asked, changing the subject.

"Not too well. I tossed and turned all night."

"Well, John, you did have quite a long day. I'm glad that Nathan slept through the night without any more nightmares."

"Yeah, me, too. That reminds me, I need to check in on him."

Mary smiled and said, "Don't worry, John. I checked on him ten minutes ago, and he's sleeping like a baby."

"Thanks, Mary. I'm glad to see he got a good rest of the night's sleep. I was worried about him after his nightmare."

Mary's face changed slightly to a concerned look, and she said, "He was having nightmares about yesterday. Speaking of which, could you tell me what happened?"

John began to tell Mary what had happened the day before. He was already getting tired of talking about it. He had first told the police, then Emily, and now he found himself once again going over yesterday's strange events. John was starting to tell Mary exactly what had happened when he was attacked when Mary asked, "You couldn't tell what he looked like?"

"No. It was as if he had a shadow over his face the entire time."

Mary looked intrigued and asked, "So, you say the burglar jumped on you and held you to your bed, right?"

"Yes."

"Well, did he try to choke you or hurt you in any way?"

Seeing that Mary wasn't going to buy into just half of the story, John said, "Mary, I tell you it was the strangest thing that's ever happened to me. If it was somebody else telling me what I am about to tell you, I don't know if I would believe them or not. After the burglar pinned me down, it put its mouth next to mine and sucked super hard. I couldn't breathe because he was taking all the air around my mouth, and at the same time it felt as if it were sucking the air out of my lungs. Isn't that strange?"

Mary looked very concerned now and asked, "What else do

you remember that was strange about him?"

"Everything was strange about him. Like I said, how fast he moved, how he made no noise, and how he was ice cold when I was in contact with him. Isn't that creepy?"

"John, I think that the whole thing sounds crazy, but I think I have an explanation for you."

"What do you mean, Mary?"

"Well John, I know you don't believe in ghosts or anything supernatural like that, but you know that what attacked you wasn't any burglar. Deep down inside, you know that what happened to you was beyond any explanation as simple as a regular old house burglar, don't you?"

John listened to Mary, but he thought, "Great, here it comes. Another one of Mary's old wives' tales." Mary had grown up in the hills of Kentucky, and when it came to the supernatural, Mary would have some type of country explanation for it. As John's thoughts focused back on Mary, she was saying, "So this boy in our town named Tommy Hagert woke up one night to find a dark figure standing in his doorway. He always slept with his door closed and locked, yet his door was wide open… and standing there staring at him was some strange dark figure. Tommy's parents slept downstairs, and his and his brother's rooms were upstairs. At first he thought it might be his brother Rob, so he said Rob's name. The figure didn't respond, and Tommy found himself frozen in fear with the shadowy figure staring down at him. Tommy went to reach for a baseball bat that was next to his bed, but as soon as he made a move, the figure jumped on him and pinned him to the bed. It then put its mouth over his and began sucking all of his air away.

"Rob was awakened in his room by the noise in his brother's room, so he went to investigate. He turned on the hallway light and walked towards his brother's room. As he came in the doorway, he was horrified to see a dark figure on his brother. The figure looked up at Rob as he entered the room and in a flash leapt off of the bed and ran by him down the hall. As it got to the end of the hallway, the figure began to lighten, and just as the dark night fades into dawn, it faded into light and disappeared. Rob looked back to the bed and found Tommy out of breath and a little shaken up but still alive."

John was now intrigued by Mary's story and asked, "So, are you trying to tell me that I was attacked by the same creature that attacked some kid you grew up with, and if so, what is it?"

Mary stopped and gave John a look as if to say, "I'm getting to that, just hang on a minute." Then she said, "Yes, John."

Just as Mary went to speak, John interrupted, "I don't know, Mary. It seems pretty kooky."

"Would you let me finish explaining, John?"

"Yes, Mary, go on. Sorry." John took a sip of his coffee and leaned back in his chair.

"Well, as I was saying, my friend Tommy got attacked, and for years he would tell this story to us around camp fires. He always swore up and down that it was true, and his brother Rob would vouch for it. Both of them were straight-shooters and never told lies. Anyway, I was at the fair one night out on a date with Tommy, and there was one of the psychic tents. I begged and begged for Tommy to go to take me to it, but he wouldn't because he didn't like that stuff. Well, eventually he gave in, and we went into the tent.

"When we got inside, there wasn't a lady behind a magic ball like you always see in the movies. There were two couches facing each other with a table in between them. It was all lit up by candles around the edge of the tent, and the psychic was sitting on the couch. She looked pretty normal, though, and Tommy and I sat across from her. She was instantly drawn to Tommy. She took his hands and started looking at them very closely. After a long, awkward silence, she looked up from Tommy's hands and told him that he was very special. She then went on to say that he had been visited by the Angel of Death and survived. She also told him that anybody who escapes Death will live a charmed life."

John couldn't hold back any longer and asked, "So you're telling me that I escaped death from some angel and now I am going to live a 'charmed life'?"

"Yes, John, but let me finish."

"Okay, okay. Go on."

"Well, Tommy did live a charmed life. I dated him for about a year, and then we broke up, but he went on to be a hero in the war. He came back and married a beautiful girl from our town. He went on to open a chain of drugstores across the entire state. He had a beautiful house, beautiful children, and I'm sure he is sitting with his beautiful grandchildren right now. Everything he came across in his life seemed to work out effortlessly for him."

John rubbed his chin, looked up at the ceiling, and, looking back down to Mary, said jokingly, "I usually don't believe in old ghost stories, Mary, but if it means I'll live a charmed life, maybe I should buy into this one."

"Well John, you can make fun of my story all you want, but I swear to God it's the truth."

"Oh, I'm just kidding, Mary. I know that you don't tell lies."

"I just wanted to tell you that story. You can take from it whatever you want, but if I were you, I wouldn't be worried about anything. The bad stuff has already happened to you so, now you can look forward to the good."

John said sincerely, "Well, thank you, Mary. I appreciate you trying to ease my worries." John then took the last drink of coffee and, standing up, said, "I'm gonna get a refill and go take a shower."

"Okay, I'll see you in a bit."

John filled his coffee cup and headed to their room to get his overnight bag. He quietly slipped in, got the bag, and went out of the room and into the bathroom. After his shower, he changed into brown khaki shorts and a blue T-shirt and headed back out to the kitchen. Much to his surprise, Emily was now up, sitting with her Mom at the table.

John took a seat at the table with Emily across from him and Mary to the left. As he sat down, he said to Emily, "Well somebody is up awfully early."

"Yeah, I didn't sleep too well thanks to somebody tossing and turning all night."

"Sorry, Em. I just couldn't get back to sleep after Nathan woke us up."

"I just checked in on him, and he's sleeping great now."

"Yeah, that's what Mary said."

Emily asked, "So what's our game plan?"

John answered, "I think we should wait until Nathan gets up and then go home."

"That's what I was thinking, too, John." Emily took a sip of coffee and smiled.

Mary said, "Well I guess I'm going to go get dressed." She stood up and walked out of the kitchen and down the hall, out of sight.

John said, "I gave my cell phone number to the police, and a detective is supposed to be calling me. Hopefully they catch this guy."

"I hope so, too, John. Well, I think I'll go take a shower and get dressed before Nathan gets up." As Emily said this, she got up from the table and took a step towards John. She leaned over, and they kissed. "I love you."

John looked into her blue, sparkling eyes and said, "I love you too, Em."

As she turned to walk away, John gave her a little slap on her butt. Emily turned and smiled and then walked down the hall into their room.

John turned slightly in his chair and looked out the window into the back yard. The sun was now getting pretty high, and the once-long shadow from the maple tree in Mary's back yard was getting shorter. He guessed that it was around eight o'clock. Then, waiting to see what time it really was, he looked at the clock on the wall. Seven fifty-five: "Pretty close," he thought.

John figured Nathan would be getting up pretty soon. After all, it was still summer vacation, and he never slept in when he didn't have to go to school. He also thought that Emily would be at least forty-five minutes before she was ready, so he decided he would go take a walk. John walked over to the door, put on his shoes, and stepped outside into the beautiful summer day.

Emily was just finishing putting on her make-up after taking a shower and getting dressed. She could hear somebody talking in the kitchen and assumed that it was Nathan. She brushed her teeth and picked up her bathroom items. Emily carried them into their bedroom and put them into her bag. As she walked down the hall towards the kitchen, she stopped and looked at a picture that caught her eye.

It was her parents on the beach in Florida. She knew the

picture well and had looked at it many times before. Her mom was so beautiful, and her dad was a handsome man.

She missed her father tremendously. Even though it had been three months since he had passed, it seemed like it had just been yesterday. She had a lot of dreams about him, and sometimes it slipped her mind that he was even gone. Last weekend when she'd been staying with her mother, her mom had run up to the store, and when Mary returned and walked in the door, Emily had caught herself in the middle of asking her mother where Dad was. Luckily, she had caught herself, because it would have really upset her mother.

She had been so close to her dad. She remembered growing up in this house with him and all of the special times they had spent together. Emily felt herself getting sad looking at the picture of her mom and dad, so she turned and walked down the hall into the kitchen.

Nathan and Mary were sitting at the table, and Nathan was telling a story about a fort he and his friend Billy were building in the woods behind their house. Mary sat smiling and nodding as Nathan went into every little detail about his fort.

Emily interrupted by saying to Nathan, "Good morning, Nathan. I see you are full of energy today."

"Morning, Mom. I was just telling Grandma about the fort Billy and I are building."

"Oh, that's good. Where's your dad?"

Mary then said, "He left this note saying he went for a walk."

"Oh, okay. I'm gonna watch the news." Emily turned and walked towards the living room. John's cell phone, which was sitting in the kitchen table, began to ring.

Emily turned back towards the kitchen table and grabbed the phone. She looked at the incoming number and, not recognizing it, flipped the phone open and held it to her ear.

"Hello?"

"Hi. This is Detective Flannigan with the Croswell Police Department. Is Mr. John Watley available?"

Emily paused for a second, and, remembering that John had told her the police were going to call him, she said, "Oh, hi detective. This is his wife, Emily, but I'm afraid John is out taking a walk right now."

"Oh, alright. Well, Mrs. Watley, I was just seeing if I could meet up with him tomorrow. Does he have to go to work?"

Emily said, "Well, he was supposed to leave on a business trip to Boston on Tuesday, so he took Monday off to get ready for it. I don't know if he is still going on his trip, but I'm sure either way he'll still take tomorrow off. So, he'll probably be at home all day."

"Okay. Well if you could tell him that I'll swing by your house in the morning tomorrow, that would be great."

"I'll tell him."

"Sounds good, Mrs. Watley. Thanks for relaying the message for me. Have a good day."

"Okay. You do the same. Bye." Emily flipped the phone shut and set it down on the table. She looked at her mom and said, "That was a detective from the Croswell Police. He's going to meet with John tomorrow."

"Well, that's good, Em. I hope they catch the guy."

"Me, too, Mom, me, too." Emily turned and walked back out to the living room to watch the news. She sat down on the couch and hit the power button on the remote. She flipped to *Channel Eight News*, which she watched every day.

John walked into the front door of Mary's house to find Emily sitting on the couch watching TV and Nathan and Mary sitting at the kitchen table. Emily was now dressed in a red shirt with white shorts and sandals. Nathan was eating cereal and was still in his pajamas.

Emily looked up at him as he came through the door and asked, "So, how was your walk?"

"Oh, pretty good, I guess," John replied.

"A detective from the Croswell Police Department called for you and asked if it was alright if he came by the house tomorrow."

"So, what did you say?"

"I told him I figured you'd be around so that sounded fine."

"Yeah, that will work. I'm not working tomorrow anyway. Did they catch anyone yet?"

"He didn't mention it." A look of concern came across Emily's face as she asked, "Are you still going on your business trip to Boston?"

"I don't know, Emily. I've been waiting to talk to you about that, and I was kind of waiting to see what the police said. It's important that I go, but I don't want to leave you if you're worried because of what happened."

"Well, John, I am worried. I mean, you did just get attacked in our house, and they haven't caught the burglar yet. But I was thinking that if you did need to go, I would ask my mom to come stay with us while you were gone."

"That would be fine, Em, but I want to make sure you're alright with that."

"John, of course I'm alright with it. It's my idea."

"I know, baby, but if you feel the least bit uncomfortable with me going on the trip, I want to know because I don't want to leave you if you're going to be scared."

"I swear to you, John, that I'll be fine. My mom would probably be thrilled to get out of the house for a while. We'll have a good time. I know this is an important trip, and I want you to go and not be worried about us, okay?"

"That sounds like a plan. Did you ask your mom yet?"

"No, but I'm sure it will be no problem. Actually, I'll go talk to her about it now."

"Okay, Em. I'm just going to have a nice rest on this soft couch." John took off his shoes and sat down. Emily got up from the couch and walked into the kitchen where Nathan and Mary were still sitting. As she walked away, John grabbed the remote control and began changing the channels. He wasn't really interested in what was on because he was thinking about his upcoming business trip. He knew Emily and Nathan would be fine when he was gone, but he was just concerned that maybe it would be better if he stayed.

On the other hand, John knew that if Mary came and stayed at their house while he was gone, it would be a great distracter for both Emily and Nathan. When Emily hung out with Mary, she got so wrapped up into her mother-and-daughter time that it really didn't matter if he was around anyway. If Mary agreed to stay at their house while he was gone, he decided he would go ahead with his trip. His company, American Molded Products, was in the middle of taking over two smaller companies. The trip to Boston was to finish the deal on one of the companies, so it was very important that he went. Two officers of the company had to be present in order to finish up all the paperwork. If he backed out, they would have to scramble to find somebody else to go on such short notice.

John didn't feel there was any reason to fear for his family's safety because if it was a burglar that he just happened to startle, the burglar probably wouldn't be coming back any time soon. If Mary was talking about a ghost or an angel, then what could he do about it anyway? It seemed to him that these things are out of an ordinary man's control, so how would be able to help them? The idea that it was some supernatural being was preposterous anyhow.

John's thought switched to the television as he flipped to a fishing show. He stopped worrying about problems as he watched a man in a boat lock into a fish. He hadn't been fishing in a long time, even though it was something he loved. Nathan loved to fish, too, and whenever they went, it was always a great time. When John got back from Boston, he would have to take Nathan over to the pier in Lexington. Lexington was a small town about five miles from their house. It sat high above Lake Huron and had a large rock pier that seemed to attract a lot of fish.

Nathan was always a bit sad before John traveled, so John was excited at the idea of telling Nathan that they would go fishing when he got back from Boston. This would get Nathan excited and give him something to look forward to when John got back. He laughed inside for a second as he thought of something that he had read once by Henry David Thoreau. It was a saying, and it went something like, "Many men go fishing their entire lives without knowing it is not fish they are after." Well maybe it wasn't fish he would be after, but it sure would be great to cook up some nice lake perch. It had been a while since he had a good fish dinner, and when he got back from Boston, he was going to make sure that it happened. Just like he always told Nathan, "No catchey, no eatey."

John's thoughts were interrupted by Emily who was now walking back into the living room. She was smiling and said, "Well it's a go. My mom is going to come over and stay with us while you're gone."

"Well that's good. I feel much better about going on the trip now."

Emily walked over to John, leaned over, and kissed him. She then said, "Well, you don't have to worry about us now. We'll be fine."

Looking up at Emily, John said, "Good, so that's all set. Are you ready to go home?"

"I sure am. Nathan just finished eating and is going to get dressed. I'll get our bags and set them by the door. Will you put them in the car?"

"Of course I will."

"Okay." Emily walked across the living room and down the hallway.

John's eyes went back to the television but quickly switched back to Nathan, who ran across the living room and jumped onto the couch next to his father. John put his left arm around him, gave Nathan a hug, and said, "Hey, Nathan. I see you slept in a little today."

"I was tired, Dad, and it's boring here. Let's go home so I can play with Billy."

"Okay, go get dressed, and we'll take off. Your mom is probably getting your clothes out right now." Hearing that they were going home, Nathan's eyes lit up with excitement, and he jumped up from the couch and ran down the hall towards his room. John heard the sink turn on in the kitchen. He figured Mary was probably doing the dishes from this morning. He turned his attention back to the fishing show and waited patiently for Nathan and Emily to get ready to go.

About five minutes passed when Nathan came walking back into the living room fully dressed. He was carrying the duffle bag John had packed for them yesterday in his right hand. He walked over to his dad and handed John the bag, saying, "Here, Dad. Mom told me to give you this."

As John reached out to get the bag, he noticed the zipper was half open and Bobo the bear's head was slightly sticking out. He asked Nathan, "You don't want to carry Bobo with you?"

"No. He's good in there, just keep it open so he can breathe."

Sitting the bag next to him with his left hand, he reached

out with his right hand and patted Nathan on the head. John said, "I'll leave it open. Bobo will be fine."

"Okay, Dad. Can I go play in the backyard?"

"Sure, Nathan. Just don't get dirty, or your mother will kill me."

Nathan, already walking towards the kitchen to the back door said, "I won't get dirty, Dad."

John had heard the "I won't get dirty" line from Nathan a lot of times, and no matter what, Nathan always seemed to get dirty. At least now he could tell Emily that he had told Nathan not to get dirty.

The fishing show John was watching had just ended, so he grabbed the remote and turned the television off. He then stood up and walked over to the front window and looked outside. Seeing both his and Emily's vehicles in the driveway, it occurred to him that they had driven separately. This whole time, he was thinking that they would all be riding back home together. He thought about it for a minute and thought it might actually be nice to be able to ride back by himself. He would be able to ride in peace and listen to whatever he wanted on the radio. Nathan would definitely want to ride in Emily's Suburban. It had a plasma television that folded down from the ceiling and had a DVD player under the seat. Nathan had a whole collection of movies that he kept in his mother's car. John hadn't wanted to spend the extra money for all of this, but the salesman had talked him into it, telling him that it would make trips much easier – and he was right. John didn't even know how they had ever gone on trips before this. He would always have at least one vehicle with a television in it.

John turned as he heard footsteps coming down the hallway. It was Emily, and she was carrying a duffle bag in one hand and a black square bag, which contained all her makeup and girl stuff, in her other. As she walked into the living room and set the two items next to Nathan and John's bag, she said, "I'm all ready to go. Where's Nathan?"

"He's in the backyard. I told him not to get dirty."

"Yeah, like that ever works, John."

"Yeah, I know," John said. Then turning and looking out the front window to their vehicles he asked, "You know we have two cars here?"

Emily walked over to the window and looked out. Shaking her head side to side, she said, "I didn't even think about that, and I really didn't feel like driving today."

"I just realized we had two cars a couple of minutes ago. I figured that you hadn't thought about it, either."

"Well, you were right, John, but what can you do? I'm going to go get Nathan and say bye to my mom." Emily turned and walked across the living room. John followed closely behind her into the kitchen. Mary was facing away from them at the kitchen sink, where she was diligently washing some dishes.

Emily said, "Well, Mom, I think we'll head home now."

Mary grabbed a dish towel from the counter and as she began drying her hands, she turned, faced Emily and John, and said, "Okay, honey, I guess I'll see you tomorrow."

Emily walked to the door and, as she opened it, said to her mom, "I have to get Nathan. *Somebody* let him go outside." Saying this, her eyes darted over to John and back outside. She then yelled out the door to Nathan, "Come on, Nathan! It's time to go."

Nathan, who was across the yard throwing sticks into the wind and then watching them fly back and flip onto the ground, dropped a stick he had been getting ready to throw and ran towards his mother. Smiling as he ran, he said, "Mom, I'm gonna watch *Lord of the Rings* on the way home, okay?"

"That's fine, Nathan." Emily left the door open for Nathan, who was quickly approaching, and went back into the kitchen and said to Mary, "Well, bye Mom. We're going to head out now."

John, who was now leaning against the doorway which separated the living room and kitchen, said, "Bye Mary. Thanks for everything."

Mary responded, "Okay, it's no problem, guys. Anytime. Now you know that."

Nathan was now closing the door to the backyard as he stepped inside. Emily said to him, "Go give Grandma a hug goodbye, Nathan." Nathan walked over to Mary and hugged her.

Mary said, "Now, you be good for Mom and Dad, Nathan, and when I come stay with you, I'll bake you some cookies."

"Okay, Grandma."

Mary then switched her attention to John and Emily and said, "You guys have a safe trip home. I'll see you soon."

"We will, Mom. Bye. I love you."

As John turned to follow Nathan out of the house, he said, "We'll see you soon, Mary."

John, Emily, and Nathan went outside, and Nathan ran over to the Suburban and jumped into the back. Emily got into the driver's seat as John got into his Buick. After starting her car and rolling down the window to talk to John, she honked the horn so he'd look over. John rolled down his window, and Emily said, "Are you going to follow me?"

"Sure. That'll work, Em," John responded.

John rolled his window back up and waited while Emily backed out of the driveway. John followed suit, and they were finally on their way back home. They made a few turns getting out of Sandusky, and slowly the houses began to disappear. They were now in the country, driving down the same rural route that Nathan and John had taken the night before.

The sun was shining brightly, and the blue sky was broken up every once in a while by large white fluffy clouds. As John followed Emily, he looked at the corn on both sides of the road. It was very high now, making it seem like they were driving down a gulley lined with green walls. John realized they were approaching where he had seen the dark man the night before. As they neared the exact spot, John slowed down and looked across the road to the edge of the field. There was a slight shadow being cast by the wall of corn. In the shadow, John saw a dark small object, and as he got closer, he realized it was a fence post with a bundle of barbed wire balled up on top of it. He wondered if maybe this was what he saw last night.

John had been tired from the day's events, and it had been dark in the country at night. Maybe all he had seen was a few deer and a fence post. Seeing the deer and worrying about them running in front of his car could have been enough to give him that strange feeling he had gotten. John hadn't told anyone else about the second sighting he had had the night before, and he definitely didn't plan on it. He brought the car back up to a little above the speed limit to try to catch up with Emily, whom he could see a few hundred yards ahead of him.

58

As Nathan watched *The Lord of the Rings* on the DVD player, he asked, "Mom, is Grandma coming to stay with us?"

"Yes, Nathan. She's coming tomorrow and staying for a few days while Dad takes a business trip to Boston."

Nathan replied, "Okay, okay," and he turned his attention back to the movie. Nathan was glad his Grandma was coming to stay with them. She made him feel special whenever he was around her.

He was also happy because he had known his dad was leaving for work, and he was scared to be staying in their house with just his mom. He had nightmares the last couple of times he had gone to sleep about the dark man, and he had remembered the dreams, which was unusual for him. The thought of these dreams sent a chill down his spine.

The way the dark man had stared at him made him feel really scared. It was as if it was looking right into his body and trying to pry its way into his head. Nathan didn't want him to get into his head, and both times he had dreamed about the dark man, he tried to push him away. It was hard, though. He could still see the dark man standing there. It appeared to be all around him trying to get into his head.

Nathan hadn't told anyone about the first dream in the car, and as for the second one at his Grandma's house, everybody knew about it because he had woken the whole house up. He didn't tell anybody what the bad dream had been about, though. Nathan didn't know why he hadn't said anything, either. For some reason, he just didn't want to bother his mom and dad with such a stupid dream.

His grandmother seemed to listen to him more, so maybe he would tell her about the dreams. She liked his stories, and maybe she would be able to tell him about his dream and what it meant. Nathan didn't usually feel that his dreams meant anything; he just thought they were dreams. These dreams were different, though. He couldn't get them out of his head and kept picturing the dark man staring at him, trying to get into his head and tell him something. Grandma would definitely know what the dreams were about, because she just seemed to know these things.

One of the reasons Nathan didn't want to tell his mom and dad about the dreams is that he knew they would tell him that they were just bad dreams, and then they would start asking him if he had watched a scary movie at Billy's house or if he had been playing a video game with some type of dark man in it. They wouldn't understand that the dreams he had been having were different. He was smart enough to know the difference between a dream that he had from watching a scary movie and some dream that seemed to be trying to talk to him. The dreams he had were trying to talk to him, and this really made him scared. Not wanting to think about the scary dreams anymore, he focused his attention back onto the television screen and tried to think about his movie instead.

The rest of the drive was uneventful, and soon John found himself pulling into their driveway behind Emily. After parking their cars in the garage, Emily, John, and Nathan entered their house through the kitchen.

Emily looked at John and said, "Everything seems to be normal."

"Yeah, nothing's broken or anything," John said back.

"Mom, can I go see Billy?" Nathan asked.

"I don't know. You'll have to ask your dad, Nathan."

Turning and looking at John, Nathan asked, "Well, Dad, can I?"

"Yeah, that's fine, Nathan, but be back in two hours, okay?" John knew that Billy was home because he saw their cars in the driveway across the road when they had pulled in.

Nathan had already turned to go back out to the garage to get his bike and ride over Billy's. As he walked out the door, he yelled over his shoulder, "Bye!"

The garage door closed, and Emily looked at John and said, "It's probably good he goes and plays some. He seems to be worried about something."

"He's probably still a little worked up from yesterday. I figured it would be good for him to blow off some steam. That's why I told him he could go and play. Well, I'll go put these bags upstairs."

"Alright. I'm going to take something out for dinner."

John walked through the living room which led to the

staircase going up to their rooms. After walking up the stairs, he walked down the hall to his and Emily's room. As he stepped into the room, he sat the bags down by the door and took a few more steps inside. He stopped and looked around the room to see if he got a bad feeling. As John's eyes met the bed where he had been attacked yesterday, they paused for a moment and then continued on. To his delight, John felt happy to be back in his home again. He had feared that it might feel creepy, but he felt fine and was thankful for this.

John walked over to the white curtain hanging in front of the sliding glass door and opened it. He slid the sliding glass door open and stepped onto the little balcony that overlooked their backyard. John looked down at the pool and then out over it to the small woods behind the yard. The grass and the leaves on the trees were bright with colors from the days sunlight. A sense of calmness came over John, and he walked back into his room, sliding the door shut behind him.

He walked over to the edge of his bed and sat down. He took his shoes off and lay down on the bed. Reaching over to his nightstand, John grabbed the remote control and turned on the television. An old Western was on, so he began to watch. He was pleased about being home and felt very comfortable lying in his bed. Before he knew it, sleep overcame him.

John was awakened about an hour later by Emily, who was in the room with the phone up to her ear. Once she had John's attention, she asked, "Do you care if Nathan sleeps over at Billy's?"

John thought about this for a second and figured it would be good for Nathan to hang out with his friend and answered, "That's fine, Emily."

Emily then said into the phone, "Hi, Jen. John said he didn't care, so you can tell Nathan he can spend the night." She kept talking to Jen and walked out of the room. Her voice slowly faded as she walked down the hall. John sat up in bed and looked at the television. The cowboy movie he had been watching earlier was still on. He felt refreshed after his cat nap, but he stayed in bed being lazy until Emily came up to the room and asked, "So, are you going to just lay around all day?"

He looked at her and answered, "Yeah, I think so. It just feels good to relax."

61

"Well, that's fine. You rest up before you're trip. I'll make us dinner, and we can spend a nice, quiet evening alone."

"That sounds great, Em."

Emily went downstairs to cook dinner, and John stayed in bed watching the television. John and Emily had a great dinner and then watched a movie. It felt good to have some alone time. The great evening together passed much too quickly, and soon they found themselves going to bed.

The next day, John was sitting at the kitchen table finishing the last bite of a ham sandwich which Emily had made for him. Nathan and Billy had come back from Billy's and were now in the shallow end of the pool talking about some type of race they were going to have. They had been racing to see who could do the most underwater laps. But as Nathan tossed a few underwater rings into the deep end, it seemed that the race was going to get more complicated. Their discussion of the new race seemed to be taking a long time, and John's mind began to wander.

John's eyes moved from the pool and over to the grass in the back yard. The grass could probably wait a while longer to be cut. If it wasn't for the thousands of dandelions, the lawn would look much better. His attention on the lawn was cut short by somebody knocking on the front door. Emily had run into town to get some groceries, so John got up from the table and made his way to the front door. He opened the door to find a tall man with a dark complexion and black hair in a suit.

John greeted him with, "Hi, can I help you with something?"

The man in the suit held his hand out to introduce himself and said, "Hi, I'm Detective Flannigan with the Croswell Police Department. Are you Mr. John Watley?"

John took the detective's hand and shook it. He said, "Yes, I'm John Watley. It's nice to meet you, Detective Flannigan. Call me John."

Letting go of John's hand, the detective said, "Well, John, I was just in the area and I have some good and bad news for you."

A puzzled look came across John's face, and he asked, "What's that?"

"Well, we think we know who broke into your house and a few other houses in the area thanks to a tip-off. The problem is, we haven't been able to locate the suspect yet."

John asked, "Why? Does he know you're looking for him?"

"No, we don't think that's it. His brother tipped us off and said the suspect was down in the city for the weekend selling some items he had stolen lately. We're expecting him back this evening, and then we're going to make an arrest. Of course, this is just between us, Mr. Watley. I'm sorry I can't tell you his name, but we have to wait until the arrest is made. I just thought you would feel better if you knew we were getting ready to get the guy."

John smiled and said, "Yeah, I appreciate you telling me this. It really is a load off of my mind. God, that's great you got somebody."

The detective then changed the subject and asked, "Have you noticed anything stolen from your house?"

"No, but we just got home yesterday, and I really haven't looked around that much."

The detective said, "Well, if you could take a look around for us and see if anything's gone, I'll give you a call when we get this guy and we'll go from there, okay?" The detective held out his hand to shake John's again.

John shook the detective's hand and said, "Okay, I'll look around. You go get this guy, alright?"

The detective turned, began to walk away, and said, "You don't have to worry about that, Mr. Watley. It's just a waiting game now. You have a good day."

John waved to the detective, who was now walking down the stairs, and said, "Okay, bye."

John went back into the house, closing the door behind him. He couldn't wait to tell Emily the great news. She would be so excited that they had somebody they were going to arrest. He knew that his whole thing would work out.

THE CONFUSION

It had been such a hectic morning for John. He had started his day at five-thirty in the morning and by six-thirty put all of his travel items in his car, picked up Brad, and drove to their office to get all the paperwork together for their business trip. Brad and John went to the airport, checked in for their flight, and waited in the long security line until finally they arrived at their departure gate to Boston.

The flight was uneventful, and John found time to catch up on a little paperwork he had been putting off. After getting their luggage and hailing a cab, John and Brad were finally on their way to their hotel. As they went through the Ted Williams Tunnel, the cab's radio, which had been on a news program, faded and crackled as the signal was blocked by the Boston Harbor above. They quickly passed through the neon-lit tunnel and popped up into the heart of Boston. Every time John traveled to Boston and emerged from the Ted Williams Tunnel into Faneuil Hall, he fell in love with Beantown. People of all sorts walked down the sidewalks going about their business. The old-fashioned cobblestone streets and small brick buildings of Faneuil Hall were a stark contrast to the modern large glass buildings which rose up behind them. Boston was such a beautiful city, and John thought it had such a great feel to it.

As the taxi made its way through the traffic and pedestrians, John looked at the vendors who were busy peddling their goods

64

to the tourists who frequented this area. This was, after all, where America made its stand and won its independence. Patriotic Americans came from all over the country every year to see the red painted trail of brick that led through the North End of Boston marking the legendary ride of Paul Revere. As John's eyes followed the bricks down the old cobblestone streets he looked up from the road at the surrounding buildings. The buildings still possessed an old quality to them, and John felt as if he could almost picture Paul Revere riding through the streets, yelling about the British coming.

John pulled his sleeve back a bit to look at his watch. It was almost one o'clock, and they were almost to the hotel. He figured it would probably be around two by the time they checked into the hotel and got their luggage up to their rooms. This would be good because he would have enough time to take a little nap and walk around town a little. John hadn't been to Boston in almost a year, and he looked forward to enjoying its charm. He loved good seafood and was planning on indulging in lots of it while he was in town.

As the taxi drove down Beacon Street along the large park known as the Boston Common, John looked out his window and took in everything he saw. One turn later, John and Brad found themselves stopped in front of their hotel, the Ritz-Carlton. John and Brad always stayed at nice hotels when they traveled for business. They often had meetings with other executives and business owners at their hotel, and it was important that they went off without a hitch. The Ritz-Carlton always catered to them, and this made John and Brad's lives much easier.

After checking in at the front desk, Brad and John took an elevator to the fifteenth floor. One bell boy escorted them, pushing a cart with their luggage on it. They came to Brad's room first, and the bell boy carried his baggage into the room. After that they headed to John's room next door, and after tipping the bell boy, John began unpacking his bags. Once he got everything unpacked, John laid down on the bed and took a short nap. When he woke up, he felt refreshed and ready to take on Boston. John wanted to walk around the city a bit and try to find something to bring back to Emily and Nathan.

As John walked down Newbury Street, a sense of inner peace slowly began to work its way through his body. He had been reluctant to take this business trip, but everything seemed to be alright at home. He probably wouldn't have gone, but Emily had insisted that everything was fine and that it would be good for John to get out and travel for work like he had always done.

The leaves on the trees were green and bright, but the evening air felt chilly as if it was fall. A cold front had just pushed down from Canada and created the unseasonably cool weather. John was warm enough, though, because Emily had packed a jacket for him. He would have never brought it and would have suffered the entire trip.

He loved having somebody watching out for him. Emily was the perfect match for John and always seemed to be looking out for his best interests. John felt that as a man, he sometimes needed to be a little more caring for her.

This is what brought him out on this particular breezy evening. John was going to find the perfect gift for Emily to take back to her in Michigan. He laughed inside at himself and how bad this sounded. Emily nurtured and looked out for him and Nathan every single day of their lives. John, like most men, was self-centered and more into looking out for himself than anyone else. This is not to say that he wouldn't do absolutely anything for Emily, but he had come to realize that he was lacking in the day-to-day niceties that made somebody feel special all of the time.

This really didn't matter, though, as long as he got a perfect gift for Emily so that he would be considered a hero to her. This was the great thing about Emily and one of the many reasons he cared for her so deeply. She realized that he wasn't very good at nurturing on a daily basis. As long as he brought great gifts home from trips and got her flowers on special occasions, he was the best thing since sliced bread in her eyes.

The cool air seemed to flow so easily into his lungs as he casually looked into a jewelry shop window. Then he spotted it: a necklace with a single diamond in it. Emily would love such a simple but elegant piece of jewelry. The necklace looked like it was cast in white gold. John would have to go inside and find out. Hopefully, they would have one in platinum, Emily's favorite. As John opened the door of the jewelry shop and walked inside, he thought this would be one of the best gifts he had ever brought back to Emily.

After sealing the deal for Emily's new necklace, John headed back to the hotel. John had told Brad he'd be back in an hour and then they would head out to eat and have a few drinks. John had been traveling with Brad on business trips for the last couple of years. Brad was a good business man and had grown to be one of John's closest friends.

Emily and Brad's wife, Jen, were best friends and hung out together a lot when Brad and John were on business trips. They lived across and just down the street from John and Emily's house. Nathan and their son, Billy, were great friends and also spent a lot of time together. Overall, John thought he was lucky for being blessed with such a great circle of friends for him and his family. John figured Emily and Jen were probably together right at that moment. Having Jen so close to Emily and Nathan was one of the reasons he had gone on this trip to Boston.

John was also reassured by the idea that Mary was staying with them, as Mary was comforting to Emily and Nathan. John figured that if Nathan was still scared, having his grandmother around would distract him. John had talked to Nathan to make sure he was alright before he left. Nathan was at an age where he was trying to be tough and grown up, so John found him hard to read. He hadn't thought Nathan was at all affected by the intruder until he had the nightmare at Mary's house.

He had told Nathan that the police had identified the bad guy and were trying to catch him. John told Nathan he would bring him back something cool from Boston and would also take him fishing when he got home. He thought Nathan would be alright; if he hadn't, John would have simply not gone on the trip. John loved his family deeply, and work would never get in the way if they needed him. To John, his allegiance was in family, country, morals, and then work. John had never had to face a conflict between any of these issues before, and if everything went right, he hoped he never would have to.

John had been thinking a lot about what Mary had told him about the whole incident. He wished he could have been the one to tell her about his conversation with the detective and that they had a suspect. What bothered him the most about what she had told him and what he kept thinking about was that everything she had said to him seemed to make so much sense. From the way she described the way the angel of death, as she had called it, moved without making noise to the way it would pin someone to the ground and suck his breath right out of him. This is exactly what had happened to John, and he found it hard to believe any human had done that to him.

When the dark figure had attacked John, it had made no noise. It didn't even seem to move any air around it, even though it had moved very quickly. Normally, John could feel if someone was approaching him, but it was as if the dark man wasn't there at all. After he had fought it off, it had turned and fled down the hallway, making no sound. It was as if the dark man had run out of the room and vanished into thin air.

Mary's story was hard to believe, but John was also having problems believing that his attacker had been human. The whole incident confused him, and he was skeptical of any theory about what had really happened. John had never been one to believe in ghosts, the supernatural, and especially not an angel of death that had been sent to kill him. Even though Mary had told him the story and he didn't feel that she would make up something like that, he was very hesitant to believe it. Mary was from the country, and John felt she believed in all kinds of crazy things.

One of the biggest flaws he could find in her story was the fact that he was still alive. If he had been attacked by some angel of death sent to take his life, why hadn't it finished the job? John's bullheaded male ego kept popping up in the back of his head, telling him that he had fought the dark man off and that this was the reason he was still alive. Deep down inside, though John knew the truth. For some reason, the dark man had just quit attacking him and left.

The dark man could have easily killed him if it had wanted to. So why didn't it just finish the job? And why would a supernatural being send a physical creature to kill somebody? Wouldn't it be easier for God or whoever sent this angel of death to just shoot John with a bolt of lightning or make him die of a heart attack? The whole thing just didn't add up to John.

Why couldn't the police have just caught someone? Then everything would have made sense in John's eyes. They had a suspect, but until he saw him, John didn't believe that any human could have done what this dark man had done to him. John had just woken up, so he did realize that the way he remembered the incident could have been a little misconstrued. He had never been the type of person that could just wake right up and start going about his business. For the first fifteen minutes after John woke up, he was clumsy and bleary-eyed.

Thinking of the way he was when he woke up made John realize that maybe it was just a house burglar that had attacked him. The burglar may not have thought that anyone was home, and when John had startled him, he may have panicked. The burglar made a split-second decision to try to get rid of the only person that knew who he was. Maybe he wasn't trying to suck John's breath out at all. John could have just been a bit confused from having just woken up. The weight of the burglar combined with John struggling could have caused him to be extremely out of breath and could have been the factor which made him feel dizzy and light-headed.

The problem with this was that it didn't make sense to John, either. There were just so many things from the incident that didn't add up, and John hated when things didn't add up. He was, after all, an accountant, and this meant that his whole life revolved around making things do just that – add up. John was a logical thinker, and he hated the fact that something in his life couldn't be rationalized.

He was approaching his hotel now. As he looked across the street, John noticed some joggers running through the Boston Common. Beyond them, some other people were sitting on a bench, throwing some food to the surrounding pigeons and ducks. As his eyes slowly moved across the park, he noticed so many people doing different activities that he stopped walking for a moment. John wanted to take in everything he saw to try to deflect his train of thought. Looking out at all of the commotion distracted John and he smiled because he liked this.

As John's mind eased into a better place from watching all of the chaos of the city, he began to be less distracted from his troubling thoughts. Feeling better inside made his thoughts turn to Emily. This was exactly why she'd wanted John to go on this trip. She could care less about the business side of it. It was just like her to tell John to go through with his trip just so he could

69

ease his worried head and forget about the attack.

This made him grasp the necklace box in his jacket pocket a little tighter. As he briefly squeezed the box, a feeling of gleam ran through him for his purchase. John was glad he had gotten Emily the necklace, and it even pleased him more thinking of the idea that she cared for him so deeply and was always looking out for him.

John began walking again towards his hotel. The day seemed to be getting better and better as it passed. As John approached the front of his hotel, the doorman opened the door for him and said, "Good afternoon, sir. A lovely day for a walk."

John nodded his head to the doorman, smiled, and replied, "Yes, it is."

After making a quick stop at the bar in the lobby and, grabbing a couple of whiskey and cokes to go, John took the elevator up to the fifteenth floor and walked down the hallway towards his room. He stopped by Brad's room, which was next to his, and knocked on the door. As John knocked several times, he said, "Room service, Mr. Crowly."

John heard some movement on the other side of the door and then the sound of the deadbolt unlocking. Brad opened the door and said, "Hey, buddy." Brad's eyes shifted down to the drinks in John's hand, and he continued, "Looks like room service in this joint is okay. Come on in."

Brad held the door open as John walked in and over to the sitting area of the room. John placed the drinks on the table and sat facing the window which overlooked the entire Boston Common. It was now beginning to get dark outside, and from up this high above the ground, the park looked extremely dark, with winding trails of lit sidewalks weaving their way through the darkness. John took the necklace out of his pocket. Opening the case and holding it out towards Brad, John said with a sense of pride, "Hey, look at this necklace I just bought for Emily."

Brad leaned over and looked at the necklace. He began to slowly shake his head back and forth and, in a half-joking tone, said, "Oh great, John. Here you go again buying something like this for Emily. Why do you always do this to me? Now I'm going to have to go out and get something nice for Jen or else guess who's going to be the bad guy?" Brad reached out with his left hand and gently touched the necklace. He leaned in a little closer to get a better look at it and said, "This looks expensive. Couldn't you have just gotten Emily a bottle of perfume or something a little cheaper than a diamond necklace?"

John replied, "Man, Brad, you are so cheap. You make a ton of money and never lift a finger around the house. Jen totally does everything for you and Billy from your laundry to your cooking. She even does all of your bills, and you're an accountant! The least you can do for her is go out and get her something nice. You know it would make your life much easier; it would thrill Jen to death. You know you can't take that money with you when you die. It wouldn't hurt you to part with some."

"I know, John, but it's like my father told me: you can't have it and spend it, too."

John had a discouraged look on his face. The one quality he didn't like about Brad was how cheap he was when it came to spending money on Jen. When it came to going out or buying toys like fishing rods and tools, Brad had no limit, but when it came to his wife, his wallet always seemed to be closed. John said, "You know Brad, it's only money. You can always go make some more."

Brad replied, jokingly, "Well, by the looks of that necklace, I'm going to have to go make a whole bunch to make up for this trip. Thanks to you, Diamond Jim."

John closed the necklace box and put it back in his jacket pocket. Taking a drink of his whiskey and coke, he changed the subject and asked, "So, what's the game plan for tonight?"

Brad looked towards the window across the Common and said, "I figured we could go get some good Italian in the North End and see where the night takes us."

John took another drink, thought about it, and replied, "Italian, yeah, that sounds good to me. But I'm going to go call Emily first. Then I'll be ready to go."

"Alright, take your time. I want to finish watching the news anyway."

John stood up, walked to the door, looked back at Brad, and said, "I'll give you a call in a little while, then." He opened the door, walked into the hallway, and headed for his room. John didn't care what Brad thought about the necklace; he was happy he got it for Emily.

Emily was putting a bag of popcorn into the microwave for Billy and Nathan. The boys were in the living room playing some shooting game on Nathan's PlayStation 2. She didn't really care for violent video games, but she let Nathan play them anyway. Emily wasn't one to buy into the idea that violent video games could make your children become serial killers. She knew that Nathan had been raised properly and could handle mature subjects such as death. He clearly knew the difference between a video game and real life. Emily felt that if parents of children who committed some brutal crime would have just spent a little more time teaching their kids the difference between right and wrong, they wouldn't have to blame a video game for their crime. Children in Emily's eyes were a direct reflection of the amount of quality time invested in them by their parents.

The popping from the microwave was now slowing, and it was quickly followed by the sound of the microwave beep indicating that its cooking cycle was now complete. Emily opened the microwave door, grabbed the sizzling bag, and placed it on the counter. As she pulled the bag open, the hot steam burned her hand. She jerked her hand away from the steam and yelled, "*Ouch, that is really hot!*"

Mary and Jen were sitting at the kitchen table looking at some photos that Emily had had developed earlier in the day. Jen looked up from a photo and said to Emily, "That microwave popcorn gets me every time."

Pouring the popcorn into two bowls that she had gotten out earlier, Emily replied, "I know. Isn't it amazing how hot it gets?"

Mary then added, "That's why I still cook popcorn the old-fashioned way, in a pan."

Emily's eyes moved to her mother, and she said jokingly, "Mom, you still do everything the old-fashioned way."

"Yes, I do, Emily, and there's something to be said for that, you know what I mean?"

Rolling her eyes at her mom, Emily teased, "Yeah, that you're retired and have all the time in the world to make some popcorn?"

Emily grabbed the two bowls of popcorn and took them into the living room where Nathan and Billy were laying on their stomachs on the floor. They were facing the television, and both of them held controllers to the video game they were playing. Billy and Nathan's eyes were both glued to the television as Nathan said, "Just shoot him, Billy, then I'll run in behind you."

Billy replied with a hectic sense of urgency in his voice, "I'm trying, I'm trying. I just can't hit him."

Emily crouched down and set the popcorn on the floor next to the boys and said, "Here's your popcorn, guys."

Without looking away from the video game, Nathan and Billy said simultaneously, "Thanks." Then Nathan asked, "Can we get some Coke, too, Mom?"

"Sure, Nathan. I'll be back in a minute."

Emily went back into the kitchen, and the cordless phone, which was sitting on the counter, began to ring. She picked it up and looked at the caller identification display. It read "Ritz-Carlton" and had a six-one-seven area code displayed. Realizing this was John calling, she looked at Jen and said, "Hey, Jen, this looks like John calling. Can you get the boys some Coke for me?"

"Sure. No problem," Jen replied and stood up from the table to walk towards the refrigerator.

Emily answered the phone: "Hello?"

On the other end of the line, John responded, "Hi, Em, how're you doing?"

"Oh, good, John. I was just getting Billy and Nathan some popcorn."

"Well, if the boys are eating popcorn, all must be well on the Western front."

"Yeah, everything is good. Jen is over, and we're just talking about taking the boys on a day trip to the zoo tomorrow."

"They'd like that," John responded.

"I think we're going to go in the morning," Emily said and then asked, "So, how's your trip going?"

"It's fine. We had a pretty hectic morning, but we made it here safely and got checked into the hotel. I just got back from a walk around town. We're just getting ready to head out on the town to get some dinner now."

"Jen said she talked to Brad before she and Billy came over."

73

Sensing Emily was discouraged because he didn't call her as soon as he checked in, John replied, "I was just so excited being back in Boston again, I just had to get out and enjoy the city some."

Emily asked, "It's kind of late for dinner, isn't it John?"

"Oh, Em, it's only eight o'clock. That when everybody eats in the big city."

"Oh, is that so? Well, be careful tonight in that 'big city,' okay?"

"Sure thing, Em. Tell Nathan I said hi, and I love you both."

"Okay. I love you too, John. Have fun."

"You too, Em. Bye."

John hung the phone up and stood up from the edge of the bed where he had been sitting. He walked over to the large window which overlooked the park below his room. John's eyes were once again drawn to the lit sidewalks that cut through the darkness of the park. He could see the flickering of headlights from the cars that made their way around the outside of the park. Traffic seemed to be much lighter now, but it was still very busy compared to what John was used to.

Looking straight down directly across the street to the sidewalk along the edge of the park, John watched people walking. Everybody in the city seemed to walk very fast and deliberate as if they were always in a rush to get to their destination. A few were carrying bags, and others were empty handed. A jogger wearing a reflective vest ran in front of the hotel and took a left into the darkness of the park. The sidewalks were well lit, and as the jogger got farther into the park, the bouncing reflections of his safety vest slowly faded out of sight.

As John stared off into the park, a tingling sensation began to build in his upper body. The sensation was familiar to John, and he quickly turned around and scanned the room for the dark man who had caused such a feeling in him before. John half expected to see the shadowy figure standing in his room. The lights were all on, and to John's relief, the dark man was nowhere to be found.

John noticed that when he had turned away from the window and looked into his room the strange feeling began to fade. As he looked back out the window, the hair on the back of his neck stood up, and the tingling sensation he had just felt intensified immediately. John's eyes scanned over the park and followed one of the lit sidewalks out of the darkness to the street directly below the hotel. His eyes stopped on a shadowy figure standing on the edge of the sidewalk. The figure was leaning against the wrought iron fence which enclosed the park. A shadow was cast over the dark man by the large oak trees which ran along the street. John stared down at the figure which he could sense was staring back at him.

John set his drink on the edge of the window and rubbed his eyes, as if they were playing some trick on him. He wondered if what he was seeing was real or if he was just freaking himself out. A lady wearing a brown hat walked directly past the dark man, but she didn't seem to notice him and passed quickly. Then, a man walked a dog past the figure, and neither the dog nor the owner paid it any attention. John thought this was really strange; he could not even believe his own eyes anymore.

He tried to convince himself that the dark figure had to be an ordinary person leaning against the fence in the shadows. He was just getting himself worked up for nothing and letting his imagination get the best of him. But then the figure darted across the road toward the hotel. Even though it was out from the shadows of the trees and in the light of the streets, John still couldn't make out any of its features, as if a shadow was still being cast over the figure's entire body.

John leaned up against the glass, looking down to the sidewalk directly below the hotel. The dark man made its way under the green awning of the entrance to the hotel and out of John's sight. What should he do? Was the dark man coming into the hotel to get him? As fast as it was moving, it could be coming up the stairs for him as he sat there.

John began to panic, rushed to the door of his room, and grabbed the handle. Should he open it or not? He would simply fall over and have a heart attack if he opened the door to find the dark man standing there before him. But John knew he had to open it and get to Brad's room before the dark man got there so he quickly opened the door.

The hallway was empty as John took a step into it and looked both ways up and down. To John's right was Brad's room and the elevators, and to his left was the stairway. The humming noise from the lights that lined the hall seemed to be much louder than it had been before. John took a right and began to walk towards Brad's room. When he was only a few feet from Brad's door, John heard the ding from the elevator as it arrived on his floor. John paused and stared down the hall at the noise of the now opening elevator doors. The doors opened completely, and yet no one came out. They stayed open for a few seconds and then closed together.

John heard a door open behind him and spun around to see what was there. A short, middle-aged, blonde man in boxer shorts and a T-shirt walked out of the room just past John's. The man was holding an ice bucket and was walking towards John in the direction of the ice machine located by the elevator on his floor. John stepped up to Brad's door and knocked two quick taps. A few seconds later, the bolt was unlocked, and Brad opened the door. When Brad saw John standing there, he said, "Well, that was fast. Did you already talk to Emily?"

John looked nervously up and down the hall one more time and, returning his attention to Brad, he answered, "Yes."

"Well, don't just stand there, John. Come on in. I'm not quite ready to go out yet, but it won't take me long."

John walked past Brad, who was holding the door open. As he passed, he said, "I need to sit down for a minute."

Looking closer at John and thinking to himself that John didn't look very well, Brad asked, "Are you alright? You look kind of pale."

John sat down in the seat and answered, "Yeah, I'm fine. I think I just need to get something to eat."

"Alright. Just give me a few minutes, and I'll be ready to go." Brad grabbed a small shaving kit out of his suitcase which was sitting on the dresser next to the television and walked into the bathroom.

John leaned back in the chair he had sat in and, with his face pointed upward as if he was looking at the ceiling, he shut his eyes and sighed deeply. His mind was racing much too fast, so he slowly inhaled and exhaled a few times trying to gather his thoughts. Was what he just saw real? Was John to believe that he just saw the dark man staring at him? He thought to himself, "Come on, John, you've got to pull it together. So you got attacked in your house and now you're mind is working overtime on this, causing all of this nonsense to go through your head. The police have a suspect, so you need to quit thinking so much and move on. You're a full-grown man, after all." He couldn't keep letting his imagination run wild with this. Why was he having such a problem letting all of this go?

The first time John saw the dark man after his attack was on the side of the road when he and Nathan had been traveling to Mary's. John had decided that the corn field sighting had just been because of all of the stress he'd been through on that day. The question was: why was he seeing things now? He had gotten up early and had been running around all day. He had rushed from his house, then to the office, then to the airport. John had never been a big fan of flying, so this was also stressful for him. Then, they arrived in Boston in the middle of a busy work day and took a taxi through the chaotic city traffic to finally get to their hotel... Maybe all these events, piled up on top of worrying about Emily and Nathan at home, had finally taken their toll on his overloaded brain.

John stood up from the chair and looked at the window again. His eyes scanned the road directly below the hotel. There was nothing out of the ordinary to be seen. The regular pedestrians lined the sidewalks, and traffic formed around the park as usual.

John thought that maybe he should talk to Brad about everything that had been going on. Brad was pretty smart and could have some good insight on the entire situation. On the other hand, John didn't want Brad to think that his trusty business partner was going crazy. If John told Brad about some dark man that he had seen twice since his attack, Brad might think that John needed some psychological help. John definitely didn't want Brad to think he was going crazy, so he decided he wouldn't talk about it.

John thought to himself that he might just need to get out tonight and relax. The last few days had been very stressful, and they seemed to be taking their toll on John's mental stability. He would block all of the recent events of his life out of his head and just go out and have a good time. He needed to blow off a little steam, and everything would be fine. John's brain had been working overtime lately, and tonight he was going to shut it down and not worry about anything.

As John thought about going out tonight, he reached to his back pocket for his wallet to see how much money he had. He figured he might have to stop and use an ATM machine. To his surprise, his back pocket was empty. He had taken his wallet out when he used his calling card to call Emily, and he could picture right where his wallet was. It was sitting on the nightstand next to the phone. Well, he had to go get it if he was going to go out tonight. John thought about how ridiculous his current dilemma was. He was frozen in his chair because he was scared of some dark man that his mind was creating. John began to get mad at the thought of being scared by some boogeyman like a little child. He decided he was done being scared.

John stood up from his chair and headed towards the door to go get his wallet. He decided not to care about any dark man anymore. As he passed by the closed bathroom, John said loudly, "Hey Brad, I'm going to run back to my room to get my wallet."

Brad's muffled voice came back through the door, "Alright, I'll be ready in a couple of minutes."

John opened the door to the hallway and looked out. He stepped into the hall and looked left and right, but there was nobody to be found. John then walked over to his door and opened it with the key from his pocket. Even though he was trying not to be scared, he was still a little shaken up inside. John pushed the door open until it abruptly hit the doorstop. He scanned his room, but there seemed to be nothing out of the ordinary. As John slowly walked into his room, his eyes caught some movement on the far wall. They quickly focused on the curtains, which were ruffling around from the heater located in front of the window.

John's eyes moved from the curtain over to his nightstand, where he spotted his brown leather wallet. Scanning the room once again, he walked along the side of his bed and over to the nightstand. He grabbed his wallet then turned to walk out of his room. As John turned, his eyes caught a movement in the doorway and darted to it. John jumped and inhaled loudly as he was startled by Brad who was standing in the doorway.

Seeing John's startled reaction, Brad said, "Calm down, John, I'm just seeing if you have any toothpaste."

John's heart was pounding rapidly as he quietly exhaled a sigh of relief. He then said, "God, Brad, you scared the shit out of me."

"Sorry, man, I thought you knew I was standing here."

John, feeling silly for getting startled so easy, replied, "I've just been a little jumpy since the whole burglar incident."

Changing the subject Brad said, "Do you have any toothpaste?"

"Yeah, I have some." John was now walking towards the doorway where Brad was standing. He went into the bathroom, reached into his shaving kit, and grabbed a tube of toothpaste. Turning to Brad and handing it to him, he said, "Just keep it until we get back tonight."

"Alright," Brad replied as he turned and walked back down the hallway to his room.

John closed the door to his room and followed Brad. As he was walking, he stuck his wallet into his back right pocket. When John got to Brad's room, Brad was already standing in front of his sink opening the tube of toothpaste. John walked by him and proceeded to the chair he had been in earlier and sat down.

John closed his eyes and tried to slow his racing mind. He had never really been stressed out before but now was beginning to realize the toll it was taking on his brain. It was a strange and unfamiliar feeling to John. He had known people his whole life who complained of stress and being at their wit's end but had always thought they were just weak-minded. Maybe after John got back from Boston, he would take a vacation. Nathan still had a couple of weeks left of summer vacation, so he could take Nathan and Emily on a little trip up north.

Brad walked out of the bathroom and said, "You ready to go?"

John stood up from the chair and replied, "Yeah, I'm pretty hungry. Let's get going."

Brad and John walked out of the room and down the hallway to the elevators. They exited at the lobby and made their way to the front of the hotel where a line of taxis waited for the hotel guests. The taxi took them to the North End where they ate at La Famiglias. After finishing a great Italian meal, Brad asked John, "So, what do you want to do now?"

John was looking at the check and said, "I don't know. I don't really feel like going out."

Brad looked surprised as he asked, "Why not, don't you feel good?"

John replied, "My stomach is a little upset." He said this even though his stomach felt fine. He just didn't feel like going out tonight.

"Well, that's fine with me, John. We can go out tomorrow night. It's been a pretty long day."

John and Brad paid their bill and went outside to hail a cab. The streets of Boston were loaded with taxis, and one soon stopped for them.

On the ride back to the hotel, John stared out the window and looked at the passing sights. He really wasn't taking them in, though, as he was deep in thought. John was upset that he had been so shaken up by a simple house burglary. What if he had a real incident? How would he handle that type of stress? John had always considered himself a strong person, but now he was questioning himself. How could such a little thing as an intruder in his house cause his whole mind to have such a meltdown? He was seeing things that didn't exist and then getting himself all worked up.

The ironic part about everything was that he had been so worried about Emily and Nathan that he never even thought it would be himself who had such a problem. Emily and Nathan seemed to have moved on from the entire incident without any problem at all, yet he was stuck thinking about the dark man until he actually made him appear. His own mind was creating a huge thing over nothing at all. John didn't know how he could stop it, but he had to figure it out.

The ride back to the hotel went quickly. After taking care of the cab fare, John and Brad headed inside. As they were walking in the lobby, Brad asked, "Hey, do you want to stop in at the bar for a drink?"

John was reluctant, but since he was back at the hotel, he felt much better. He replied, "Sure, why not?"

They walked into the bar, and John said, "Hey, I'm going to go use the bathroom. Will you get me a whiskey and coke?"

Brad answered, "No problem."

Brad headed for the bar as John took a right and headed for the bathroom. After relieving himself and then washing and drying his hands, John headed to where Brad was sitting. Brad was taking a drink and looking up at a baseball game on the television. Seeing his drink sitting in front of the empty bar stool, John asked, "So how's that whiskey and coke treating you?"

Brad looked towards John and took the drink down from his mouth. He swallowed and replied, "Pretty good. Yours is right there." Brad nodded his head in the direction of John's drink.

John sat on the stool next to Brad and took a drink of whiskey and coke. He then said, "That's just what I needed."

"You know, John, whiskey and coke probably isn't the best thing in the world for an upset stomach."

John replied, "I know. The truth of the matter is, my stomach feels okay. I just didn't feel like going out tonight."

"You didn't have to make up having an upset stomach if you felt like staying in. We're friends, John. You can tell me the truth." Brad took another drink and looked back up at the television.

John thought about what Brad said for a minute and figured Brad was right: he could tell him what was wrong.

John looked at Brad and said, "I have had some problems ever since I was attacked."

Brad asked, "What kind of problems?"

John cleared his throat and said, "Well, I've been worried a lot and stressed out. I just don't feel like myself. You know what I mean?"

Brad answered, "Yeah."

John continued, "It's weird because I've never felt like this before, and it's tough. I just keep thinking of the same thing over and over again. I just want to get it out of my head so I can move on. You know what I'm saying?"

"Yep."

John continued, "I mean, what do you think, Brad? Do I seem stressed out?"

Brad answered, "Yeah, a little. You were kind of acting strange before we went to dinner. Then you just wanted to get back to the hotel. That's not like you at all, John. When we travel you're usually the one who keeps me out all night."

John said, "I know, so you can tell I'm a little stressed?"

Brad answered, "I can, but I wouldn't worry about it if I

were you. You know, with everything that has happened to you, I didn't even figure you would have gone on this trip."

"Well, I wouldn't have, but the detective said they had a suspect they were getting ready to arrest, so I figured everything would work out. Emily insisted that I went, too. So that's why I came. I'm starting to wish I would have just decided to stay home, though. My mind could have definitely used a rest."

Brad replied, "Well, maybe once they catch this guy you won't be so stressed anymore."

John thought about this for a second and replied, "Yeah, you know, I bet I will feel a lot better once they catch him. You're probably right."

Brad tilted his glass high in the air and drank the rest of his drink. After drinking it, he said, "Why don't we have another drink? That'll probably help you."

John said, "What the hell; it probably can't hurt me any, huh?" He finished his drink as Brad waived the bartender over to get them another round.

Nathan and Billy were in the woods behind Nathan's house working on their fort. Billy looked over to Nathan and said, "We're out of nails. Go run up to your house and get more."

Nathan, who was leaning a piece of plywood against a tree, said, "Okay, no problem." He took off running toward his house. He knew where his dad kept a lot of nails in the garage.

As he was zigzagging through the trees, the shadows from the high sun above the large oaks trees flickered in his peripheral vision. Something to Nathan's left caught his eye, and he looked over at it. He was shocked to see the dark man he had dreamt of running about one hundred feet from him in the same direction. Nathan stopped, looked over, and the dark man went behind a large oak tree. Nathan walked a little left and then right, trying to get a better view behind the tree in the distance.

He didn't see anything, so he began to run in the same direction towards his house again. As Nathan took off running again, he saw the dark figure running parallel to him. Nathan stopped again, but the dark man once again stopped behind a large tree.

Nathan tried to look behind the tree again by walking a little left and right. He could see most of the way around the tree but still couldn't see behind it.

Nathan yelled, "Billy, is that you?" Nothing but silence followed. Nathan was beginning to get scared now and took off toward his house in a sprint. As he was swerving in and out of trees, he looked to his left and again saw the dark man. The dark man took off much faster than Nathan and darted ahead of him to the open field which was in between the woods and Nathan's house. As Nathan approached the edge of the woods, he could see the dark man in the field, now running toward Nathan's house.

Nathan ran to the edge of the field and then stopped, watching the dark man, who ran around the front of his house and out of sight. Nathan was now terrified and didn't want to go home.

A loud clap of the thunder broke the silence, and Nathan jumped and let out a loud scream. Clouds blew in from the horizon towards Nathan's house, and it quickly became dark outside. The clouds brought a downpour of rain with them. Nathan began to get cold as the wind picked up and the temperature dropped. What was going on? Nathan was scared and confused. He crossed his arms and began to shiver as his clothes became soaked from the downpour. The wind began to howl and he could hear it saying his name: "*Naaaathaaan.*"

He could feel the dark man around him, trying to get in his head. It was trying to talk to him, but Nathan blocked it out. The lights were on inside his house, and he could see his mother vacuuming inside. He was alarmed to see the dark man standing behind his mother. She was busy vacuuming and didn't see it.

Nathan tried to run to his house, but his feet were slipping on the wet grass. He looked up from his feet back to the window, and the dark man was still standing there, staring out at him. Nathan's feet slipped in the muddy grass, and he fell hard onto the ground.

Nathan jumped up in bed as he awoke from his dream. He looked around his room and down to the trundle bed where Billy was sleeping. Billy had stayed over and was breathing heavily as he slept.

Nathan was a little scared and said, "Billy?" and then paused for a minute. He then said a little louder, "Billy, you awake?"

Billy moved a little but didn't wake up.

Nathan then said much louder, "Billy, wake up!"

Billy woke up, looked over at Nathan, and asked, "What's going on?"

Nathan, not wanting Billy to know he was scared, said, "I just had the craziest dream."

Billy replied, "Yeah, well I'm sleeping. Why don't you tell me about it tomorrow?" Billy closed his eyes and rolled over.

Nathan lay silent. He wasn't as scared as he had been the last time he had dreamt of the dark man. He tried to think of good things as he closed his eyes to try to go back to sleep. Soon, sleep came again for Nathan.

John fumbled his key until he got it to fit into the door of his room. He and Brad had quite a few drinks down in the lobby bar. Brad had just gone into his room. John opened the door and staggered into his room. He closed the door harder than expected and was startled as it slammed shut. He walked to the bathroom and grabbed some aspirin from his travel kit. He poured himself a glass of water, put two aspirin in his mouth, and drank the entire glass of water.

John took the glass, refilled it, and gulped one more glass. He always took a couple of aspirin and drank lots of water after drinking liquor. Somebody had told him of this trick in college, and he had been using it ever since. He set the glass down on the counter and leaned over the sink. The water was still running from when he had gotten his drink. He cupped both of his hands together and splashed some water on his face.

Standing back with his eyes closed, he reached over to the towel holder and grabbed a small wash cloth. He figured this would work fine and dried his face off with the wash cloth. John opened his eyes to see his reflection in the mirror. His eyes seemed bloodshot, and he thought he looked pretty drunk. He laughed quietly at the drunken man staring at him in the mirror.

John didn't feel stressed at all anymore. He actually felt confident and strong. John thought, "Why couldn't the dark man show himself now?" He was in a scrappy mood and thought, "I'd love to hand out a can of whoop-ass. For that matter, I'd hand out a whole barrel of whoop-ass to the dark man."

He half-jokingly looked under the sink and said in a quiet whisper, "Come out, come out, dark man. Where are you?" John then peeked into the shower. John figured, "The dark man doesn't even want any of this because he knows what I'd do to him."

As John turned to walk into the room, he knocked into the sink and hit the bottle of aspirin which was on the edge of the counter. The bottle slowly tumbled in the air, and aspirin flew everywhere as it hit the bathroom's marble floor. John looked at the pills, stepped over them, and said, "You see what you did, dark man? You went and made me spill my aspirin. If I find you, I'm gonna rip you to pieces."

John stumbled out of the bathroom and into the main area of the room. He looked all around for the dark man. He had his fists clenched up in the air, and as he took a couple of jabs, he said, "You want some of this, dark man? Come and get it." John was now punching the air in front of him. He stopped punching and put his arms down. He sighed and said, "That's alright, dark man. You just keep coming around me, and one of these days, I'll get a hold of you."

John collapsed on his bed. He looked over to the phone and saw the message light blinking. He sat up on the side of the bed and picked up the phone receiver. He leaned over and looked on the phone's base to see how to get his messages. After studying it for several minutes without finding where to get his messages, John hung up the receiver and lied back in bed.

He thought to himself that he would just get the message in the morning when he was sober enough to figure out how to work the phone. Thinking of the morning reminded John he needed to arrange a wakeup call. Well, this was simple enough, so he picked up the phone and dialed zero.

The phone rang several times, and a man answered, "Good evening. Front desk. How may I be of service, Mr. Watley?"

John paused and thought about what time he needed to get up.

After a moment, the man at the front desk said, "Hello? Sir, are you there?"

John finally said, "Oh, yeah, sorry about that. I was just

thinking about what time I need to get up."

The man responded, "Not a problem, Mr. Watley. What time would you like to receive a wakeup call?"

John replied, "Eight."

"Okay, sir. Is there anything else I can do for you?"

John thought and said, "Nope. I just needed the wake up."

"Excellent. Have a good night, sir."

John responded, "Okay, you do the same." John hung up the phone and laid his head back down on the pillow. The room was spinning, so he left the light on. John quickly fell asleep.

THE PROPHECY 4

John was surrounded by darkness that seemed to be rushing all around him. What happened? He was just sitting by his pool on a warm summer's day watching Nathan swim. In the blackness, a ringing noise kept blaring out around him every couple of seconds. He turned but couldn't find where the ringing was coming from. His mind seemed to be melting together with the darkness and racing back to his thoughts. He heard more ringing. Where was the noise coming from? Slowly the darkness began to fade into light, and John's thoughts came together.

He opened his eyes to see the white fabric of the hotel's pillowcase. As he scanned the room, John realized the phone was ringing. His head was throbbing, so he quickly reached over and grabbed the phone off of the nightstand. Holding the phone to his ear, John said sleepily, "Hello?"

A peppy girl on the other end of the phone responded, "Good morning, Mr. Watley. I am calling to give you your eight o'clock wake up."

John paused for a moment and said, "Okay, thanks." He hung up the phone and lay his head back down on the pillow. He stared at the red numbers of the alarm clock next to his bed that read 8:01.

The message button was flashing on his phone, so he picked up the receiver again and dialed the message service. He remembered vaguely trying to retrieve the message last night but in his drunken stupor couldn't **figure** out how to use the message system. The automated service told him he had one new message, so he pressed the appropriate button to hear it. Emily's voice came to life and said, "Hi John. I tried to call your cell phone, but I just got your voicemail. Anyway, Detective Flannagan called and said they caught the guy who broke into our house. The detective said he'd give you a call on your cell phone. I just wanted to let you know the good news so you wouldn't be as worried. Anyway, everything is good here. Nathan and I are fine, so don't be worrying about anything. We love you."

John held the phone to his ear even though the message was over. Emily's message was now setting in, and John became a little happier hearing such good news. He finally hung up the phone and lay his throbbing head back down on the cool, soft pillow. John remembered that he had a couple of aspirin followed by a few glasses of water the night before. A friend of his in college told him this trick, but it never seemed to work. Nonetheless, John continued this ritual every time he drank in the hopes of it one day working.

His head was pounding, but he could handle a little headache with the good news he just got from Emily. He wanted to call her to get more details but figured she might not be up yet. Besides, if he was going to make it to his meeting by nine, he didn't have any time to waste. As he stood up to go to the bathroom, he couldn't help but feel happy. This was great; now that they caught somebody, his mind could be at ease. This would stop it from creating the dark man anymore. All he needed was a little closure on the whole incident, and since they caught somebody, John figured what more closure could he ask for.

John got into the shower, and as the warm water ran over his head, he massaged his head, trying to wash his headache away. He was reminded of what his father, Frank, always said: "This, too, shall pass." John's dad had died ten years prior. Frank had smoked since he was seventeen years old and had died within three months of being diagnosed with lung cancer. John wondered for a second if his father would still be alive if he had not smoked.

Nathan had never even known his grandfather. This upset John because he had learned a lot about life from his dad. He wished he could teach Nathan about life as well as his father had taught him. Since the death of Emily's dad three months ago, John became the only male role model in Nathan's life. John took this role very seriously. He felt it was very important to teach children how to be good people in life. This is not to say John didn't feel that a solid education in school wasn't important, but he felt that the way people live their lives is just as important. He always tried to teach Nathan to be good and to treat others the way he would want to be treated. John's dad had taught him this, and so far it had been working pretty well. Frank had also taught John to never let the little things get him down. This is why he said, "This, too, shall pass." Frank told John that the big financial problems in life like house payments and other bills would always be there, so people never really let these problems get them down. The little problems in life, that occur unexpectedly could bring a person down. His dad always said to just wait them out, and eventually everything would be all right again.

John had his eyes closed while he rinsed shampoo from his hair. As the last of the shampoo was washed away, he opened his eyes, stepped out of the shower, and began to dry off. John wrapped his towel around his waist and walked over to the sink. As he reached for his shaving kit, the phone began to ring. John knew it was probably Brad due to the two rapid rings that identified a room-to-room call. He picked up the phone and said, "Hello?"

Brad responded with, "Morning. How are you feeling today?"

"All right. I got a headache, but besides that not too bad."

Brad then asked, "So how long until you're ready to go?"

John answered, "Give me about fifteen minutes, and I'll be good."

"Okay. Well, give me a call when you're ready. I'll be in my room waiting."

"I'll call you in a bit. Bye."

"Talk to you soon, John."

John ended the phone call and grabbed his electric razor from the shaving kit. After shaving and brushing his teeth, John got dressed in a black suit with a red tie. He walked over to the mirror and looked at himself. He was satisfied with his appearance, so he called Brad. After telling Brad he was ready to go, he walked into the hall. Brad was waiting for him, so they went downstairs to the street to get a taxi.

Emily finished drying off from her morning shower with a large white towel. She stuck her legs through the small holes of a pair of white silk panties she had folded neatly on the counter. The leg holes expanded as she pulled them up her tan legs until they were snugly in place. Emily was excited that they had caught the burglar who had attacked John. She didn't tell John, but she had been scared and didn't feel comfortable with him going to Boston. Even though her mother had come to stay with her and Nathan, she still didn't feel completely secure without John at home. But since they caught the guy, Emily didn't have to be scared anymore.

She hoped that John got her message. Emily had been worried about him ever since he was attacked. John hadn't been himself for the last couple of days. He had been quiet as if he was in some type of deep thought. This worried Emily because in all the years she had known John, he was never quiet. John had always been an easy-going, funny person, and this is what Emily loved so much about him. Now he just sulked and didn't say much.

Emily knew that John's routine had been messed up. Like most men, John did the same things on the same days, week after week. John liked his routine, and Emily could see he was upset by being knocked out of it. This was one of the major reasons she had pushed to have him go on his business trip. She knew that he enjoyed traveling and that it would help to push him back into his routine. Emily figured that if John would have stayed home, he would have just continued sulking around the house until they caught the burglar. She thought that John might be a little worried on his trip but figured Brad would keep him pretty entertained. Now that they caught the burglar, John could finish his trip with no worries and come back home. She figured he would be back to his old self once he got back.

Emily walked out of the bathroom over to her dresser. She grabbed some white shorts and a bra from the drawer and put them on. She went to her closet and put on a maroon shirt. She and Jen were taking the boys to the Detroit Zoo. Emily had asked her mother to go with them, but Mary said she wasn't up for it.

That was okay, though, because even though she loved spending time with her mom, Emily and Jen would have a much better time by themselves. There would be a lot of walking at the zoo, and Emily had noticed her mother couldn't walk all day anymore. Seeing her mother getting older made Emily sad.

Emily had never thought her parents would get old, but the death of her father really opened her eyes. She had never really seen her parents for their true age, but in the last few months, she could definitely see her mother aging more. Since the death of Emily's father, it was as if Mary had given up on life. Emily used to go to her mom's house, and they would walk for a couple of miles. The last time they had gone on a walk was about six months ago, before her dad got sick. She had a hard time believing that her mother's health had deteriorated that much in such a short period of time. Emily figured that her mom might be depressed and that she would get back into the real world again soon. At least Emily hoped so.

Mary seemed to be more like her old self when Nathan was around. This is one of the reasons that Emily had asked her to come and stay while John was gone. Well, she hoped that her mom would get out of this depression. As Emily realized she'd been daydreaming, she realized she was late, so she quickly put on some makeup.

Through the crack in Emily's partially open door, Nathan asked hurriedly, "Mom, are you ready yet?"

Emily responded, "Yes, Nathan, I'll be done in a couple of minutes. Go downstairs and watch some TV."

Emily heard her mom's muffled voice yelling from downstairs, "Nathan, let your mom be. Come on down here, and finish your cereal."

Nathan yelled back downstairs, "Okay, Grandma!"

Emily heard the sound of Nathan running down the hall. She finished getting ready then went downstairs.

Emily walked into the kitchen and said, "Come on, Nathan, let's go." She turned her head toward the living room and yelled, "Mom, we're leaving now."

Mary got up from the couch, walked over to the kitchen, and said, "You kids have a good day. Nathan, you be good for your mom."

Nathan was now turning the knob to go into the garage. He looked back at his grandmother and said, "I will be, Grandma. Bye." He opened the door and walked into the garage.

Emily walked toward the open door and said to her mom, "We'll be back around dinner time. Are you sure you don't want to go?"

Mary responded, "I'm fine, Emily. You go on ahead. I'm going to make some dinner for you, so don't eat on the way home, alright?"

"Okay, Mom. Bye." Emily walked into the garage.

Mary turned around and walked back into the living room. She sat down on the couch and took a drink of her coffee. She was tired, so she stretched out on the couch, pulling the throw blanket over her. Mary had been sleeping a lot since the death of Steve. She still woke up early, just like she and Steve had done for their entire lives. When Steve was around, she always stayed up for the entire day. Now, though, she didn't really see the point of being awake so much. The day seemed to pass much faster while she was sleeping. Mary curled up on her side, and soon sleep overcame her. The Zoloft Mary had been taking for her depression made her sleep very soundly.

Mary awoke to the sound of the telephone ringing. She reached over the coffee table and grabbed the cordless phone. She pushed the Talk button and said, "Hello?"

John replied, "Hi, Mary. Is Emily around?"

Mary answered, "No. She and Jen took the boys down to the zoo today. They should be back around five."

"Okay, Mary. Well, I will be back in a couple of hours."

Mary answered, "Okay, John. Bye."

Mary set the phone down and thought about the conversation for a moment. Did John say it was only a couple of hours until five? Her eyes darted to the clock sitting above the television. It read 3:12. Mary couldn't believe she had slept for almost the entire day. If she was going to get dinner ready, she needed to start working on it. Mary got up from the couch and walked into the kitchen. It took Mary about 45 minutes to prepare the chicken she was making for dinner. She set the thermostat of the oven to 400 degrees and placed the tin-foil-covered chicken and stuffing on the top rack. After setting the timer for one hour, she poured herself a glass of orange juice and looked out at the overcast, cooler day. Mary figured the chicken would be done by the time Emily and Nathan got home, and she had made extra in the anticipation of Jen and Billy also coming to dinner. She was looking forward to hearing all about their big trip to the zoo.

Brad and John were riding in a white Lincoln Town Car heading to Salem for the evening. The shuttle service vehicle was driven by a dark-haired, skinny young man. John figured he was around 25 years old. He was friendly and had shaken their hands earlier; telling them his name was Greg.

One of their business colleagues had invited them up to his house in Salem for a party that evening. John didn't want to go, but Brad had talked him into it. They were getting up to Salem a little bit before the party so they could check out the downtown area.

They made a few turns down some side streets and suddenly came to a small downtown area. The street was fairly modern, but the buildings surrounding them seemed very old. The driver of the shuttle car looked back in the mirror at Brad and said, "Here you go, guys. Downtown Salem, just what you wanted."

Brad looked ahead at the driver and responded, "Just go ahead and drop us off right here".

The driver eased the Lincoln to the curb by the sidewalk and stopped. He looked over the back seat, handed a business card to Brad and said, "You give me a call about 45 minutes before you want to be picked up and I'll head right on up here."

Brad took the card, and then responded, "Alright, we'll give you a call".

John and Brad opened their doors and stepped out of the car. As the Lincoln drove away, they began to walk down the sidewalk. The downtown area was littered with small shops and restaurants to serve the steady flow of tourists who came to see the town that had become famous from killing a bunch of young girls for being witches. John looked at Brad and asked, "So, what now?"

"I figured we could check out some of these souvenir shops. I need to find a gift for Jen and Billy, and I thought I could find something original in Salem. Jen has already got enough Cheers T-shirts for a lifetime." Brad smiled at his own joke.

John laughed and responded, "I don't know, Brad. Nobody can have enough Cheers T-shirts around."

Brad walked up to a large storefront window, stopped, and after looking inside, said, "I'm gonna check this place out, John."

John looked in the store but wasn't interested, so he said, "I'll sit on the bench and wait for you."

Brad was opening the door as he turned and said, "Alright, buddy. You sure you don't want to trade the necklace in on some nice witchcraft stuff?"

John answered, "Nope, I think I'm good."

Brad responded, "Your loss then," and walked into the store.

John looked up and down the sidewalk, walked over to the wood bench in front of the store, and sat down. The bench was cool, as was the evening air. As John leaned back and settled onto the bench, he looked up the street. There were a few people looking in the shops and enjoying the beautiful evening. John loved the fall and was happy to see that it may start early this year.

As John's eyes slowly moved down the street, he was happy to see nothing out of the ordinary. He was expecting to see the dark man, but he seemed to have disappeared from John's mind since he had received the good news from Emily this morning. John let out a huge sigh of relief. He was feeling normal again now, and this felt good. He was hoping that everything would be okay, and with the capture of his attacker, all seemed to be well.

John still hadn't talked to Emily, so he reached into his pocket and pulled out his cell phone. Quickly scrolling to the number and then pushing send, John put the phone to his ear. It rang twice, and Emily's familiar voice came through the small phone. "Hello?"

"Hi, Em. How's my favorite little blonde this beautiful evening?" John said in a chipper voice.

"Hi John, I'm doing fine. By the sounds of it, I take it you got my message?"

"I sure did. They got the guy. That's great news. So what

else did the detective tell you?"

"He said the burglar was from down in the city and had just moved up here a couple of months ago. Apparently, the house he had been renting is full of goods from around the area. When you get back, you're supposed to go meet with the detective to see if you can find anything that was stolen from our house. I've looked over the entire house but can't find anything missing."

"He didn't have time to grab anything, but I'll give the detective a call. So how is Nathan?"

"He's great. We were down at the zoo today, and Billy and Nathan loved it. They are in watching television now. Mom, Jen, and I are just going through some old photos I found..."

Emily was still talking, but John's eye was caught by a red light coming from the shop across the road about a hundred yards away. John squinted a bit to try to see better. A couple walking arm in arm walked by the shop. As they walked by, they slowed and looked in. The couples' faces glowed red from the light from inside. The couple quickly lost interest and continued walking. Had that light been on the whole time he had been here? John had looked up the street before and not noticed it. On the other end of the phone, Emily's voice got louder. "John, hello, are you there?"

John paused and said, "Yeah, we must have a bad signal, Em. Sorry."

"Well, anyway, everything is going well here, John. Why don't you give me a call tomorrow? I'll be home all day."

John's eyes were staring back down the street at the eerie red light. He then said, "Okay, baby, I'll do that. I love you."

"Love you too, John," Emily replied.

John took the phone from his ear and put it back in his pocket. He got up from the bench and took a couple of steps down the street toward the red-lit storefront. He felt as if something were calling him, pulling him toward the store. John paused for a second and then looked into the store where Brad was. Brad was at the register putting change from his purchase into his wallet. John figured he would wait for Brad and then get him to walk down to the store with him.

With a big smile on his face, Brad walked out of the store. He held a small bag up and then said, "Well, it's no diamond, but I think I did alright."

John replied, "That's good. You've got to keep the little lady happy." Looking away from Brad, John nodded his head toward the store with the red light and said, "Let's cross the street and walk down that way."

"All right, John," Brad said as he looked down at his watch. He then continued, "Tom's house is down that way, and we should start heading there. I thought we would have more time than this, but the ride here was longer than I expected."

John naturally looked at the time on his cell phone and stepped toward the edge of the road, saying, "Well, let's get going. I want to look at that shop down here." John looked both ways up and down the street for traffic and crossed. As he got to the sidewalk on the other side of the road, he paused and waited for Brad. Brad got to the sidewalk and said, "John, slow down. We have ten minutes until we have to be at Tom's house, and it's less than five minutes away."

John and Brad walked together toward the red-lit shop. As it approached, John sped up his walk a little, stopped and looked into the storefront. The window was covered by a red curtain with a light behind it. Marked in white printed letters on the front window was only one word: "Psychic."

Brad caught up with John and asked, "What's up, John? You want to go see the psychic and get told a whole bunch of crap about you?"

John looked at Brad and responded, "No, I just saw this red light from down the road and wanted to see what was up with it."

Brad continued to walk past the red shop and said, "Let's get to the party and have some drinks."

John turned and started walking with Brad, saying, "Alright, let's go."

They proceeded up to the next side street and took a left. Tom Tablen's house was just up a little hill and on the left. All the houses on the street were quite large with huge wrap-around porches. Large oak trees lined the well-lit, nicely manicured street. Brad knew the directions to the party well, so he led the way up the sidewalk and on to the front porch. By the amount of cars parked in Tom's driveway and in front of the house, it appeared it was a pretty big party. A low roar of people's voices and the occasional laugh could be heard as Brad and John stepped onto the front porch. John rang the doorbell, and a few seconds later, a tall, middle-aged woman answered the door. As she held the door open for John and Brad, she said, "Hi, I'm Tom's wife, Cindy."

No sooner than she said this, Tom came walking down the hall saying, "Brad, John, glad you could make it. I see you've met my better half, Cindy."

Brad smiled and, holding out his hand to shake Tom's, he replied, "Yes, we met." Then, looking from Tom to Cindy, Brad continued, "You have a beautiful house."

Cindy smiled and responded, "Oh, thank you very much. We love our house." Tom put his arm around John and led them into the living area. As they walked down the hall, he said, "Come on into the party, guys. We're gonna have dinner in about an hour. Let's have a drink."

The dinner party ended up being just what John had expected. Everybody loaded up on cocktails before dinner in Tom's large living room. There was a fire going in a stone-covered fireplace. After a few drinks, the party of about sixteen people moved into a large dining room with one of the biggest tables John had ever seen in a house. Everybody comfortably fit around it with a few spots to spare.

The dinner was a typical fancy dinner with salad, soup, and bread, and the main course was lobster. It was a bit messy to eat, but John loved New England lobsters.

Cindy had hired caterers for the party. Two young men in suits served the food and made sure everyone's wine glasses were always full. Tom was a great host and kept everybody amused at dinner with some funny stories about their children. John was happy that the conversation hadn't switched to business yet. John had a rule that he lived by, and that was never talk about work unless you are at work. He absolutely hated talking about work on his off time. This was the reason he had been so hesitant to come to the dinner party. Brad had talked him into coming by telling him there wouldn't be much business talk. Thus far, Brad had been right, and John was having a good time.

After dinner, Tom invited anybody who wanted to smoke a good cigar to come with him. Brad and John both enjoyed cigars so they and about five others from the party joined Tom in a large den in the back of the house. Tom told everybody in the den about the two large smoke-eaters which filtered the air in the room. The den was lined with cherry bookcases full of books. They complimented the large, overstuffed, dark leather sofas and chairs that furnished the room.

John was sitting in one of the large chairs smoking an Arturo Fuentes cigar. He held the cigar in his right hand and a whiskey and coke in his left. He was starting to catch a good buzz from all the drinks. John was really enjoying himself and was pleased Brad had talked him into going.

John enjoyed seeing the way people lived in other places besides Croswell, Michigan. It wasn't that Croswell was such a bad place; it was just that it was, after all, the Midwest. His friends back home would never have a party this fancy. Most of the parties he attended back home were barbecues. None of his friends would ever sit in a fancy den smoking cigars for entertainment. At most of the barbecues he went to in Michigan, the entertainment was horseshoes. The only thing that people usually drank was Busch beer, and one never had to worry about the conversations switching to business. Most of John's conversations back home with his friends involved hunting or fishing.

John had gone to a small college in Michigan called Olivet. A professor in one of his accounting classes had once told him that to be successful, you must have a little bit of knowledge on all of the issues. John took this seriously, as he did most things. He read the *New York Times* everyday and always watched the evening news. The amazing thing is that this secret his professor had told him seemed to work very well.

Brad wasn't from around Croswell and was well educated. He kept up with all the local, state, and world news also. This was the main reason John enjoyed his company so much. John still had friends that he had grown up with, but they seemed limited in their activities. They would go up north to hunt or canoe for a weekend. A big vacation for them would be going to Cedar Point all the way in Ohio, and the thought of traveling to Boston would be totally insane for most of them. He respected his friends for being this way, though. John actually was kind of jealous of them. John could never be happy just staying in one place. He loved to travel and felt that he had just about been everywhere in the world.

"Hey, John." Brad was standing in front of him.

John came out of his daze asking, "Hey, Brad, what's up?"

"Not too much. You were just sitting there staring. You feeling alright?"

John smiled and stood up. He put his hand on Brad's shoulder and said, "I'm feeling great, as a matter of fact. I'm gonna go take a little walk and smoke this cigar."

Brad responded, "Okay, do you want to go back to the hotel or something".

John smiled again and said, "No, I'm fine. I just need to go out and enjoy some fresh air."

"Alright." With this, Brad turned to walk back to the group gathered around Tom who was now showing off pictures of a new boat he had just bought.

John grabbed his jacket and slipped out the door without anybody noticing. He didn't figure anybody would even realize he was gone. John walked off the brick walkway leading to Tom's house and onto the main sidewalk. He stopped, took a large puff from his cigar, and blew the smoke up into the calm night air. John smiled at the billow of smoke rolling up into the streetlight. He turned and looked toward the main street. Traffic seemed slow as a car would cross only every couple of minutes. The red light that John had seen earlier was dimly coming around the corner.

John had wanted to check out the shop earlier, but Brad wasn't into it. For some strange reason, John felt as if the shop was calling at him to come to it. John figured he had some time, so why not go check the place out. He wasn't much into psychics, but he did believe in listening to that little voice in the back of his head. He felt that when people feel they should do something, they should follow through. He felt the need to go to the shop, so that's exactly what he was going to do. There was no traffic, so John crossed the street and began to walk down the sidewalk. As he approached the main street corner, he picked up the pace. He felt a strong pull toward the shop as he turned right onto Main Street. The red light gleamed out of the front window of the shop now approaching on the right. John walked in front of the shop and turned to faced it. There was a lamp closely behind the red cloth hanging over the window. Besides this light, the shop seemed to be dark inside. There was no sign on the door, so John assumed by the shop's appearance that it was closed.

John figured it wasn't that big of a deal. He hadn't known what to expect on his little walk. Maybe his walk was just that, a simple walk on a beautiful New England night. As John turned to walk back toward Tom's house, he noticed a silhouette of a person moving around in the shop. Maybe it was open after all. John stepped up to the door and pulled on it. To John's surprise, the door was open, so he walked in.

John took a look around at the dimly lit shop. The front of the shop was quite normal, but toward the back, the only lighting was provided by candles. There were a few sitting areas lit with candles and a table in the middle. The sitting areas were separated by cubicle walls normally seen in offices. The only difference was that these cubicle walls were covered in red cloth instead of the standard gray or black.

As John peeked around one of these walls, he was startled to find an older woman with gray, wild hair sitting quietly on a couch. She appeared to be reading a book, but as soon as John's eyes came into contact with her, she calmly looked up from it and said, "Hello, how may I help you?"

John stood there silent for a moment. What was he to say? He wasn't even sure why he had come in here himself. Unsure, John responded, "I don't know what you can help me with, if anything. I was just out for a walk and wanted to check out your shop."

The woman sat down her book and said, "It was the red light, wasn't it?"

John thought about this and responded, "Yes, actually, I think it was."

"Ahh, I knew it!" The woman explained, "I told you that red attracted people!"

John looked around, confused about who the woman was talking to. He didn't see anyone else so, he asked, "Who did you tell about the red?"

"Oh, nobody. I just talk to myself a lot. Never mind that. Why don't you have a seat? Would you like some tea or coffee?" The woman gestured with her hand toward the small kitchen area in the corner.

"No, thanks. I don't need anything to drink," John replied.

With a hand gesture toward the chair across from her, the woman said, "Well, why don't you have a seat then?"

John hesitated, and the woman, seeing this, said, "It's alright, honey. Go ahead and sit down." Then, holding her hand out to shake, she continued, "My name is Jenny."

John took her hand and said, "Nice to meet you. I'm John."

Jenny's hand was warm and inviting, so after she introduced herself, John felt much more comfortable. He walked over to a large cushioned chair and sat down.

Jenny's eyes moved up and down John, and she said, "You know, I get a lot of people like you in here."

With a puzzled look on his face, John asked, "Like me? What do you mean by that?"

"You know, John. The type of person who doesn't believe in psychics or the paranormal but has to come in here anyway. It's as if you cannot resist the curiosity of my red window. Well, John, this is a business, so I'll tell you straight up, my fee is one hundred dollars." Jenny calmly looked at John to see his reaction.

"For one hundred dollars, what will you provide me with? Do you have a magic ball or something?" John was a little buzzed from the cocktails earlier, and when he drank, he tended to get a little obnoxious.

Jenny laughed and replied, "Oh, John, of course I have no magic ball. I just know things about people. I don't need a magic ball because as soon as I meet someone, I know more about them than they do themselves. Like you, for instance, John. Do you remember when you stopped earlier with your friend?"

"Yeah, but you've probably been sitting here all night, so you could have easily seen me. Just telling me that you saw me earlier isn't going to convince me that for one hundred dollars you aren't going to tell me a bunch of bullshit," John replied.

"John, it's late, so why don't we cut to the chase. When I saw you earlier, I saw more than just a man. I could see a man who was carrying a huge burden. A burden he is not able to understand, but I can. If you let me, I can tell you more about it."

"Okay," John replied as he reached into his back pocket for his wallet. He took out one hundred dollars and handed it to Jenny. He figured, what the heck, it was only a hundred dollars.

After all, John had felt a pull toward the shop earlier, so there must be something to what she was going to tell him.

Jenny took the hundred-dollar bill and put it into her pocket. She then looked at John and said, "Could you let me see your hands?"

John leaned forward to the edge of his chair and put his hands out. As he was doing this, Jenny leaned forward in her chair. She then reached out and took John's hands. Jenny had her fingers on John's palms as her thumbs gently rubbed the top of his hands. Her head was leaned down looking at John's hands. Jenny sat for several minutes in the same position without saying a word.

John was beginning to feel awkward, so he asked, "Jenny, are you okay?"

Jenny looked up for a second at John and calmly shushed him. Her eyes moved back to John's hands as she regained concentration. John sat quietly as Jenny remained silently focused in deep concentration. Jenny's hands felt warm against his at first, but the longer they sat there, the hotter they felt. John thought at first that it was because they had just been holding hands too long, but it wasn't that sweaty awkward heat that occurred when this happened. The heat was intensifying rapidly. John figured if it got much hotter, it would be painful. Not wanting to interrupt Jenny's concentration but worried he would soon get burnt from Jenny's hot hands, John said quietly, "Jenny, it's getting really hot."

Jenny didn't look up or even recognize John's attempt to communicate with her. She just kept staring down at John's hands in silence. The heat was now uncomfortably hot to John. He gently pulled back from Jenny, but she firmly grasped his hands. John, beginning to feel panicked, said, "Jenny, hello, is anybody there?" The heat was now painful, so John tugged harder and said, "Jenny, let go." Jenny still held his hands firmly, so John pulled back hard and broke her grasp. She sat back hard onto the couch and still said nothing.

John, surprised by the whole situation, said, "Jenny, are you okay?"

Jenny's eyes were closed now as she slowly rolled her neck around as if she were stretching. Her eyes opened, and a smile came across her face. She looked at John and said, "That wasn't so bad, now was it, John? You lasted much longer than most people do. You're a very strong energy source."

John was still stunned by the whole incident and asked, "What was that? What just happened? Was it normal?"

Jenny let out a little laugh and answered, "It was perfectly normal, John. The heat that you felt was our energies connecting and communicating."

John touched his hand to his face as if he was seeing if the heat was real. The touch was hot, and he asked, "Well, what did you find out during our little energy encounter?"

Jenny sat silent for a moment. She rubbed her chin and replied, "John, I don't really even know where to start. Most people that come into my shop have little problems they are dealing with. Yours, on the other hand, is a very complicated situation. I will tell you what I know about what has been going on with you lately, but as far as what you need to do, I don't have the answer."

With a confused look on his face, John asked, "What are you talking about?"

Jenny looked John in the eye and replied, "You know what I'm talking about, John. The dark figure that attacked you and has been following you lately. Remember, John?"

John's face went completely expressionless as shock set in. Until now, he had been the only one to see the dark man. He had written it off as mental stress from being attacked earlier in the week. John cleared his throat and replied, "Yeah, I remember. I just don't know what to say."

"You don't have to say anything, John. Let me try to explain everything as clearly as possible. Then, if you have any questions, I will try to answer them. Okay?" Jenny asked.

"Okay."

"The dark figure you have encountered lately is called a Gatherer. A Gatherer is a source of energy that has come to get another source. The energy it is coming to get is a part of it on the other side. In order for it to move on, it must become whole again. I know this all sounds pretty strange, John, so let me try to explain it better. You see, when we aren't in these physical bodies we are given to live on earth, we exist in the form of energy. Once your body dies, you return back to your natural energy form. The problem with existing in the form of energy is that you live forever and you know all the answers that we can't figure out on earth. In

103

order to experience emotions and having to face one's own mortality, we must take a physical life form. The earth was created as sort of a playground for us so we could experience these things. The problem that had to be addressed is how we experience these if we know everything. What we came up with was to split up your energy into a few different bodies in order to weaken the knowledge it contains.

So, you are John, but you may only be one fifth of your true form. Your energy could have split up to form five different humans, all experiencing different mortal experiences. When you split up energy into several forms, a problem arises when the individual energies return from mortal existence. If all the energies aren't done with their mortal lives, the energies who return into pure energy form go into a type of in between world. The stronger the energy – say for example, four of your five energy parts had ended their mortal experience and reunite into one, waiting in the in between world – it would be able to make some type of physical presence known amongst us."

John interrupted, "So, you are saying the dark man is actually my energy trying to..." John formed his fingers into quotations in the air, "'gather' me, the remaining one fifth of it, so it can be whole again?"

Jenny took a sip of a glass of water she had next to her and replied, "I use you as an example only, John, in order to show you what makes a Gatherer. No, I think if the Gatherer was after you, it would have gotten you by now. Gatherers don't see like we do. They only feel energy. I think the Gatherer was looking for energy close to you. You've confused and probably weakened the Gatherer some, but it will gain its strength and be back. Energy moves in waves, and this is what a Gatherer sees. Your family probably has similar wavelengths as you. Thus goes the saying, we're on the same wavelength. Do you understand what I'm getting at, John?'

John thought for a second and responded, "So, you think it is trying to get somebody in my family?"

"Yes, John, I think it is looking for somebody who is very close to you. Your energy is very strong and overshadows whoever it is looking for. With you being such a powerful source of energy in addition to being similar to the energy it is looking for, I can see how it accidentally tried to gather your energy instead of whoever it was really after. It got confused. Next time, it will make sure it gets what it is looking for."

John was just realizing what this meant and asked, "So, who is it after, and how can I stop it?"

"John, I do not know who it is after. As for stopping it, that is impossible. We are unable to compare to the power of natural energy in our mortal bodies. You are much too weak to mess with a Gatherer. The only reason you survived the last encounter is that once the Gatherer connected with your energy and saw that it wasn't the right one, it quit attacking. Do not be foolish enough to try to believe that you actually defeated the energy."

John had thought much about the attack and knew that Jenny was right, so he responded, "I realize that I could have been killed easily by this Gatherer. It's just that if it is going to try to get Emily or Nathan, of course I'm going to try to stop it. I can't just sit by and watch something hurt my wife or my son. I don't care how powerful it is, I will stop it from hurting my family."

Jenny shook her head then responded, "No, no, John. You do not understand. You will not even be given a chance to defend anybody. It will simply attack whoever it is trying to gather when you are not around. You can't be around your wife and son every moment forever. Once it gets what it is after, it will leave, and you will be left with whoever it did not kill. You cannot stop it. There is nothing you can do, John."

"But, I..." John was interrupted by his cell phone ringing in his jacket pocket. He looked down at it. It was Brad. John had been gone for over an hour now.

Jenny looked at John and said, "You can answer it, John. I could use a break anyway."

John was pale. There was so much he needed to find out. Was all this true? He flipped his phone open. "Hello?"

Brad's slightly slurred voice came loud through the speaker, "What the hell, John? I said I could cover you for a walk. How much longer are you gonna be? Where the hell are you, anyway?"

"Oh, it's just a nice night out. I'll be back soon. I'm just taking a walk."

"Well, hurry up. We still have to make our rounds and say goodbye to everybody. I'm gonna call the taxi service and tell the guy to head back up here. Okay?" Brad asked.

As John was talking to Brad, he walked back up by the front of the store. John looked at his watch. He had at least 45 minutes, according to what the driver had told him. That gave him plenty of time, so he said, "Alright, Brad, I'll see you in a few minutes."

John turned around and looked back into the store. Jenny wasn't where she had been, so he walked over to the sitting area. Her water was still there, as was the book she had been reading earlier.

A door in the back of the store opened, and Jenny came out. She was wiping her brow off and walking toward John. He looked at her and asked, "What happened? I thought you left like in a scary movie or something."

"No, John. I just had to go to the bathroom, my friend," Jenny replied. "I'm not feeling well, John, so I will need to be closing up soon. I know you have many more questions, but I do not have the answers you need. I'm going to warn you, John. Do not mess with the Gatherer or try to interfere, or it will cause you and any of your energies in mortal form to have a lifelong of torment. You need to go on living your life like normal, John. Whatever's going to happen is going to happen. You must not try to stop it. Do you understand, John?"

"No… I mean, this is just so much so fast. How do I even know what you're saying is real or if it's just a bunch of bullshit?" John asked.

Jenny was now walking around the store blowing out the candles. She responded, "John, you have seen the Gatherer. You were even attacked by it. You know what I'm saying is for real. You are a smart person that has been placed in a very difficult situation. Gatherers are very tricky, John. If you get in one's way, it will cause you and all of your energies torment for the rest of all of your existences. Please, John, just try to live your life normally. Do not interfere. I have told you everything I know about it." Jenny picked up a jacket that was on a chair and put it on. She walked to the front door of the shop. "I must close now John. Come on, and I'll let us out."

John walked towards the door. As he stepped outside followed by Jenny, he asked, "This has been so much. I don't even know what to think about everything that has happened to me.

Now you come along telling me that it is coming to kill somebody I know. I mean, what in God's name am I supposed to do, Jenny?"

Jenny was now locking the dead bolt on the door. She turned, looked John in the eyes, and responded, "There is nothing you can do, John." She then pointed towards a red Honda sitting on the side of the road and continued, "Well, this is me. I'm sorry I couldn't tell you more, John. Bye." Jenny opened the driver's door and got into the driver's seat.

"Wait. I have more questions."

"That is the problem with you, John. That is why I am rushing off. I can see, and I realize that the situation is out of your control, but you can't. I am scared that by telling you this, I will condemn myself to a lifetime of torment."

Jenny was getting frustrated at John not listening to her and said, "I have to go now. Please, this is all I know."

John didn't know what to do or say as Jenny pulled the door shut. A second later, the Honda started and pulled onto the empty street.

John stood staring at the taillights until they faded into the distance. "Great, this is just great," John thought. "Now what do I do?" Was he to believe what Jenny had just told him? John turned back towards Tom's house and began walking. He was mad at himself now for even going to the psychic's shop. What had he really expected? Now he was really confused. Jenny had known so much about what had been happening recently, but she had left him with so many unanswered questions. If what she had been saying was real, what could he do to protect his family? He didn't know, but he felt he had to come up with a plan.

John turned left onto Tom's street and began walking up the hill. He stared down at the uneven sidewalk deep in thought about what he had just been told. John had been given so much information that he was in a little shock. As he approached Tom's house, he took out his cell phone and called home.

The phone rang several times until Emily answered. "Hello?"

John paused for a second, delighted to hear her voice. He responded, "Hi, Em, what's up?" Her voice was recognizably tired and she answered, "John, it's eleven thirty. What's up is I'm sleeping."

John turned on his sweetest voice, "Calm down, baby. I just couldn't get a hold of you earlier, so I just wanted to give you a call and let you know I love you."

Emily's voice became a little clearer, "And you're drunk, John. I've told you a million times not to call me drunk late at night. I'm going back to bed, John, so call me in the morning, alright?"

John was left speechless and responded, "Okay, baby. Sorry to wake you. I love you."

"Oh, it's okay, John. I love you, too. I'm just tired from being at the zoo all day. Call me in the morning, okay?"

"Okay, Em. I love you," John said again. "Goodnight."

Emily responded, "Good night, and I love you too."

John put his cell phone back in his pocket and headed up the small walkway to Tom's house. He felt a little better now that he heard Emily's voice. He slipped around to the back of the house and into the door from the den, looking around he closed the door behind him. Brad, Tom, and a few others were sitting around the den. The room was smoky.

Tom, seeing John come in, stood and said, "John, where the hell you been all night?"

"I just took a little walk, Tom. I see you're feeling pretty good." John could tell everybody in the room was pretty drunk.

Tom laughed and, holding his glass in the air, said, "I'm feeling good. Make yourself a drink, and come on over, buddy."

"Alright, Tom, that sounds good," John said and walked over to the large, dark wood bar in the corner. He stepped behind it, grabbing a bottle of whiskey which was sitting up on the bar. The group of guys had returned to talking to each other. Brad was loudly boasting about the Detroit Pistons' recent NBA championship. John smiled at the sight and especially the sound of Brad's slurred voice talking shit. John's smile turned to a slight pucker as he took a shot of whiskey he'd poured for himself. He sat the shot glass down on the bar then grabbed the whiskey and coke he'd just made. Feeling a little better after the shot, John casually walked over to an empty chair amongst the circle of his business colleagues.

Brad looked over at John as he was sitting down and said, "Ain't that right, John? We love the Pistons, huh?"

John smiled and replied, "We've got to cause the Lions

sure as hell ain't winning anything anytime too soon."

Everybody laughed at John's cheap shot at his own football team. Tom started to ask some other people if they were ready for the Patriots' opening but John's thoughts were drifting away. He was worried. What if Jenny was right? What would he do? He got up, walked back over to the bar, and did another shot of whiskey. Still feeling the weight of the world on his back, John poured another shot and slammed it down. All he could think of is what the dark figure had done to him and how horrible it had been. He would not let Emily or Nathan be put through that.

"Hey buddy, slow down," Brad walked up behind John, put his hand on John's shoulder, and continued, "You alright, man? I saw you over here pounding shots all by yourself. What the hell is wrong with you? The other night you were all freaky, and look at you now. You need to pull it together."

John turned to face Brad and responded, "I know, man. I'm sorry I've been so weird lately. I just... I mean," John paused, looked to the right, and then shook his head back and forth. "Brad, I've just had a few strange things happen to me lately, and I kind of freaked out. I'll tell you about it back at the hotel."

"Okay, well let's say bye to everybody. The taxi should be here anytime. If you need some air, let's go outside and wait," Brad suggested.

This sounded good to John, so he smiled and responded, "Okay, let's go."

John and Brad kept their goodbyes short and sweet. They were soon standing on the front sidewalk of Tom's house waiting for the taxi.

"So what took you so long earlier?" Brad asked John.

John paused a second, thinking of how much he wanted to tell Brad, "I just ended up walking a lot farther then I realized. Then it just took me awhile to get back. Heck, I bet I walked five miles." As John was finishing his little lie, a car turned off of Main Street and headed up the hill to John and Brad. John, recognizing it, pointed and said, "Hey, here's our ride." The white Lincoln eased up to the curb and stopped. Brad opened the rear door and slid all the way across. John got in immediately after, closing the door behind him.

The familiar face of Greg, their driver, smiled back at

109

them and asked, "So, how was the party, guys?"

Brad responded, "Good, we're feeling great, Greg. We're drunk and we're tired and we want to go home." Brad's voice was now singing.

John laughed at Brad's joke. Greg seemed to be oblivious to Brad's reference to the movie Jaws. They were now turning back down Main Street, heading back towards their hotel. John stared at the red light of the psychic shop he had been in earlier. He was slightly turned towards Greg and Brad who were deep in conversation. Greg was telling Brad how he was trying to make it as a photographer but had to drive a taxi on the side when business wasn't good. John couldn't quite put his finger on it, but something in Greg's voice didn't sound straight. Then, through the cloudiness of the recent shots John had taken, he realized that Greg sounded like he was probably gay. As John listened, he nodded his head, yep, that was it; he definitely had a little sugar in his coffee.

Getting bored with Brad and Greg's conversation, John looked out his window. He was starting to feel the shots from earlier. His troubled mind was ill-at-ease as he stared at the passing street lights, coming then fading away until the next. They seemed to be fading in and out in a rhythmic pattern. John leaned his head to the glass on the window and shut his eyes. The cold glass felt good against the side of his head.

Brad, seeing John leaning against the window, asked, "Hey, John, you alright, man?"

John responded without moving or opening his eyes, "Yeah, I'm just gonna get a little nap in."

"Alright," Brad added as he looked back towards Greg to continue their conversation.

John was awakened the next morning by the phone ringing. He fumbled around with it, put it to his ear, and said, "Hello?"

Brad responded, "Good morning, John. How're you feeling? You were pretty drunk last night."

John, not feeling too bad, responded, "Alright, I guess. Shit, I don't remember anything except for leaving Tom's in the taxi and passing out. How'd I get up to my room?"

Brad paused for a second and asked, "You don't remember anything after Tom's?"

John answered, "No, why? What the hell happened?"

Brad responded, "It's no big deal. We walked up to your room, and we had another drink. Then you just started telling me all kinds of crazy stuff about how the burglar that broke into your house wasn't a burglar, that it was some kind of creepy thing that kept following you around. Then you were saying how it was going to come back again to finish the job, and when it did, you would be there waiting. I wouldn't worry about it, John. I actually found the whole story quite entertaining. Shit, if you could get it down on paper, you might even be able to make some money for it. It was just drunk talk. Your secret is good with me, man."

"Yeah," John paused. He didn't know what to say. "Sorry, man, I was really drunk. I don't remember saying anything like that to you."

"Oh yeah, man. You told me all kinds of stuff. I hope it was just drunk talk. Was that all it was, John?"

"Yeah, of course that's all it was." John was getting defensive now. "I was just shit-faced making up some stupid shit. You know what I mean? You always get drunk and talk shit. So the shoe is on a different foot now. Whenever you get loaded and talk crap, I don't say shit to you about it."

"John, settle down. I'm not saying anything about what you were saying. I'm just kidding around with you, man. Calm down. Hey, if it makes you feel any better, from now on, I'll never mention last night or the conversation again to you or anybody. Alright?"

"Yeah, that's a deal." Changing the subject, John asked, "So what the hell are we doing today at work?"

"You don't remember Tom's whole spiel last night about the new warehouse and docking facility?" Brad paused, thinking of last night, and continued, "Oh, of course not. That's right; you were down with that psychic smoking pot or some crazy thing. Shit, sorry, we weren't supposed to mention last night again, huh?"

John was now shaking his head back and forth, thinking he would never live this one down. He replied, "No, you're not supposed to mention it ever again, but I guess you just find it too funny, huh, Brad?"

Sensing John was getting defensive again, Brad backpedaled, "Sorry, I just couldn't help it. I won't mention it again. Anyway, we're supposed to go on a tour of our new shipping facility at noon. We've get a few hours until then. You feel like getting something to eat?"

John touched his queasy stomach then replied, "Not just yet. Let me take a shower and give you a call back, alright?"

"Alright, see ya." Brad hung the phone up. John laid back down on the soft feather bed and pillow. He stared at the ceiling, trying to remember talking to Brad last night, but the memory seemed to elude him. Oh well, he didn't care what he'd told Brad. Brad would, no doubt, tease him about his drunken stupor he'd been in, but this was just because Brad was usually the one getting drunk and John was the one doing the teasing. What the hell, if you hang out with somebody long enough, eventually you're going to freak out in front of them. John didn't care. His thoughts were drifting back to earlier in the night.

He was now thinking of what Jenny had been telling him about the recent events in his life. Was he supposed to believe everything she had been saying? The hard thing about it was that everything Jenny had told John made perfect sense. John liked for things to add up and make sense, but if he was to believe what she had told him, he would have to believe that something was going to try to kill either Emily or Nathan. When he wanted things to add up, he definitely didn't mean like this.

Remembering calling Emily last night and realizing she had blown him off, he fumbled around the nightstand for his phone. As he did, he looked at the clock which read nine-thirty am. Well, she would easily be awake by now, so he flipped his phone open and entered his speed dial number. The phone rang four times until the answering machine picked up. Not wanting to leave a message, John snapped his phone shut and placed it back on the nightstand. Oh well, she could be off doing anything. That was definitely nothing to get worried about. He was sure that she and Nathan were were out doing something; they were probably in town at the grocery store. That was right; it was Thursday. Every Thursday morning, Emily and Jen went grocery shopping. Since it was summer vacation, they brought Nathan and Billy with them.

The boys would hang out at a small arcade across from the

grocery store while Emily and Jen got their shopping done. John was glad that he made enough money so Emily didn't have to work. Nathan and Emily's relationship was great due to all the time they spent together. Nathan respected and loved his mother, and this made John very proud of him. John had a great relationship with his mom and was grateful for it. He hoped that Nathan would one day be able to reflect back on his relationship with his mom and feel as special about it as John felt about his own relationship with his mother.

Thinking of his son and wife was making John sad and upset. He sighed loudly, trying to blow the heavy feeling out of his chest. John was homesick, and he did not like feeling that way. All the years he had been traveling, he had never been this sad from being away from his family. John had missed them before and talked with them a lot on the phone, but he had never felt so unhappy as he did now thinking of Emily and Nathan.

John was in such deep thought that the sound of his cell phone ringing made him jump. He reached over, grabbed it, and looked at the viewing window. It read his home number and "Home." Thinking for a second that Emily must have felt his sadness and called him, he flipped the open and said, "Hello."

"Hi, John. I was just calling you back." Emily's voice sounded as if she had just woken up.

"Yeah, I assumed you were out shopping with Jen like you do every Thursday. Were you still sleeping?" John asked.

"Yes," Emily paused.

John asked, "What's wrong. Are you sick?"

"No, I had problems getting back to sleep after you woke me up. Then I finally got back to sleep, and Nathan woke me having a nightmare," Emily replied and continued, "It was just a really long night, John."

"Is Nathan alright now?" John had been concerned about Nathan right after the attack, but he thought that Nathan was fine now.

"Yeah, he's sleeping right next to me in our room… just like when he was little."

John paused and then said, "Hmm, what was his dream about to get him so worked up?"

"I really don't know. He was so hysterical, and when I

finally got him calmed down, he fell back to sleep. I'm sure he is just still traumatized by the whole burglar incident. I thought he was over it by now."

"I did, too. So he didn't say anything about why he was so upset?"

"No. He must be having a dream about the break in, though, because he did say that the dark man was coming. I tried to tell him that they caught the bad guy and he was in jail now, but..."

John interrupted, "Hold on, did you just say he said the dark man was coming?"

"Yeah, that's what he said when I got him settled down," Emily answered.

"Did he say anything else, Em?"

"No. He was just muttering about the dark man coming before he went back to sleep, and he's been sleeping soundly ever since."

"Em, I should have never gone on this trip so soon after such a traumatic incident."

"John," Emily interrupted, "Nathan had a nightmare the same night of the incident, and he was fine. We talked about this, remember? I mean, didn't we decide that Nathan was fine and it would be okay for you to go on your trip?"

"I know, Em. I just can't help but feel like maybe I should have stayed home. You know little events like a burglar breaking in could scar Nathan for the rest of his life. I don't know... I just think maybe I should have never left."

Emily's voice softened, "John, honey, it was just a nightmare. I mean, come on, you had nightmares when you were a kid, and so did I. Everybody has them. Don't be so hard on yourself. He would have had it whether you were here or not."

"Yeah, yeah, I guess you're right, Em. I just can't help feeling guilty because I'm away, and you're there by yourself dealing with our problems."

"Oh, aren't you so sweet," Emily said, her voice changing from sweet to sarcastic. "You must still be drunk from last night, huh, honey?"

"Ha ha, Em. I appreciate your support." Emily's joke had fortunately lightened the mood.

"Speaking of sweet, hang on a second," Emily said. John

could hear Emily talking away from the phone, and then her voice returned. "Well, I've got to go, John. Nathan just woke up, and I want to talk to him."

"Alright, Em. Tell Nathan I said hi. I'll give you a call later. Love ya."

"Love you too." Emily hung up the phone.

John flipped his cell phone shut and stared up at the ceiling. He really didn't feel up to playing businessman today. His mind was nowhere close to being able to work. Why was Nathan having dreams about the dark man? What was even stranger was that Nathan referred to the image in his dream as the "dark man." That was exactly what John had been referring to as the night before, until Jenny had told him it was a "Gatherer." Regardless of its name, he wondered if it was possible that the same "Gatherer" that had been following him around was haunting Nathan in his dreams. John wished he could talk to Jenny about it more to ask her if this was possible. There was no way he would be able to make it back up to Salem again, though. And in any case, Jenny had told him everything she knew on the subject. At least that was what she had said.

John wasn't sure what to think about the whole thing. The more he thought about it, though the more John realized that staying in Boston another day wasn't going to help to resolve the issue. John sat up in bed as if a light bulb had just appeared above his head. That was it: John decided he was going to go home. He didn't need to go on any tour of a warehouse. What John needed was to get back to Michigan and be with his family.

Better yet, John decided he would surprise them. It was pretty early on a Thursday, so John figured he could get to the airport and get right on a flight. Well he better call Brad and let him know what his plan was. John picked up the room phone from the nightstand and dialed Brad.

After one ring Brad answered, "Hello?"

"Hey, Brad. I won't beat around the bush or anything, but I'm thinking about heading to the airport and going back home a day early." John phrased this in a 'what do you think about this?' tone.

"Why, what's wrong, John? Is everything alright?" Brad asked.

"Yeah, I just got to thinking about how we weren't really doing shit at work today and thought, what the hell, I should just head back home."

"John, what the hell is up with you? Is this about all that crazy talk last night about the Gatherer or whatever the hell you called it? I tell you what, maybe you should go home and relax for while. You haven't been right lately, John. But you might as well wait until tomorrow. By the time you go to the airport and get on the standby list, you won't get home until the middle of the night. Why don't you calm down and just go on the nice tour to-day... then, when you get home, you can take a week off to relax a little."

John paused, taking in all that Brad had just said, and re-plied, "No, I'm going to head home today. We'll just tell the boss that Nathan was sick. I just need to get home. I don't know what the hell I said last night to you, Brad, but I assure you that every-thing is fine with me. I am going to take the next week off, though. I just haven't been myself since the attack. It's nothing to worry about. I give you my word on that."

"Well, it sounds like your mind is already made up. If you want to go home so badly, go for it. I'll cover for you. Like you said, we'll just say Nathan got sick and you had to go home. It really doesn't matter. I just think you're going to have trouble get-ting on a plane. If I were you, I would just wait until tomorrow, but I'm not... So, when are you heading to the airport?" Brad asked.

"I'm going to get dressed and go get a taxi right now. So, I guess I'll see you back home. Oh shit, I forgot. I drove to the airport. Well, don't worry about it. I'll make arrangements to get you tomorrow. Anyway, I'll give you a call tomorrow and let you know. I've got to get to the airport now."

Sensing John was anxious to go, Brad said, "Yeah, you bet-ter get going. Sounds like you really want to get home. Don't leave me hanging for a ride tomorrow. I don't want to be stuck in Detroit."

"Don't worry, man. One way or the other, we'll get you a ride. Well, I'll talk to you later."

"Okay, bye." Brad hung up the phone.

John returned the phone onto the receiver then sat up on the edge of the bed. He was mad at himself for even coming on this trip. What the hell was he thinking, anyway? John felt that Nathan still hadn't gotten over the whole incident. Of course he hadn't. Nathan was only eleven. What had ever made John go on this trip? He got up and began to collect his clothes from around the room.

John was mad at himself for leaving his family at such a bad time. As John flung his suitcase onto the bed and began filling it with items, he shook his head and said out loud several times, "Shit, shit, shit!" He was a full-grown man, and he was still shaken up from the whole thing, so what the hell did he expect from an eleven-year-old?

John had to realize that even though Nathan was getting big now and seemed to be more mature and independent, he was still a growing boy with much to be taught. John should have stayed home with his family after such a horrible event. He should have shown Nathan that when a family is faced with troubling times, they need to come together for strength.

As John quickly brushed his teeth and threw on some deodorant, he spit the water from his mouth then looked at himself in the mirror, shaking his head back and forth as if to say, 'No, no, you idiot, that's not the way it is done.' He thought, "You can't really show your son how families come together in times of need when you're not even in the same state."

He grabbed his bathroom items, carried them over to the open suitcase, and tossed them in. John made one more final walk around the room, looking for any items he may have left behind. Not finding anything else, he walked back to the suitcase and zipped it shut. John grabbed his cell phone and wallet from the nightstand and thought, "Well that's everything." He grabbed his suitcase and walked over to the door to the hallway.

As John walked to the elevator he looked at his cell phone. It read ten twenty-five. He figured it would probably be noon when he could get a flight back to Detroit, getting in at about two o'clock. By the time he found his car in the huge parking garage, it would be about two thirty. Even with a two-hour drive back to Croswell, John figured he'd be getting home about four thirty, and that was with him planning for a lot of extra time. As the elevator door opened and John stepped in, he thought that would be perfect as he would be home in time for dinner.

THE 5 RETURN

John gripped the steering wheel tightly as he came around the sharp corner of the interstate to find a wall of brake lights as far as his eye could see. It was cold out, and his windshield wipers clapped steadily trying to keep up with the constant flow of rain from the dark, overcast sky. John was mumbling a series of swear words as the car came to a stop.

When John had not been able to get on any of the stand-by flights earlier in the day, he had feared coming into Detroit at a later time would put him in the middle of rush hour. This was exactly where he currently found himself. Trying to keep an eye on the stop-and-go traffic, he glanced down at the clock on the radio. Shit, John thought as he realized it was almost six o'clock. This meant that he wouldn't be getting back up to Croswell for at least another two hours. With the traffic the way it was now, it could possibly even be three.

John shook his head from side to side thinking of how Brad had warned him to just wait for their flight the next day. Brad had said that it was only one more day, and by the time he would get on a flight without a reservation, he wouldn't be getting in until the middle of the night. Well, John figured he would be getting home by at least eight o'clock, which he really didn't consider to be so late. Nonetheless the stop-and-go traffic definitely made him see Brad's point of view.

John had been sitting in the uncomfortable airport all day

long trying to get on a flight back to Detroit. He had gotten so frustrated at one point John had even considered renting a car and just driving home. A friend of his, who had been stationed in Boston in the United States Coast Guard, had once told him that you could make the drive from Detroit to Boston in twelve hours if you cut through Canada.

John had considered that at ten in the morning after not getting on either of the first two flights that had left for Detroit. He was glad he hadn't now, since he would still be home a few hours earlier after waiting another two more flights before he got on one. Even with all the frustrations of today, John knew it was all worth it and couldn't wait to see Nathan and Emily. He had felt an overwhelming urge to get home and be with his family since he had awakened and realized that what Jenny had told John could be so serious, if true. The thought of Jenny telling him that there was nothing he could do kept running through John's mind and bothering him. From what he had understood from Jenny, John had confused the Gatherer the first time. Once the Gatherer gained enough strength to appear in the mortal world again, it would get whoever it was really after.

Shit, John didn't know if what Jenny had told him was real or not. He just figured no matter what the truth was he just needed to be close to his family right now. He knew there was something odd about whatever had attacked him, and deep down inside he thought that it would probably return. John had seen it several times since his attack and had even begun to doubt his own sanity. The more he reflected back though, the more he realized that the sightings were real. It was as if the Gatherer had been following him looking for somebody else. John figured it had to be after Emily, because when it first attacked him, the Gatherer had come from the direction of Nathan's room. If it had been after Nathan, it probably would have gotten him then instead of coming to John and Emily's room.

Jenny had mentioned that Gatherers didn't see the same as humans. John wondered if maybe it could smell and had been drawn to the room by Emily's strong presence there. John wasn't sure of why the Gatherer had come to his and Emily's room, but he was sure that it had been coming for Emily. He didn't know how, but he was going to figure how to stop the Gatherer. He couldn't

119

just sit around and let something mess with his family. John didn't know how anything could be worse then the torment of allowing something to cause somebody in his family harm.

John was so worried about Nathan. Nathan's continuing nightmares were actually one of the final deciding factors in his returning home. Emily had told John that Nathan said the dark man was coming over and over again before he had fallen back to sleep. John was curious to talk to Nathan and find out more about his dream. The biggest question in John's head was why would Nathan be having nightmares about some dark man?

Nathan had never seen the attacker and had been sleeping when John had seen it in the cornfield. The only thing John could figure was that Nathan was just remembering the description of the burglar John had given to the police. After all Nathan had listened to every detail John had told the police. He wasn't sure what was going on in his family right now, but he needed to get home and get everything back to normal.

At this rate though he would never get there, John thought as he held the Buick at a staggering twenty miles an hour in the bumper-to-bumper traffic. It should break up soon though, he thought as he neared a major artery that broke off to one of the largest suburban areas around.

John was happy that he would keep heading north past the artery. He had no interest in living in the 'burbs. He liked life out in the country just fine. He was happy because he knew that in a couple of minutes he would be able to get back up to the speed limit and make some real time.

Emily was putting away the groceries she had just gotten from her and Jen's recent trip into town. Once they arrived home the boys went to Jen's to play some video games. That was fine with Emily anyway, since she was still tired from being up last night. Nathan and Billy had seemed to be extra loud to her today. Emily noticed that Jen had realized she was at her wit's end and had suggested that Nathan come home with Billy to play.

Jen told Emily to just go home and relax a little. Emily was thankful for having such a good friend so close to help her out. As

Emily put away the last of the groceries, Mary walked into the kitchen.

Seeing her mom, Emily said, "Hi, Mom. How are you today?"

Mary replied, "I'm fine, Em. I just heard you here, so I thought I would come in and help. What are you doing?"

"Well, I just finished putting away the groceries, and now I'm going to chop up some onions and potatoes for this roast." As Emily mentioned the roast, she motioned toward the large chunk of meat she had laying on the counter.

Mary walked over to the sink and began washing her hands saying, "Em, why don't you go relax some. I'll take care of dinner. You look exhausted, and I know you didn't get much sleep last night."

"Well, Mom, if I wasn't so exhausted, you would probably get more of an argument from me. But I am tired enough that I will happily let you cook dinner tonight.

"Go lay down in the living room and rest some, Okay?" With this, Mary looked at Emily and gave her a very loving smile.

Emily smiled back and said, "OK, thanks, Mom. I'm so glad you came and stayed with us." Emily turned and headed into the living room. She was exhausted from last night. She walked over to the couch and laid down on it. As Emily pulled the blanket from the back of the couch and curled up on her side in a ball, she had a warm feeling rush through her. Emily felt like a little girl again taking a nap as her mom cooked dinner in the kitchen.

The couch seemed to be so soft to her as she squirmed around a little getting more comfortable. Emily was listening to the rhythmic sound of her mother in the other room dicing the onions. She closed her eyes and slowly drifted to sleep.

It seemed like she had just dosed off when Emily was startled awake by the phone ringing. Opening her eyes and looking at the phone on the coffee table, Emily leaned over then picked it up and said, "Hello."

"Hi, Emily. This is Brad."

"Oh, hi," Emily responded then paused. She was confused as why he would be calling her from Boston. Emily almost instinctively assumed something happened to John and continued, "Oh my God, Brad. What's wrong?"

"Nothing, nothing. Calm down," Brad said trying to reassure Emily everything was fine. "I just called to tell you John is on his way home. Everything is OK. I was just a little worried about him."

Intrigued Emily asked, "Why? What would make you worry so much about John to call me? And why is he on his way home?"

"I don't know why he's going back home. All he told me was he hadn't felt right since the burglary, and since we weren't doing anything at work today he figured he would head back home and surprise you and Nathan. I mean, I don't mean to ruin his surprise or anything; I just wanted you to know that he was acting a bit strange before he left. I mean, what do you think? Am I overreacting? Was I wrong to call you and tell you this, Emily?"

Emily thought about what Brad said and responded, "No, no, Brad. I don't think you were wrong at all for calling me and telling me about John. You are just being a concerned friend. We all know John has been acting a little odd since the attack. What makes you so concerned about him now?"

Brad said, "Well, it's just weird of John to up and leave in the middle of a business trip, and the whole time he was acting strange."

"Brad, I don't get it. I mean you knew John was acting odd before you left. I told you that. I mean something had to happen in order to make John leave in the middle of a business trip. I don't think John would ever leave in the middle of something because he was just feeling odd. Did something happen to him, Brad?"

Brad paused and answered, "Well, I don't really know what, if anything, happened, Emily. All I know is that last night John got pretty shit-faced and told me some odd things."

"You're worried about him because of something he said to you when he was drunk?" Emily interrupted.

"Hang on and let me tell you the whole story, all right?" Brad waited for an answer.

"Yes, now get on with it, Brad."

"Well, as you probably already know, last night we went up to Salem to a business colleague's house for dinner." Brad paused, putting together the rest of the night in his head.

"Yes," Emily replied, waiting for the rest of the story.

"After dinner all of us guys were sitting around, you know, bull shitting and stuff, when John comes up to me and says he is going to step outside and get some fresh air. So he goes outside, and before I know it he's been gone for over an hour. So I call him, and he comes back. This is where he gets weird on me. After he's back he wanders over to the bar, and I watch him start slamming one shot after another."

"Why didn't you stop him, Brad?" Emily interrupted angrily.

"Hang on a minute. I did go over and stop him. I didn't want John all drunk at our colleague's house. Well, anyway, he falls asleep in the taxi ride home, so I think, well, this will be nice and easy; I just help him up to bed then I can get some sleep. But when I got John to his room, he comes to life and wants me to have a drink with him, which I agree to, of course. Then he starts talking about the burglary and how it wasn't a person but some type of dark energy source who was coming to kill him."

"What?" Emily interrupted again, "Are you kidding me, Brad? You are taking him serious after you yourself said he was so drunk he could barely talk."

"Well, no. I just wrote the whole thing off as drunken talk until this morning when he told me he was heading home. I mean John may have been drunk last night when he was telling me all that stuff, but I've known John long enough to be able to tell, drunk or sober, whether or not he is serious about something. I'm telling you, Emily, John really thinks that there is some kind of creature following him around."

"Well I don't know if John was serious or not, but I do know that he has been acting strange lately, and I'm glad he's coming home." Emily responded.

"I don't know what to make of it all," Brad said. "I just know John definitely needs to relax. You know, he was just telling me a couple of nights ago about how stressed out he had felt lately. He was also telling me he was going to take some time off of work. I think that would be a great idea, and you should talk him into a little vacation. There are still a couple of weeks left of summer vacation for Nathan, so why don't you get John to take you up to your cabin?"

"I don't know what to make of it either, but I will definitely try to get him to take some time off. When do you think he'll be back?" Emily asked.

"I would imagine probably within a couple of hours. He just called me and said he landed a little bit ago. Actually more like three hours, if he is in rush hour."

"OK, Brad. Well, thanks for calling. John is lucky to have a friend who cares so much about him. I think everything will be fine though," Emily said.

"I hope so. Oh yeah, Emily, don't forget to act surprised when you see him, and please don't tell him that I called you about this. I feel awkward about this entire phone call. I don't want to betray John's trust. If you tell him, I will never tell you anything again."

"Oh don't worry, Brad, I won't tell John anything about our little talk. I will just casually bring up the idea of taking some time off. I won't break your little manhood code of trust." Emily's tone switched from being serious to joking.

"Ha ha!" Brad laughed sarcastically at Emily's comment. "All right. I'll talk to you soon, Emily."

"OK. Bye, Brad." Emily then hung up the phone.

Emily had been propped up on her elbow the whole conversation with Brad. She leaned over to the coffee table and set the phone down. She returned her head to the soft armrest of the couch.

Emily's half-asleep mind tried to digest everything that Brad had just told her. Well, this was great, like Nathan's nightmares weren't enough. Now she had to see what was wrong with John, if anything. She realized he was acting a bit strange. That was why she had wanted him to go to Boston. It bothered Emily that Brad would be so worried about John. John must have been acting pretty strange to get Brad this worried. Regardless of everything, Emily had to get John to relax. He had been working such long hours lately; then there was the whole burglar incident.

This was just a bad year for her entire family, Emily thought. She had just come out of a period of months of being depressed due to her dad's passing. Her mother seemed to be so deep into a depression that Emily didn't know if she would ever snap out of it. It was as if her mother's sadness was almost aging her closer towards death. Emily didn't know if it was possible to actually die of a broken heart, but she felt her mom might not ever recover from her dad's death.

On top of all this, her son and her husband were now having problems. Maybe Brad was right. A vacation up at the cabin would be so nice now. They hadn't been up to the cabin this entire year. Usually they spent a couple of weeks there in the summer. John and Nathan would go fishing at sunrise. Emily loved sitting on the porch drinking her morning coffee waiting for them to return. Once they got back she would make them breakfast, and they would talk of their great fishing tales.

They had bought the cabin about five years ago. John had talked Emily into it by promising long weekend trips. The first year they had it they actually did use it, probably ten separate trips. But over the years they had gone less and less. The one trip they never missed was a long summer trip there. This year was the only exception to their ritual.

When John got back, Emily was going to talk him into going to the cabin for a while. He had been working a lot on the big Boston deal, but now that it was over John needed to relax. There were still two weeks of summer vacation left, so she was going to talk John into going to the cabin for the whole time.

She was sure John would want to spend some time fishing on Fife Lake. She knew he had been dying to take some time off and go on vacation. John was just too responsible of a person to do this until everything was wrapped up at work. Emily figured the real reason John was coming home early was so they could leave on a surprise vacation. She wasn't too worried about John. He was a strong-minded person who knew when he needed to take a little break from it all.

John would be getting home soon, so Emily figured she better get up and get ready for him. She would love to do something special for him, a kind of surprise to put on top of his surprise of coming home early. Emily sat up and grabbed the phone. She had the perfect plan. She punched in a few numbers then held the phone to her ear.

The familiar voice of Jen came to life at the other end of the phone, "Hello."

"Hi, Jen. I just found out John is coming home early to surprise me, and I would love for it if Nathan could spend the night?" Emily asked.

"Yeah, that's no problem. Is everything all right, and is Brad coming home, too?"

Emily paused, then answered, "Everything is fine, Jen. Brad is staying until tomorrow. I was thinking of trying to get John to leave in the morning to go up to our cabin for the rest of summer break. Don't mention it to Nathan though, because if John agrees, maybe we'll pick him up tomorrow morning and surprise him."

"That sounds good, Emily. Are you sure everything is all right though? I mean, why is John coming back early and then you guys are rushing off up north?" Jen sounded baffled at the idea.

"Well, you know how I told you John has been acting strange for the last week now? I just feel he's been a little stressed out because of everything being so hectic at work. Then we had that whole incident last week. He's just been working too much lately. So as the head of this family, I made a decision to go on vacation," Emily said.

Jen laughed a second then said, "Well, Emily, sounds like you have a plan. Don't worry about Nathan tonight, but I think you're forgetting one little thing."

Intrigued, Emily asked, "What's that?"

"Mary."

"Oh, yeah, my mom," Emily said as if a light bulb had just gone off over her head, "She won't mind. I think she is ready to head back home anyway."

"Well, that's good, Emily, because you won't have a very romantic night with your mom sleeping in the room next to you."

"You're right there. Well, I'm going to let you go, Jen. I have to go talk to my mom then go get some things ready for when John gets home."

"OK. Bye, Emily."

"Bye," Emily replied, as she hung up the phone.

John had to flip the wipers on high as the extra drizzle kicked up by the eighteen-wheeler he was passing blocked his sight. As he came nose-to-nose with the semi, John could make out the sign for his exit. He stepped on the accelerator, pulling ahead of the semi enough to cut across ahead of it and onto the Wadhams Road exit ramp. His heart was beating quickly from having to make such an evasive driving maneuver just to not miss his exit.

That was just stupid of him, John thought. He drove this same route every single day. John didn't even remember seeing the sign a mile before the road indicating its approach. His mind just wasn't right. He looked down at the clock on the radio, which read seven-forty-five. Well, at least he would make it home by eight-thirty. That was still early enough to enjoy the evening.

John slowed to a stop at the end of the exit ramp. He turned left and headed onto the bridge crossing back over the expressway. As he neared the top of the bridge the now-setting sun turned the clouds on the horizon a dark orange. The headlights on his car switched on automatically as the Buick descended the other side of the bridge then down in to a tree-lined gorge. It was getting dark early tonight due to the overcast sky above. The clouds made it easier to drive this stretch of road. It was refreshing to be able to drive without the sun blaring in his eyes.

John brought the Buick up to his usual cruising speed, fifty-nine miles per hour, and then switched the cruise control on. He yawned and shook his head from side to side vigorously trying to make himself more alert. John thought maybe some music would help as he reached over and turned the radio on. It was now getting to be dusk, and this is when deer moved around the most. It was very important for John to be wide awake.

The weatherman on the radio was saying that it was supposed to get colder. This made John annoyed because he wasn't ready for the long Michigan winter to begin just yet. He had been working so hard lately it seemed like summer had just begun.

The dusk slowly turned into darkness as John made his way into the heart of the thumb of Michigan and closer to his home. After being in the well-lit city for a few days, the night that had fallen upon John seemed to be extra dark. His eyes squinted at the small lighted area that his headlights provided for him to navigate with. It was as if they could barely cut their way through the surrounding darkness. Luckily, there wasn't much traffic so John was able to use his high beams most of the drive.

As he got within a few miles from home his headlights lit up three sets of eyes ahead in the distance on the right-hand side of the road. John instinctively slowed the Buick and drifted out over the centerline giving the deer plenty of room if they decided to make a run for it. As he got closer John could make out the outlines of one large doe and two small fawns. The scene was so familiar that it made John's mind flash back to the road going to Mary's house, when he had seen the Gatherer before.

John slowly passed the deer waiting for the creepy tingling sensation to come. His eyes were scanning all sides of the road in search of the ominous dark figure. The deer passed though and nothing happened, much to John's surprise. He watched the deer in his rearview mirror till they faded into the darkness.

John was happy he hadn't seen the Gatherer again. A great flow of joy was rushing through him so he reached down and turned up the radio as the Golden Earring song, "Radar Love," came on.

"We got a thing it's called radar love!" John bellowed out along with the radio. He felt happy to be getting home and also to have not had any more sightings of the dark man.

As John sang along he could begin to make out his house ahead in the distance. As it neared he could see the front porch light brightly cutting a hole in the darkness, but it didn't appear that any other lights were on. John began to lose interest in the radio due to the excitement of getting home, so he reached down and shut it off.

John was now within a few hundred yards of his house, and there still was no sign of any light except for the brightness from the porch ahead. Well, John thought, this was going to be the worst surprise ever, since no one was home. Maybe he should have phoned sometime earlier and let Emily know he was coming. He slowed the car then made a right-hand turn into his driveway.

John's eyes looked around the driveway but Mary's car was nowhere to be found. He hit the garage door opener, and the door began to open. He could see Emily's vehicle still in the garage, so he figured they all must be somewhere in Mary's car. Oh well, at least it would still be a surprise once they got home. It was almost eight-thirty, so Emily should be home soon. She usually didn't stay out late. This would give John a chance to get all of his stuff put away and relax a bit before they get home.

As John got out of the car and walked to the door leading into the kitchen he pushed the close button on the garage door.

It noisily came to life as he walked into the kitchen. John was shocked to find a single candle burning on the counter with a note in front of it. Not able to read the note John took a step closer, leaned down, and squinted in the dark candlelight.

The letter said, "Try to surprise me, John. You got to get up pretty early to pull the wool over old Em's eyes. Why don't you blow out this candle and come upstairs to get your special surprise." There was the imprint of Emily's lips puckered in red lipstick in place of a signature.

John shook his head from side to side with a grin from ear to ear. Emily always seemed to be one step ahead of him. He leaned over, blew the candle out, and left the kitchen. As he entered the living room he could hear music coming softly from upstairs. The oak staircase was dimly lit from the chandelier hanging high above it.

John couldn't make out what the music was that was coming from his bedroom. As he neared the top of the stairs he could tell that it was some type of slow jazz. He really didn't care what the music was anyhow. John could feel himself starting to get worked up as he walked down the hallway towards the half opened bedroom door. Emily must have seen him pull in the driveway and just came into the hallway and sprayed her perfume before he had entered the house. Her smell was very strong and seemed to be pulling him down the hall.

A strange flickering light could be seen coming through the half-open door and dancing on the hallway wall. As John pushed the door open, the light from the many candles Emily had spread around the room made his eyes dilate to adjust. His eyes moved across the room to the bed where Emily lay on her side propped up on her left elbow. The strange light from the candles made her skin seem dark in contrast to the white bra and panties she was wearing.

Emily was staring at John as he walked into the room. Once he made eye contact with her she said, "Hi there. Had a long day at the office, honey?"

John stopped and stared at his beautiful wife for a few seconds. Emily hadn't done something like this in years. As John looked her up and down, he felt a tingling sensation in his groin area growing stronger and stronger. His eyes darted back to the white lacey edge that curved sharply up from the silky triangle

129

of her panties then crossed high over her rounded smooth hips. John continued staring at Emily for a long time until she broke the silence.

"Are you going to just stand there drooling all night, or are you going to come over here and visit with me?" Emily asked.

Feeling kind of embarrassed for standing there speechless for so long, John reached his right hand into his jacket pocket and walked toward the bed. He held out the jewelry box containing the necklace and said, "Why don't you open this before we get started?"

John sat on the edge of the bed then leaned over and gave Emily a quick peck on the side of the cheek. He sat the jewelry box into her open hand and said, "I missed you so much, Em."

Emily looked up at John and responded, "I missed you too, baby. Can't you tell?" Emily made a gesture down her body with her free hand and smiled sincerely at him.

John nodded his head towards the jewelry box and asked, "Are you going to open it?"

"Yes," Emily responded as she looked down at the tiny box and opened it. Emily's eyes got big and she smiled brightly as she saw the necklace John had gotten for her. She sat up on her knees and hugged John tightly saying, "Thank you, John. This is so beautiful."

"I knew you would love it, Em." John responded as he pulled her in tightly to his own body. John was now getting very aroused so he began to kiss Emily's sweet-smelling neck.

Emily laid her head back in the air and ran her fingers through John's hair. Her breathing was beginning to quicken, and John could hear her getting aroused.

John gently pushed Emily down onto her back. He continued kissing around her neck then slowly moved down her body. He paused briefly and gave each of her breasts a kiss through her bra as he moved across them to her flat, hard stomach. As he approached Emily's belly button she began to squirm a little. Her breathing was becoming much deeper now, and on her exhale she was beginning to sigh. Her fingers, which were once running through his hair tightened a little, and he felt his head being pushed down toward her womanhood.

John was now kissing the top edge of Emily's panties. As he moved down slowly Emily opened her legs and allowed his head to move directly in between them. He pushed her thighs up onto her stomach and kissed the damp silky cloth directly above Emily's pleasure zone.

As he did this Emily's fingers pushed a little harder into his head, and she begged excitedly, "Yes, John, yes, please quit teasing me."

John could feel the moisture from her arousal through her panties. He pushed the material to the side with his hand and held it, then began to lick around her clitoris.

Emily's fingers grasped harder and harder as she came closer to climax. Her moaning was increasing as John began to lick faster and faster. Finally she exclaimed, "Oh yes, yes, there you go, baby. I'm cumming, John, I'm cumming." As Emily said this she pulled his face tight into her vagina.

John slid back up Emily's body and began to kiss her passionately on her mouth. Emily's hands were now fumbling with John's belt and zipper. She managed to get them undone and took his now hard penis into her hand. John was much too aroused for anymore foreplay, so he pushed Emily's hand out of the way and moved his hips close to hers. John pulled Emily's panties to the side with his right hand and guided his throbbing penis inside of her with his left.

As he pushed deeper inside of Emily, she pulled his chest tightly against her and looked him in the eye then said, "Fuck me, John, fuck me hard."

Emily saying this got John super aroused so he pinned her legs up against her chest and began to pump her hard. The bed was banging loudly off the wall, and Emily was yelling, "Yes, yes. Oh yes, here it comes, baby, harder, harder."

John was nearing his climax. Emily was beginning to get near hers, too. John pushed extra hard a few times then Emily yelled, "Yes, yes. I'm cumming baby. Don't stop now. Harder, faster, faster."

John was more aroused now at Emily having an orgasm, and he began to cum deep inside of her. As Emily felt the hot load of cum being deposited deep inside of her, she began to have another orgasm. This made her dig her nails in John's back. She was now yelling, "Don't stop. Fuck me harder!"

John gave her a few more hard pumps then rolled off to her

side. He was out of breath and covered in sweat. Emily put her head on his shoulder and cuddled up next to him.

John looked at her and said, "My, oh my. I sure do have a little bad girl on my hands."

Emily acted embarrassed and put her face into John's shoulder and shook her head no.

John kissed the hair on top of her head then said, "It's all right, baby, everybody gets to be bad every once in awhile."

Emily looked up at John and said, "I love you."

John looked back at her then replied, "I love you too, baby. I sure did miss you. I think somebody really missed me, too."

Emily nodded her head as if agreeing then continued, "I did miss my special man. I love you and don't want you to leave again."

"Don't worry, Em. I'm not going on any more trips anytime soon."

"Good," Emily responded.

John stared up at the ceiling and let out a long sigh then said, "It sure is great to be home." John and Emily lay peacefully on the bed as John stared up at the dancing shadows on the ceiling. The candles made John feel relaxed, and he was glad that he had made the trip home.

As he leaned his head over and looked at Emily, he laughed to himself thinking of how stupid Brad had thought it was for John to go home early. John would be willing to bet that Brad was sitting all alone in his hotel room with nobody cuddling him, especially not a beautiful little blonde like Em.

John's thoughts switched to wondering how Emily found out he was coming home. He looked at her and started to ask, "So how did you . . ." John stopped, seeing Emily's eyes were closed and she was sleeping. Oh well, John thought. It wasn't important how she found out anyway.

With Emily sleeping and John himself feeling tired, he softly eased his shoulder from under Emily's head. He got up from bed, pulled his pants up, and zipped them shut. As he walked over to the dresser to blow out the candles, he noticed his jacket was still on. He smirked thinking of the quickie he just pulled off. Just like they say though: a quickie but a goody.

He and Emily hadn't had sex like that in years. It made him

feel great so they were going to have to do it more often. John couldn't get the image of Emily looking up at him and begging for him to fuck her. God, he forgot how much he loved it when she was a bad girl.

John switched on a small lamp that was next to the chair. He leaned over and blew out all of the candles Emily had lit. Getting a pair of shorts and tee shirt from the dresser John removed his clothes he had been traveling in all day. The new clothes felt clean and fresh, helping him to relax after such a long day.

As John turned to walk into the bathroom, he glanced over at Emily who looked so innocent lying in bed in her white bra and panties. She was on her side with her knees tucked up in the fetal position as she peacefully slept. John smiled then shook his head at how innocent she could look and yet Emily could be so bad. It was just like one of those naughty little Catholic girls to be able to look like an angel and yet be so bad at the same time.

John walked into the bathroom then relieved himself in the toilet. As he walked out he switched the light off and headed over to the bed. To John's surprise Emily was now lying on her back with the covers pulled up over her.

Seeing her awake John asked, "What happened? Did my little innocent girl get embarrassed laying there in her underwear?"

Emily nodded yes and asked, "Could you grab me some pajamas from the dresser, John?"

As John switched directions and headed for the dresser he asked, "What drawer?"

"Third from the bottom."

John opened the drawer and grabbed a pair of silk shorts and matching top. As he closed the drawer he asked, "Is green all right for my baby girl?"

"Those are fine John."

As John turned to sit on the chair next to the dresser he lightly tossed the pajamas to Emily. John sat down as he watched Emily slip into them, then get up and walk toward the dresser. Emily opened the top drawer, grabbed another pair of panties, and walked past John toward the bathroom.

As she walked away from John he let out a whistle, "Witt woooooo."

Emily looked over her shoulder, smiled, and disappeared

behind the bathroom door. John sat patiently until the door opened and Emily reappeared. She crossed the room to where John was and then lightly sat down on his lap. As she rested her head on his shoulder he began to gently nibble on her ear lobe.

John whispered into Emily's ear, "Are you ready for round two, bad girl?"

Emily turned and gave John a peck on the lips then said softly, "No, baby, I'm still a little sore from being treated so roughly in round one. Anyway, I just put some dry panties on, and I'm all through for the night."

John kissed Emily on the cheek and asked, "Oh, did my poor little Em get rode hard and put away wet?"

"Yes," Emily said innocently as she pushed her face into John's shoulder as if she was just so shy and innocent.

They sat there cuddling silently for a couple of minutes until John asked, "Hey, where is Nathan?"

"Spending the night over at Billy's" Emily replied.

"Wow, well thanks for a great welcome home party," John said.

"No problem, baby." Emily kissed John on the cheek, got up off his lap, and walked over to the edge of the bed. As she turned and sat down she continued, "You know what I was thinking that we should do this week, John?"

"No, what?"

"Well, I just think you've been working so much lately and with all of the recent events and Nathan having nightmares that maybe we could really use a nice family vacation. So what do you think about heading up north for the week?"

John smiled and laughed at this, then responded "Great minds think alike, Em. I was just thinking the same thing. Now that the whole Boston thing is wrapped up. We haven't even been up to the cabin this whole year."

"I know, but you've just been so busy lately, John."

"Well, I'm not busy anymore, Em. I told Nathan when I got back I'd take him fishing. He will probably be really surprised when I tell him where we're going fishing. So when do you want to go?" John looked at Emily with a gleam of excitement in his eyes.

"That's where my surprise gets even better John. I have all of our stuff already packed. I say we go in the morning."

John's excitement turned into a smile as he responded, "Yes, that would be perfect. Nathan doesn't even know I'm home yet, right?"

"Nope, I never told him." Emily let John figure out what she had already planned.

"Then we'll surprise him in the morning. He will be super excited because I'm home. Then when I tell him we're heading up north to the cabin he will be ecstatic." John nodded his head at such a great plan. Realizing that Emily was the mastermind behind it all he looked at her and said, "Nathan and I sure are lucky to have somebody so great looking out for us."

Emily was blushing a little as she responded, "Well you guys are my two special little men. I'm just so glad that you want to go, John."

John stood up from the chair he had been sitting in and walked over to the bed. He sat down next to Emily and said, "I love you, Em," John leaned over and gave Emily a gentle kiss on the cheek.

Emily turned, looked John in the eyes, and replied, "I love you, too. But if we're going to make it out of town at a decent time tomorrow morning, I still have some things to get done. I still need to call Jen, too, and let her know we'll be over in the morning to get Nathan."

"Oh shit," John said, remembering that he had to pick up Brad from the airport. "Will you ask Jen if she can get Brad from the airport tomorrow?"

Emily stood up and began walking towards the hall. "Don't worry about it, John. I'm sure Jen won't have any problem picking up her own husband from the airport. Why don't you lie down and watch some TV? You need to relax after traveling all day. I'm sure you're exhausted."

"Well, I'm not going to argue with that, Em. John grabbed a couple of pillows and stacked them up and lay on his back looking up. He reached over with his right hand, grabbed the remote, and turned the television on. He flipped to the Guide station to see what was on. As the shows rolled by on the screen, John looked for something that interested him.

His eyes slowly drifted from the television to the ceiling in a daze as he thought of the long day he had. It had definitely been worth the long wait at the airport, all of the traffic, and the rainy weather. He was exhausted, but at least he was sleeping in his own bed tonight. His family was safe, and he was close enough to ensure this remained true in the future. John was beginning to think everything was all right. Maybe the whole thing was just a bunch of bullshit. What if John's recent paranoia was all made up in his head? John didn't know what to believe anymore. He was just going to go up north to the cabin and relax. He was going to keep his family close to him until he knew everything was all right.

Nathan and Billy lay on the floor on their stomach with their necks bent up as they both stared at the television. Each of them was holding PlayStation controllers in their hands. They could pretty much play as long as they were quiet. The volume was turned all the way down on the small color television in Billy's room. Billy's parents' room was downstairs on the other end of the house, so Nathan and Billy always took full advantage of this.

It was summer time anyway, so Billy's mom wouldn't be checking to make sure they were asleep, but they were still extra quiet out of habit. They always stayed up late and played video games. Nathan had a television and PlayStation in his room too, so they did this when they spent the night there also. They were masters at staying up late playing video games and at creeping around the house getting snacks.

Nathan, who felt hungry, whispered to Billy, "Hey, let's go downstairs and get something to eat."

Billy was getting tired so he responded, "No, it's too late. Let's just go to bed."

"Well, if you won't' go downstairs, then let's at least play one more game. It's not very late," Nathan replied.

"OK," Billy hesitantly responded as he moved the arrow to the start position on the game.

As the game started Nathan was happy that he had managed to get Billy to stay up longer. He was scared of going to sleep because of all the recent nightmares he had been having about the dark man. The thing that scared Nathan the most about the dark man was that he felt as if it was trying to get inside of his head. Nathan didn't want anything inside of his head, so he wasn't going to go to sleep. Last night the dark man had told him he was coming, and this really made Nathan scared.

Nathan quit daydreaming and focused on the game. He only had one man left and he had to keep him alive in order for the game to continue and Billy to stay up.

"Shoot!" Nathan exclaimed slightly over whisper level as his man was killed.

"Shhh," Billy hissed, holding his fingers to his mouth. "Don't wake my mom up, Nathan."

"I'm not going to wake her up. She's all the way on the other end of the house. Anyway, let's play again."

"No, I'm getting tired, aren't you?" Billy asked.

"I'm not tired at all so come on let's play another game." Nathan pleaded with Billy.

"No, I'm not playing anymore, Nathan. You can keep playing by yourself. I'm going to go to sleep." After saying this Billy laid his controller on the floor and fluffed his pillow up. He laid his head down and closed his eyes.

"Come on, Billy." Nathan pleaded. Let's stay up all night long. We haven't done that in a long time."

"I don't want to stay up all night. Now leave me alone. I'm trying to sleep." Billy rolled over and put his back to Nathan.

Nathan let Billy sleep and continued playing video games by himself. After a few games he began feeling tired, and his eyes kept closing. Nathan's head nodded in sleep, but he quickly awoke and jerked back straight. Well there was no way he was going to be able to stay awake all night by himself, so he poked Billy in the back and whispered, "Billy, hey are you up?"

There was no response from Billy so he poked him again, "Billy, hey Billy?"

Billy rolled over looked at Nathan then asked, "What, what's going on?"

"Nothing, hey get up. I got to go to the bathroom, and I don't want to go by myself." Nathan responded praying for something that would awaken Billy and keep him awake for a while. Once he got him awake, Nathan figured he could talk him into something in order to keep him up. Billy's eyes were closed again as if he was asleep. Nathan reached out and shook his shoulder and said, "Billy, are you up? Hey, Billy."

Billy opened his eyes and stared at Nathan and asked, "What do you want now? I'm trying to sleep."

"I have to go to the bathroom. So come on, get up. I don't want to have to go all by myself," Nathan pleaded his case.

Billy asked, "What's up with you? You are acting all freaky."

"Huh, me?" Nathan responded pointing his hands on his own chest then he continued, "I'm not acting all freaky. I just have to go to the bathroom and don't want to go all the way down there by myself. I never make you go to the bathroom by yourself when you stay at my house. So why should I have to at your house?"

"Hey, I'm not saying I won't go down there with you. I'm saying that you just want me to go so I'll stay up with you. For some reason you want to stay up all night, and I just don't want to. So do you really have to go to the bathroom or not?" Billy asked Nathan.

Nathan let out a sigh then said, "No, you're right. I was trying to keep you up. I just ... I just ...."

Billy continued, "You just what?"

Nathan paused, thinking, and continued, "No, I can't tell you. You'll think it's stupid."

"Come on, just tell me," Billy pleaded.

"Well, OK. I'll tell you. As long as you promise not to tell anybody."

"OK."

Nathan continued, "And you have to promise you won't tease me."

"OK, Nathan. I promise. You know I won't tell anybody or tease you. So come on, tell me."

Nathan exhaled deeply then said, "OK. Well the thing is ..." He paused, embarrassed by his problem and not wanting to sound stupid. He gathered his courage then continued, "Well, I've been having this nightmare lately. The thing about it is that it's so real, and when I wake up I remember everything so perfectly. No matter what I think about before I go to sleep I still have it. So that's why I'm trying to keep you up. The truth is that I'm scared to go to sleep." Nathan's eyes focused on Billy studying his face waiting to see if Billy was going to make fun of him or if he believed that Nathan was truly scared.

Billy shook his head as if he was saying "My oh my, you silly boy" then he said, "That's it. Your big secret is that you're having some nightmares?"

"I knew I shouldn't have told you," Nathan responded. "You promised you wouldn't tease me."

"No, hey, I'm not teasing you. I just know a secret about nightmares. If you do it, then I guarantee you won't ever be scared again."

Nathan was curious now, so he asked, "What is the big secret?"

"My dad told me about it. I'm surprised yours hasn't told you. But anyway, it's easy. The trick is that whenever you have a bad dream you have to say over and over again, 'You're not real. You're just a dream.'"

Nathan interrupted, "What? That's it? That's not going to work. I thought you had some great secret and that's it? Just saying that to the dark man in my dreams would make it laugh at you."

"Dark man?" Billy inquired. "What is that? The thing you've been having nightmares about?"

"Yeah, I keep seeing it again and again. Every single night I go to sleep it is in my dreams. I don't know how to get rid of it. I mean, I know dreams aren't real, but this thing is just different. The dark man that I dream about, it's just different."

Billy was awake now so he asked, "What do you mean it's different?"

"I don't' know how to explain it. It's just that most dreams I had before that I got scared if something was trying to get me and hurt me. The dark man that I keep dreaming about ... " Nathan stopped thinking about what he was saying then continued, "It's just the dark man isn't really trying to hurt me."

"Well then, what's the problem? Why are you scared to go to sleep if some dream you're having isn't even scary?" Billy asked.

"No, no. I mean the dark man is bad, and every time I dream about him it's dark out and scary. I always end up alone with the dark man." Nathan paused again. "It's just that I feel like the dark man is here for a reason."

"I don't know what to tell you, Nathan. I mean, if I was having a dream about some dark man but it wasn't trying to hurt me, then I think I would just ask it what it wanted and why it kept coming into my dreams," Billy said.

Nathan thought about this then said, "Well, I want to talk to it. I just don't want to let it inside of my head so I can."

"What do you mean let it in your head? If it is in your dreams then it's already in your head. So you might as well find out what it wants."

"Yeah, you're probably right. I just worry that it is trying to trick me." Nathan said.

"It's only a dream. Dreams can't hurt you. That is why saying 'You're not real. You're just a dream.' works. But I don't think you should be scared to go to sleep. I promise you that if I see you're having a nightmare, I'll wake you up, OK?"

"OK," Nathan replied. "I am getting pretty tired."

"That's nice. I'm wide awake now so let's play another game." Billy turned onto his stomach and grabbed the controller which was lying on the floor in front of him. As they began playing Billy asked, "Aren't you happy? You got me to stay up now."

Nathan was happy Billy was up, but as the game continued on, his eyes began to shut and soon he found himself getting tired. As his neck crooked over to the side Nathan found himself falling asleep and his controller dropped to the floor. All three of his men were killed before Billy died once.

Billy looked over at Nathan whose eyes were closed, but his head was still looking up at the television. Slowly Nathan's head started falling to the side. Once it was almost down to his shoulder Nathan's eyes flipped open, and he quickly snapped back to staring at the television.

As he did this Billy laughed and said, "You really need to go to sleep. You're trying to play, and you don't even have any players left."

Nathan looked at Billy, put his controller down, and laid his head on his pillow. As he did he said, "Good night."

"Yeah, good night. Thanks for waking me up," Billy said to himself jokingly then continued playing his game.

Nathan's mind slowly went from thinking about not

getting killed on the video game to a calm darkness. The darkness had engulfed him relaxing him, easing his burdened mind. He had been so scared of going to bed that he forgot how great sleep could be.

In the darkness he could hear the rhythmic beat of his heart. Nathan could also hear the calm, easy sound of air rushing in and out of his lungs as he slipped into a deep sleep. The blackness around him was so dark he could not see anything. He was not scared, though. Nathan still had a deep feeling of calmness rushing through him.

He could not feel or hear his body anymore. Nathan could only feel a tingling sensation that pulsated on and off softly and rhythmically all around him. He felt as if he was slowly spinning and descending downward. The spinning feeling slowed but Nathan felt as if he was still moving downward.

Nathan began to wonder how far down he was going when he came to a soft stop on a cold surface. He could feel a cold tingling sensation on his back. Nathan could feel his body again as the cold tingling moved around the bottoms of his legs. His eyes were still closed but as he slowly regained his senses, Nathan could feel that he was lying on his back with his arms outstretched as if he were getting ready to make a snow angel.

The cold under his body didn't seem to feel cool enough to be snow. Nathan began to wiggle the backs of his hands and fingers feeling the cool surface he was on. He was regaining a sense of his body but still felt as if he couldn't open his eyes. A sense of peace ran through Nathan as he listened to the sounds of the warm breeze which he could feel blowing gently across his face.

Nathan rolled a piece of the cool material in between his thumb and index finger. He could instantly tell by the texture that it was grass that he now found himself laying in. Gaining control over his vision, he opened his eyes. Nathan was lying in a grass field staring up at the dark blue sky. White fluffy clouds drifted high above him. They were bumpy and contorted in all different sizes and shapes as they made their way across the smooth dark blue backdrop.

Nathan held his hand out above him, reaching upward toward the sky. As he did his eyes moved from the clouds and focused on his hand which he slowly opened and spread his fingers.

He then turned his hand back and forth, closely inspecting it. Nathan exhaled deeply, staring at his hand as if he had never seen it before. As he breathed out he made a low sigh, "Ahhhh."

He lowered his hand down then leaned up on his left elbow. The grass was soft and cool. It felt refreshing and as far as Nathan looked it was all he could see. There were small hills of the thick grass all around him. As he completed looking around in a circle, Nathan's eyes met with a single oak tree off in the distance. Nathan stood up and began to walk toward the tree. He looked down and laughed a little at the grass which was tickling his bare feet. The tree was only a few hundred yards away from Nathan as he climbed the slow rising slope which led up to it. The tree was large and cast an enormous shadow underneath its canopy. The leaf-covered branches gently swayed back and forth in the soft, blowing wind.

Nathan now walked faster toward the tree. He didn't know why but he felt as if something was at the tree that he needed. As he made his way, Nathan glanced over his shoulder and was surprised to see something odd far off in the distant horizon. He stopped, turned, and squinted trying to see farther. The entire horizon seemed to be moving up and down as if it were liquid. As Nathan put his hand above his eyes to shield the glare from the bright sun, the waving horizon seemed to be moving nearer to him. As it got closer he could see that it was a sea of what appeared to be black water rushing toward him. It was as if a tidal wave of darkness was rushing toward him.

Remembering the tree on top of the hill, Nathan turned to run toward it but was frozen in terror at what he saw. There sitting on the first branch of the tree was the dark figure that had been haunting him. Nathan instantly got a tingling sensation throughout his body, and his hair stood up on the back of his neck. He could feel the dark man rushing all around him, trying to get inside of his head. Nathan was pushing it away as usual but as he looked back over his shoulder a sudden sense of urgency rushed through him. The raging sea of darkness was almost halfway from the horizon to where he was now standing.

As Nathan turned back and looked at the dark man sitting with its feet dangling from the branch, he knew he must face it. Nathan panicking, yelled, "What do you want?"

The dark man sat there in silence. Nathan couldn't see any eyes, but he could feel the dark man focusing in on him. The sense of the dark man around Nathan was beginning to intensify. It was now pulsating around him trying desperately to get into his head. Nathan, glancing back at the raging wall of darkness that was rushing toward him, decided to let the dark man in and trust him.

He quit blocking the dark man's thoughts. The dark man's calming voice suddenly came alive in Nathan's head. "Come to the tree, Nathan! Hurry!"

As Nathan started sprinting towards the tree, he could hear the raging sea behind him. It sounded loud like he was at the beach in a storm. He was too scared at how close it was and too focused on running as fast as he could toward the tree, to look back.

The dark man's voice came to life again in his head. "Hurry, Nathan! Run! Do not let it get you!"

Oh God, it must be close, Nathan thought so he glanced over his shoulder. Nathan was horrified at the sea of darkness rushing toward him because it wasn't just dark water but seemed to be alive.

Nathan got an extra burst of speed from the sight that he had just seen. Among the sound of breaking waves Nathan could hear the screams of what seemed to be people yelling out from inside the darkness.

Nathan was only a few feet from the tree as he looked back again. The darkness was getting ready to engulf him, and he didn't think he was going to make it. He turned back toward the tree to see the dark man hanging out from the branch it had been sitting on earlier. It had one of its arms outstretched toward Nathan. The dark man's voice came into Nathan's head again, "Jump, Nathan! Jump! I will save you."

As the darkness engulfed his back foot, Nathan leaped toward the dark man reaching his hands up toward it. The dark man's tight grip wrapped around Nathan's right wrist and began to pull him upward. The dark matter that engulfed his foot stretched out from the sea of darkness, hanging onto Nathan's ankle. The dark man pulled strongly upward until the dark matter stretched up then snapped and dumped back into the sea.

The dark man lifted Nathan high above him to another branch then sat him down. The voice came into his head again.

"Climb, Nathan! You must climb higher!" As Nathan climbed up he looked down at the raging dark sea that was all around him. Faces that seemed to be in agonizing pain were trying to emerge from the dark liquid mass. It looked as if a dark smooth cloth was tautly pulled over the faces. From their gaping mouths, muffled moans and cries echoed out in the air around them.

Nathan looked out around the tree in all different directions, but all he could see from horizon to horizon was the dark ocean of terror. Nathan was still climbing upward, but the branches were getting smaller now, so he had to move slower. The dark sea's level was rising rapidly beneath Nathan. The dark man was crouched down near the edge of the rising dark sea, staring at it as if he was communicating with it somehow. As he stared into the dark sea, he looked back up at Nathan, and his voice came into Nathan's head, "It is too strong. I can't stop it! We must climb." The dark man climbed up a couple of branches higher then stared down into the sea again.

When the dark man quit looking at the ocean of rage that had surrounded him and climbed up the tree, the ocean appeared to rise much faster. But now as he stared down into it, the rate of rising began to slow. Nathan was nearing as far as he could go up the tree now. The limb he was currently standing on was bending and swaying from his weight and the wind.

The dark man scooted up onto Nathan's branch. The branch bent down much more, and the bark on it went taut and began to tear right at the elbow where it separated from the bigger branch it grew from. The dark man reached high above his head and grabbed a few tiny limbs. They were much too small to hold him, but it relieved a little stress from the branch they were standing on.

As the dark sea rose within feet from the branch they were on, Nathan yelled, "Do something! It's going to get us!"

The dark man crouched down onto the branch he and Nathan were sharing and looked down at the dark water again. Nathan looked at the dark man as it trembled trying to concentrate on the rising ocean. The added weight of the dark man strained the branch again, and it began to crack. Suddenly a large gust of wind picked up and the branch snapped completely. The dark man was heavier and fell below Nathan. As the dark man fell toward the ocean, it separated around him. The ocean now formed towering walls around the dark man as he fell hard onto the grassy covered earth. Nathan's back slammed hard against the earth as he landed. The jolt of the fall made Nathan's body jump. As it did Nathan's eyes came open, and he found himself lying in Billy's room on the floor. His sleeping bag was pushed off of him, and he was breathing rapidly. His heart was racing from the nightmare he had just had.

Nathan looked over at Billy who was sleeping next to him on the floor. He was usually terrified after a nightmare with the dark man but wasn't scared at all now. His eyes slipped shut again.

THE STALKING

Nathan and Billy slowly made their way down the carpet-covered stairs of Billy's house. Billy had told Nathan before they left his bedroom that they would have to be extra quiet in order to not wake up his mom. As they walked, Nathan recalled that Billy told him this every single time he spent the night. What the heck, did Billy think he wanted to wake up his parents or something?

About three quarters of the way down the stairs, Nathan stepped down extra hard. The noise made Billy stop instantly, causing Nathan to bump into him almost knocking him down the rest of the stairs. Billy scowled back at Nathan and then held his index finger up to his mouth and quietly shushed Nathan. Nathan shrugged his shoulders then nodded his head in the direction down the stairs urging Billy on. Billy turned back around, and they continued to the bottom of the stairs into the living room.

They simultaneously sat down on the couch. Billy took the remote control and switched the television on. As the television came to life, the volume blared out loudly. Billy frantically pointed the remote of the TV trying to lower the volume. Once the volume was turned all the way down, he looked over at Nathan shaking his head with a big smile on his face as if he was saying that was stupid, huh. Billy switched stations to the cartoon network then eased the volume up so they could hear.

Nathan was staring at the television but his thoughts wandered. He was thinking of the dream he had last night. It was so strange because for the first time since he had been having night-mares about the dark man he had not been scared, or at least not horrified like he had been during all the rest of his dreams. He had listened to what the dark man was saying. Every other time he had dreamed of the dark man, Nathan could feel him all around his body trying to talk to him. Nathan felt as if he was trying to force himself into his head, but Nathan had always pushed him away. Well, last night Nathan finally let him in, and it wasn't so bad. He wasn't sure who the dark man was but he felt as if he was trying to help him in some way. Nathan didn't know how the dark man would help him, but every time he dreamt of him, they communicated better and better.

Nathan was happy because he had been scared to go to sleep lately because of his reoccurring nightmares of the dark man, but after last night he wouldn't be scared any more. All he could remember from last night's dream was the dark man telling him that he was here now. In his previous dreams, Nathan was scared because the dark man kept saying that he was coming. Not knowing what was coming, was what really made him feel scared.

Last night, once Nathan finally let the dark man in instead of fighting him so hard, he felt at ease about him. It was as if he was just scared of him because he hadn't really known him. But now that he saw the dark man was actually trying to help him, he was relieved. Nathan was still a little skeptical of the dark man, though. He felt that the dark man was most likely trying to help him, but he did have a little doubt as to the dark man's motives. Nathan figured now that he wasn't scared of him and could understand the dark man better, he could figure out whether or not he was trying to help him or hurt him. He was pretty confident that the dark man was trying to help him, though. Nathan's thoughts were interrupted by the sound of a door opening. Billy and Nathan stared at the doorway leading to the downstairs hall at the sound of approaching footsteps. Jen turned and stood in the doorway looking at the boys and said, "Eight- thirty, guys. You decided to sleep in a little today?"

Smiling at his mom, Billy responded, "We were up late playing video games."

Jen asked, "What do you guys want for breakfast?"

The boys said in unison, "Cereal." Then looked at each other and laughed.

"All right, all right," Jen said as she walked away toward the kitchen. She continued, "Billy, come in here and get it."

Nathan and Billy continued sitting on the couch for a couple of more minutes. Cupboards closing and other sounds were coming from the kitchen. Then Jen said, "Billy, come and get your guys cereal."

Billy yelled back, "Hang on until a commercial, Mom!"

"OK."

A few minutes later a commercial came on, and Billy jumped off the couch then made a squealing sound as if he were a car spinning its tires, taking off rapidly. "Urrrrrr." He then started into the kitchen. Nathan smiled as he heard Billy's mom yell at him, "Hey, slow down, Billy!" Billy made another obnoxiously loud peel-out noise as he came around the corner back into the living room, the sound of Jen's voice followed him, "You'd better slow down, Billy. I will be so mad if you spill the cereal."

Billy handed a bowl over to Nathan then sat down next to him. He hollered out, "Thanks, Mom!"

Nathan and Billy were sitting on the couch, staring at the television in a daze when the doorbell rang. They didn't care who it was. They were deep into their cartoon. The door from outside could be heard being opened through the doorway into the kitchen. Somebody came in from outside, and muttered talking could be heard in the kitchen. Then out of the corner of his eye, Nathan saw somebody step into the doorway.

His eyes naturally moved over to the doorway. He was totally shocked at the sight of his dad standing there. He paused for a moment. Then all at once he realized that's who was at the door. Nathan leaped up from the couch and yelled, "Dad!" He then ran around the coffee table and hugged John.

John responded, "Hey, buddy. I knew you'd be surprised." He hugged Nathan tightly, then continued, "There's more too, Nathan. You better get dressed 'cause remember how I told you when I got back I would take you fishing?"

Nathan took a step back from his dad and asked, "Yes?"

"Well, you need to get out of your pajamas because we are heading up north to the cabin for a vacation."

Nathan jumped in the air, "When are we leaving? And

what do I need? How long are we going for?"

John grabbed Nathan's shoulders and said, "Calm down, Nathan. We have everything in the car that you need. Why don't you finish eating breakfast then go upstairs and get dressed. Take your time, though. We'll be in the kitchen talking to Jen."

Nathan took a couple of deep breaths and relaxed. He then said, "OK, Dad."

Nathan turned and walked back over to the couch to finish eating his cereal. As he got near Billy, he looked at him with a big smile and said, "Did you hear that, Billy. I'm going up north!"

John looked down at the time on the radio, which read 9:30. He figured they would be up to the cabin by 1:30, if all went well. He looked over at Emily who had her eyes shut and her seat tilted back. She had just shut her eyes so John didn't figure she was sleeping yet. As John made his way down the rural country road, he thought about what he would be doing if he hadn't left Boston early. He laughed to himself in his head thinking that he would probably be nursing a hang over. That's probably what Brad was doing, and John wasn't jealous a bit. He glanced back in the rear-view mirror. Nathan was staring at the television, which was flipped down from the ceiling of the Suburban. John couldn't tell what he was watching, because he couldn't see the picture. Nathan wore headphones, which blocked the sound from the rest of the car. As John glanced back in the mirror at Nathan, their eyes met quickly, and Nathan smiled at him. John smiled back and continued driving through the farm country. It would still be a few hours of driving until they got far enough north to be in the big woods.

The big woods is what John referred to any part of northern Michigan. His father and all of his dad's buddies always referred to northern Michigan as just that. John remembered how he had once asked his dad why they called up north the big woods, and he responded by taking John out back. John and his dad stood looking out over the open farm fields around them for a moment until his father had asked him what he saw. John said, "Nothing." His dad said, "Exactly. As far as you can see in each direction, all you see is farm fields. Of course these are some tiny two-or even ten-acre woods around here, John, but if you go up north the woods go as far as you could walk all day. That was the way this whole state used to be, but now all that is left is up north. That's why I call it the big woods, because it is the way the woods should be." John could still hear his dad's voice talking about the big woods. John's dad had loved northern Michigan and had passed it on to John. He hoped that someday Nathan would be able to show his own son the wonders of the big woods.

It felt great to just leave everything behind and head up north for the week. John reached down with his left hand and let the chair back a tad. There, that was just what he needed. Now he could enjoy the ride a little better. He sighed loudly as he drove. John was thinking about work and everything else that had been going on in his life lately. He was excited to be going to the cabin where work didn't exist.

Actually, John thought he might just turn off his cell phone once he got to the cabin. Why did he need it anyway? There was nothing John could do for anybody at work from all the way up in the big woods. When he got a chance, he would have to change his voicemail in order to say he would be out all week. Then once that was done, he really could turn off his phone and just relax. Well, at least work seemed like it would be easy enough to get rid of for the week. John really hadn't thought of the other crazy part of his life lately. Maybe the whole dark man thing had just been stress related. John hadn't seen the dark man in a couple of days. Nathan had dreamt about him but that was just a dream. You couldn't go around making decisions in life by what you dreamed about. So, as far as John could see, everything was good. They slowly made their way out of the farmland and into the beginnings of up north. Along the sides of the road were mostly woods, but there was the occasional farm.

The land was beginning to change, too. The once-flat earth was beginning to get some nice rolling hills in it. As the Suburban made its way through the landscape, John noticed it had to kick down a gear now to climb the steep hills. As John's cell phone began to ring, he thought, how ironic. He was just thinking of shutting that off, too. He grabbed the phone and looked at the incoming call number. It was from around his house, but he didn't recognize it as anybody he knew so he flipped the phone open and said, "Hello." A man on the other end of the phone responded, "Hi, this is Detective Flanagan with the Croswell Police Department. I'm looking for Mr. Watley."

"Oh, hi, detective. This is John Watley you are speaking with."

"Well, it's nice to finally catch up with you. We've been playing some phone tag," the detective laughed.

John laughed and said, "Yep, yep. We sure have."

The detective continued, "Anyway, Mr. Whatley, what I'm calling for is that everything that was taken into custody from the suspect's house has been claimed by other people in the area whose houses were broken into. So I don't know if you were missing anything or not?"

John paused, thinking, and responded, "No, I looked around and my wife looked, and we can't seem to find anything missing."

"Which leads me to the other reason I called you." The detective paused as if getting his thoughts and continued, "I don't think the burglar was in your house long enough to steal anything, and as far as the assault, you said you wouldn't be able to identify anyone?"

John answered, "I couldn't identify one little piece of what the suspect looked like. It's just like I said in the report. It was as if a shadow was over the burglar's face."

"Mr. Watley, the suspect is wanted back in Detroit for some very serious felony charges. We still have him for some burglaries but as far as the assault case goes, I think we would have a hard time prosecuting him. But what I'm trying to say is it really doesn't matter what we do up here anyway. Once he goes back down to the city, he is going to be in jail for a long time. You see, without a positive identification, we won't be able to prosecute the suspect for attacking you. But I just wanted you to know he was going to get what was coming to him anyway." The detective paused and then continued, "And without anything stolen from your house, I don't think there is anything else we can do for you."

"No, no, it sounds like you are pretty much through with me. I'm glad to hear that the suspect is going to go to jail anyway. Even though it's not for what he did to me, at least he is still going to get punished. John paused while thinking more about what the detective had said and then continued, "This kind of works out better for me anyway."

"How is that?" The detective inquired.

"Well, I know for the safety and sake of my family, the criminal is going away, but at least I don't have to get all wrapped up in some trial. So you could kind of say I'm gonna get my cake and get to eat it too." John tried to lighten the mood with a joke.

The detective laughed and said, "Well, Mr. Watley, I'm glad you're not upset we have to drop the charges against this guy."

"No, I'm not mad as long as I can be assured he has been taken off our streets and won't be let out so he can terrorize somebody else, then I am pleased at how the situation has ended," John said.

"OK, Mr. Watley, well I guess if everything is all right, you have a good day. Hopefully, next time we talk it will be under better circumstances," the detective said to John.

John laughed and responded, "Yep, that's for sure. OK. Bye."

"Bye, Mr. Watley." The detective hung up the phone.

John flipped his cell phone shut and put it back into the cubby on the dash where he kept it. John didn't really know what to think about what the police had just told him. He looked over at Emily whose head was positioned so she was noticeably sleeping now. He wanted to tell her about what the detective had just told him but now that he realized she wasn't awake, he figured it could wait. It didn't really matter if he told her anyway, because it had no effect on their lives.

The only way it would have affected them was if John would have had to testify against the burglar in court. John was actually happy how everything had worked out. The bad guy was going to go to jail for what sounded like the rest of his life, and John didn't have to do anything. It was just like his dad always said, "This too shall pass." As John drove down the hilly tree-lined road toward the cabin, he smiled. It did pass and everything seemed to be just fine. His dad was pretty wise.

When John went through stressful periods in his life was when he missed his father the most.

Thoughts like these were exactly why John took being a father so seriously. His dad had been a great father, and John had many great memories of his dad. John referred back to his father's advice still to this day.

John had been reflecting a lot lately. Since his attack, John focused his thoughts more about life and how he should live it. He had a great life, but sometimes he didn't feel he was as fatherly to Nathan as his dad was to him. Would Nathan look back upon John one day with as much admiration as he had for his father? John's mind continued to wander on such issues, and the drive passed quickly.

They were getting pretty close to the cabin when John broke from his thoughts and looked over at Emily. He was surprised and happy to see her awake, so he looked over at her and asked, "How long have you been awake?"

"I don't know, probably about twenty minutes."

John was shocked, "What twenty minutes? So what you've just been sitting there in silence for twenty minutes now?"

"Well, John, I was looking at the scenery too." Then she turned on a country accent and finished, "You know how us flat-landers don't ever get to see anything like these fancy hills they have up here in the big woods."

John laughed and then looking over at Emily responded, "Hey, you finally remembered to call it the big woods."

"God, John, how could I forget? I heard stories of the big woods from your dad for years, and since he has gone you seemed to have taken over the big woods tales."

"Well, we're pretty close now. Aren't you excited?" John asked.

Emily hesitantly said, "Yes, I just hope there aren't any surprises around."

John paused, realizing Emily was referring to the dead mice they had found in previous years. He responded, "Why don't you and Nathan wait outside while I make sure the coast is clear for my princess?"

"Ok, but you don't have to be so snotty about it, John. I can't help it if I don't like dead mice," Emily said matter of factly, then reached down and switched the radio on.

John glanced back in the rearview mirror at Nathan who was sleeping in the back seat. He was gonna tell him that they were getting close but figured he would let him sleep.

Nathan opened his eyes as he awoke. His right eye was covered by the pillow, and his left eye focused hazily on a wood wall next to him. As he breathed in slowly through his nose, Nathan could smell the familiar scent of their cabin. That's right; they were going up north and he had fallen asleep in the car on the way up here.

As his mind shook the haze from sleeping off, everything came back to Nathan very quickly. The dark knotty wood wall he was facing began to look familiar. Nathan rolled over on the hard bed in his room at the cabin. As he sat up and put his feet over the edge of the bed, Nathan couldn't help but feel excited at his surroundings.

The floor felt cold and hard as he stepped down off the bed. Instead of a doorway leading into the main cabin area, Nathan's room had a blue cloth hanging where a door should be. Nathan pushed it aside and walked into the living room and kitchen area. To Nathan's left was the small kitchen that looked like it had been set up with somebody's antique white sink and stove. The short fridge next to them had a big silver handle which had to be pulled hard in order to open.

The black wood stove which was in the middle of the room was burning. Nathan heard his mom's voice to his right and looked out the front window toward the lake. Nathan saw his mom and dad sitting in lawn chairs looking out at the calm lake.

He rushed through the living room and out the wooden glass-paned door onto the front lawn. As Nathan came through the door, he said, "WOOWW!" looking out over the lake.

His dad smiled and said, "Pretty great, huh buddy? The best thing is that it's loaded with fish, and tomorrow morning we are gonna catch 'em up."

"Good," Nathan said staring out across the large lake.

"Nathan, go get some shoes on before you come out here; get a sweatshirt on too, it's cold," Emily commanded Nathan.

"OK, Mom," Nathan said as he turned back and quickly walked inside.

John sat staring out across the lake. Emily looked at John and said, "Well, so much for sitting here and just relaxing. What are you gonna do, go fishing or something?"

"Yeah, but just off the dock. We're gonna head out fishing on the boat in the morning."

Emily stood up and walked toward the cabin door. As she opened it she said, "Well, I'm going to start fixing dinner. I'll holler at you guys when it's ready."

"OK, Em."

The door shut softly behind Emily as she disappeared into the cabin. John heard her muffled voice as she was saying something to Nathan. John looked out over the lake. He took in a large deep breath then got up and walked over to the storage shed on the side of the cabin. He grabbed his keys out of his pocket and opened the padlock. As he opened the door to the locker, he was startled by a fishing rod which fell as the door opened. He caught the pole and leaned it against the cabin. John grabbed another fishing pole and tackle box and closed the shed back up.

After a short inspection of the rods and tackle, John carried them back up by the front of the cabin and sat all the gear down next to the lawn chair he had been in earlier. He waited a couple of minutes for Nathan and then figured Emily was making him change into some warmer clothes, so he carried the tackle box and poles to the end of the dock. Nathan ran out of the cabin.

Emily watched Nathan and John fish for a couple of minutes then moved back over to the kitchen where she was preparing dinner. Emily was happy at how well the trip had been going so far. She had been so worried about John. She had noticed how strange he had been acting but what had really convinced her that he was so stressed out was Brad's phone call.

John had told Emily earlier about the phone call he had received from the police while she had been sleeping. It was disappointing to her at first that the person who attacked John would not face charges for it. But once he explained that the bad guy was going to jail for a long time because of charges from down in the city, she was pleased.

Now that she thought about it a little more, it was great because she didn't know if John's mind could handle going through some long, drawn out court case. She thought he was having enough problems dealing with this midlife crisis he seemed to be having. Hopefully this little getaway would relax his burdened mind so he could get back to being himself again. He had just been so quiet lately, and that was not like John at all.

As she glanced back out the window at John and Nathan out on the dock, she smiled thinking that this was exactly what John needed, some relaxation.

Emily put the casserole she had prepared into the oven and set the timer on an hour. She went and sat down in the small recliner which was next to the wood stove. The cabin still felt damp, but the fire which was going in the wood stove was drying it out quickly. The evenings up here were much cooler than downstate. She leaned her head over to the side, staring out the window at the water. It was calm like glass. The only ripples were coming from John and Nathan who were both casting out and then slowly reeling back in. Her eyes drifted upward to the deep blue sky. There were no clouds so as the sun fell, closer to the horizon it got colder and colder.

The boys came in from fishing, and they all enjoyed a family meal next to the fire softly burning in the wood stove. Emily had asked them where the fish were, and John had gone on to explain that tonight was just a warm up for in the morning when they went out in the boat fishing for real.

After dinner, Nathan and John went out to the storage building in the back of the cabin and got the small aluminum boat with the fifteen-horse engine out for in the morning. John easily dragged the boat to the water's edge.

After setting the boat off and getting all of their equipment in it, John retrieved a minnow trap from the storage garage. He put some of the leftover casserole in it and lowered it off the deep end of the dock. John tied the line off to a dock cleat.

Well, that was it, John thought. In the morning they were gonna catch some fish. John and Nathan had gotten everything done in the nick of time too, as the sun slowly dropped below the pine tree-lined horizon on the west side of the lake.

John reached over and grabbed the alarm clock next to his bed as he held it up so he could see it better. It read 4:35. He was up now so he might as well not try to go back to sleep for 25 minutes more until 5:00.

John could hear the sink running in the bathroom. The sound of Emily's puking had awakened John. He and Nathan were getting up early anyway to go fishing. John rubbed his eyes and got up from bed. He staggered over to the bathroom door which was closed and knocked on it gently saying, "Hey, Em, are you OK?"

Emily's half whispered voice came back through the bathroom door, "Yeah, John. My stomach was just upset, but I feel better now."

"OK," John replied as he walked over to the wood stove and held his hands by its moderately warm top. He opened the door to find only a pile of red hot ambers surrounded by gray ash. John grabbed a couple of logs out of the wood rack and threw them on the hot coals. He left the door slightly ajar to give the fire a little more air in order to get going. John had grown up with only two wood stoves in their farmhouse to heat it. Throughout the years, he had mastered the art of running a wood stove. He could tell he was a little rusty though by last night's harsh temperature rise right after he had stacked the stove before they went to bed. He closed the vent a little. That way once he closed the door back, it wouldn't burn so rapidly. Once you got good with a wood stove, you could keep a house at relatively the same temperature throughout the day. At night, you had to really put a lot of wood in the stove and close the oxygen off so it would smolder all night. The cabin would be slightly colder in the morning but it wouldn't be as cold as it was now. Oh well, John thought as he walked over to the counter to make coffee. Tonight he would definitely keep it warm in here.

As John was finishing filling the coffeemaker with water,

he heard to door open up behind him. John turned and saw Emily who walked over to the wood stove and held her hand over it.

As Emily did this, she said, "Brrrrr, this is one thing I hate about this cabin. There is no furnace. It is always like you are freezing or you are burning up. There is no happy medium."

John looked at Emily and shook his head saying, "Well, maybe you can try to run the wood stove. You would probably burn the place down so I wouldn't be complaining. Maybe you should go back to bed, if you're in such a bad mood."

"I think I will," Emily said as she walked over to the bedroom entrance. She stopped and continued, "Just go fishing and don't worry about me, John. I'm sorry; I just have a bad stomach ache."

John hit the start button on the coffeemaker and replied, "It's all right, Em, go back to bed. I think you could use a little rest."

"OK, good luck fishing." Emily said as she walked through the doorway into their bedroom.

John went and sat in the recliner next to the woodstove. He could hear the crackling of wood burning through the vents in the stove. Every time John restarted the woodstove, he was amazed at how fast one would relight. That was just like Emily, John thought. Just because she wasn't feeling good, she picked on something like keeping a woodstove going. Emily knew John thought he was good at running the woodstove, so Emily deliberately picked on it. If there was a bad trait about Emily, John thought it would definitely be how spiteful she could get when she didn't feel well. Oh well, that's why John tried to avoid her when she was sick.

Hopefully, she would be better by this afternoon when they got back from fishing. John didn't want to deal with a week of Emily not feeling good. Especially up here at the cabin where there weren't very many places to hide.

John could tell by the increased speed of the percolating coffee pot gurgle that the coffee was almost done. He got up and poured himself a cup. After some coffee, John packed his and Nathan's lunches and some sodas in a small cooler. John went out on the dock, put the cooler in the boat, and pulled the minnow trap from the bottom. He smiled and poured the twenty or so medium-sized minnows into the boat's small live well.

All that was left to do now was to go get Nathan up, which John suspected would be pretty easy. Nathan always woke up easily when there was something fun to do like fishing.

As John turned to walk off the dock to the cabin, he was surprised to see Nathan coming toward him all dressed in his favorite red-hooded sweatshirt and blue jeans. John was happy to see Nathan up, and he instantly became proud thinking he had gotten up and ready all by himself.

As Nathan stepped onto the dock John said, "Hey good morning, buddy. I'm surprised to see you up this early on your own."

Nathan seemed a little tired still but responded, "Mom woke me up but I was just lying there from her puking earlier."

"Oh, so you heard her this morning?" John asked.

"Yes," Nathan responded. "As little as the cabin is, how could you not hear her? Is Mom OK?"

"Yes, Nathan. Don't worry about your mom. She just has a stomach ache. She is gonna go back to bed and by the time we get back she will be in good enough shape to cook up all the fish we are getting ready to catch." After saying this, John playfully pulled up the red hood on Nathan's sweater and continued, "You might need this up. You know how fast Old Bessie here is." John motioned down at the small aluminum boat.

Nathan laughed, then hopping into the boat on the forward bench seat he said, "Well, let's see how fast she'll go."

John hopped into the back of the boat and then flipped the choke to the start position. He pumped the bulb coming from the red plastic fuel tank a couple of times. A few pulls on the ripcord later, John and Nathan found themselves slowly pulling away from the dock. The sun was starting to rise behind them. John was happy because it would burn the low haze that lay about four to six feet above the lake. The haze was thick as they slowly idled their way out into the lake. John had to stand up every once in a while to see out above it.

As they made their way closer to the center of the lake, the wind was blowing a little stronger and the fog cleared up. John looked back behind them at the layer of fog that hugged the tree-lined, wind-sheltered beach. Now he could see so he twisted the throttle on the outboard to full. The boat was light and quickly came up onto a plane. Fife Lake wasn't a very large lake. It was about a mile and a half wide and was shaped in almost a perfect circle. John knew this lake well. He had grown up spending the summers in his parents' cabin on the lake. John was reminded of his family's old cabin from the large oak tree that stuck up on the shoreline on the foggy horizon ahead of them. He would have loved to have kept that cabin in the family for sentimental value, but John was just starting a family when his parents had sold it. John regretted not buying it at the "family price" his parents had offered it to him for.

The funny thing about the whole cabin-buying thing was five years after he turned down buying his parents' cabin is when he talked Emily into buying a cabin on the lake. They then ended up paying four times as much as they would have if they had gotten his parents'. Oh well, John thought. See there: his mind was thinking about business. That was his problem: he could never quit thinking about numbers. That was the real sentimental value of his parents' cabin to John: lost money. No, no that was a horrible thought. John was saddened by his thought and hoped his father couldn't somehow hear.

As they approached the fishing area, John slowed the boat. The boat came off its plane and pushed waves ahead of it as it dropped down into the water. John flipped the engine off and then looked in all directions to make sure he was lined up on the hole.

It was a large area that rose up almost thirty feet above the sixty-foot bottom. John's dad always told him straight off the big oak at our cabin then line up with the old hotel. The old hotel was torn down now. In its place was a ten story condominium complex. It looked out of place on the lake at first, but over the last couple of years several more had gone up around them and made the north shore of the lake look pretty modern.

The north shore was where the small downtown area had once been. Now it was littered with yuppie coffee shops and a couple of breweries. John used to love coming up here to escape hanging out with pretentious business people. That was the reason he had always stayed living up in the thumb of Michigan instead of down in one of the richer suburbs. John could talk the talk with these fancy people, but he still believed in good old-fashioned country etiquette. Now that Fife Lake was growing like this, it was

160

losing its charm. He had loved it when the only place to eat in town was the small mom-and-pop pizza place or the large log cabin bar called the Fife Lake Inn.

Now if you walked downtown, the Fife Lake Inn had been turned into a fancy steak house and the old pizza place had been turned into a coffee shop. What really disgusted John was seeing all the fancy dressed families loading out of their Mercedes. They were all up for the weekend from Chicago. God, John hated that.

The boat was drifting very slowly on the calm water. Nathan had already rigged a minnow and lowered it to the bottom. John was busy staring at the north shore. He glanced back to the east where his cabin was and wondered how long before he would be driven out of here. The big woods his dad had talked about had changed for the worse.

John retrieved a minnow from the cold, live-well and hooked it through it's belly. The minnow started wiggling frantically around the piece of metal which had just been pushed through its intestines. As John threw his bait into the water then began to let line out, he thought, "It's OK little guy, your pain will be over shortly."

Only a few seconds after his weight hit the bottom, John felt his bait bouncing around scared. John thought easy now, let them take it; don't be like all those other no-fish catching friends of yours. The erratic bouncing of the minnow began to intensify.

Nathan seeing his dad's tip of his pole bouncing around yelled, "Dad, you got a fish. Hook it, hook it!"

Just then the fish swam off with his bait and John's rod bent, setting the hook deep in the fish's lip. John's rod bent and moved around as he reeled the fish slowly to the surface. As he reeled, he looked over at Nathan and said, "See how I did that, Nathan? Never yank a fishing rod. If your bait is hooked properly the fish will hook itself."

Nathan was looking over the edge into the water and asked, "What is it? Is it big?"

As John caught a glimpse of the fish coming up in the clear water, he said, "It looks like a nice yellow belly." John continued reeling the fish to the surface then flipped it over the edge onto the boat floor. John smiled and continued, "Yep, look at that, Nathan. That's probably a fourteen-inch perch." John reached down, grabbed it and pulled the hook out of its mouth. He held the fish up and said, "Boy, that's a beauty." Then flipped the door to the open live well and threw it in.

John baited his line and sent another minnow wiggling down to the bottom. It sat on the bottom for about a minute when John felt it get scared and start bouncing. He let the bait and fish do a little dance, then began to reel up another perch.

Nathan who was watching his dad intently asked, "What are you doing, Dad? What's the trick? I want to know!"

As John slowly reeled up another perch, he said Nathan, "Reel up your line, and I'll show you a secret way to hook your bait."

"OK!" Nathan exclaimed as he began to reel his line in.

Nathan got his line in, and John showed him the secret belly hook. A lot of people would tell you that hooking a fish in the belly would just kill them faster but John didn't want his bait to be sitting on the bottom, swimming around and hiding from the perch. He wanted his bait to hit the bottom and be flopping around like crazy. John always pictured a minnow that was gut-hooked as a filet mignon to fish. How could they resist something so tempting?

Nathan got his line back down, and John walked him through hooking an elusive yellow-belly perch. With both of them catching fish now, they would have dinner in no time. The fog had now been burned off of the entire lake by the now-high sun.

As John took off his flannel shirt due to the increasing temperature, he noticed a large storm front that was heading toward them from the west. The clouds were tall and dark and moving quickly toward them. John pointed up at the clouds and said to Nathan, "You see that, bud, we've got to get moving. We want to beat that home for sure."

Nathan looked up at the clouds and responded, "Yeah, that looks pretty bad."

Nathan and John both reeled up quickly, and John started the outboard engine. He brought the small boat up on a plane and made a large circle turning until they were pointed toward the east shore. Once John zeroed in on home, he headed directly toward their cabin. The small outboard hummed loudly as John held it wide open.

John glanced back over his shoulder at the approaching storm head. John had run away from storms on this lake countless times. The weather in Michigan always had the capability of turning bad, combined with the lake being down in a valley surrounded by tree top hills, made it impossible to see a storm until it was already on you.

The bite had turned off about a half an hour ago, so it was just as well they left. Now they could say they would have caught so many more fish if that stupid storm hadn't come. As it was, John figured they probably had a dozen nice-sized perch. They would definitely have enough for a feast tonight.

John looked back at the storm, then back to the approaching shore. John figured they were going to make it just fine. He had been out on the lake before when it turned bad quickly and the bite was on so they waited and waited. John could still remember being huddled in the front of his dad's boat soaked in rain with lightening starting to flash all around.

Although they weren't going to get caught today, John could see the rain now starting to pelt the other side of the lake. As John got closer to the on-coming beach, he yelled up to Nathan, "Scoot back there, buddy. We want to get up as far as we can."

"Ok," Nathan replied and moved back to the bench seat .

John reached back and shut the motor off then flipped it up out of the water. The boat slowly came to a halt on the sandy beach with the bow well onto land.

As it came to a stop, John glanced back at the rain and said, "We've got about five minutes until that rain gets here, so you throw the fish in a bucket and I'll pull the boat farther up and pull the plug. All right, Nathan?"

"All right, Dad," Nathan replied walking to the front of the boat to get the bucket.

As Emily lay on the couch in the cabin, she trembled because she was cold. It seemed so freezing in here. Emily thought she must have a fever as she looked over at the wood stove which was burning warmly.

As Emily's eyes moved around the cabin, it seemed awfully dark. She wondered if she had slept all the way into nighttime. Even in her delirious, sick state she thought that would have been impossible. Emily looked out the cabin's front windows. She was looking from down on the couch up toward the sky and could only see black, rolling clouds. Emily got a chill in her spine and a tingling sensation slowly moved up her body as she stared up at the clouds. She wondered if the boys were OK but then realized the feelings she had coming over wasn't that. It was as if somebody was staring at her. Emily's eyes came down from the window and moved over toward the direction of the wood stove. As they came into the doorway that led into the small entrance to the cabin just behind the stove, she felt as if something was staring at her from inside of the dark space. She squinted into the darkness looking to see if somebody was there.

Emily had a creepy feeling running through her body. The hair began to stand up on the back of her neck.

Emily let out a small scream as a large noise came from the darkness where she was staring. The door from outside was flung open by Nathan who was carrying a white bucket. The darkness disappeared from the outside light coming in. He walked into the cabin's main living area and turned on the light. As Nathan spotted his mom on the couch, he said excitedly, "Mom, you should see all the perch we got." He held up a bucket and began to walk over toward her. Emily said, "Nathan, go set the bucket in the sink for dad. I'm sick, so if you would, please try to be quiet and turn the light back off!" "OK, Mom," Nathan replied as he sat the bucket in the sink and walked back outside.

Emily sat up on the couch and took a few deep breaths. Her heart was pounding rapidly from the scare she had just got. The creepy feeling that had been running through her had now left. She glanced outside at John who was walking up the front lawn towards the cabin.

As she looked out over the lake, Emily could see rain over halfway across and heading toward them. With the rain came dark clouds and what looked to Emily as a very bad thunderstorm. Now that Emily was awake she could make out the sound of thunder in the distance.

Emily's heart rate was beginning to return to normal as she glanced back at the now lit up entryway. She physically shivered and pulled the blanket up around her shoulders. Emily thought to herself that she must have been hallucinating earlier when she thought somebody was staring at her. She had taken some Ny-quil this morning when she was done throwing up. Nyquil always made Emily have weird dreams.

Emily thought her fever may be high enough to be causing her to hallucinate. She was lucky enough to find the old bottle of Nyquil in the medicine cabinet or she would never have gotten any sleep.

Well, anyway, she was just glad that at least she wasn't sick to her stomach anymore.

John came walking into the cabin, sat the tackle box down in the entryway, then turned and looked at Emily across the dark room. He stepped into the main living area and switched on the light over the kitchen table. As he did, John noticed Emily sitting on the couch and said, "Hey, Em, are you feeling any better?"

Emily's sick voice responded, "Yeah, I haven't thrown up since this morning, but I've had a fever ever since."

John was now a little more concerned, because Emily was usually pretty healthy. It was normally he or Nathan that was sick. Whenever Emily got sick it was usually a pretty serious bug. John walked over to Emily on the couch and held the back of his hand up to her head. He was shocked at how hot she felt. John pulled his hand back and said, "God, you're burning up, Emily. When was the last time you took your temperature?"

"I haven't because we don't have a thermometer here."

"Oh," John said. He paused, thinking, and then asked, "Have you taken anything to break the fever?"

"Just Ny-Quil", Emily answered, as Nathan sat opposite from her on the couch. Emily switched her conversation to him and said, "Nathan, I'm sorry if I bit your head off earlier. I just don't feel well, and you startled me."

Nathan shrugged his shoulders and responded, "OK."

John turned, walked over to the kitchen area and retrieved a few Tylenol from a bottle in the cupboard. He filled a glass of water from the sink, returned to the couch, gave them to Emily and said, "Here, take these Tylenol so your fever will break."

Emily responded "OK," then took the medicine.

He kissed Emily on the forehead and said, in a southern drawl, "We're gonna clean these fish. You try to get better, OK? We got a big 'ole fish dinner for us, and we want you to be able to enjoy." John walked over to the kitchen with Nathan following.

John sharpened a fillet knife he kept up here just for perch. As he meticulously filleted what ended up being sixteen- perch, he explained to Nathan how to do it. Nathan was too young to handle the sharp knife yet, but when John allowed him to, he wanted Nathan to have some good knowledge for what he was doing. The big perch were easy to clean because of their size. The challenging ones to fillet were the small ten-inchers. If one didn't know what they were doing on these small fish, it was almost impossible to get any meat off of them big enough to even cook. John's dad had taught him well, just as John figured he was teaching Nathan. John threw all the fillets into a bowl and all the carcasses he got into the garbage. John had wanted to bury them but the pouring rain was going to make that impossible. Well, maybe it would stop raining before they started stinking then John would get a chance to bury them. As John finished wiping off the counters he looked over at Nathan and said, "Well, now all that's left to do is eat them." John pulled the silver handle on the small fridge and put the bowl of fillets onto the shelf.

He closed the door and looked over at Emily who lay on the couch, shivering. He hadn't noticed how pale she was earlier. John walked over by her and put his hand on her forehead.

Emily who seemed to be in a half asleep-half awake zone looked up at John and said, "Hi, honey."

John pulled his hand from her hot forehead and responded, "It's been 45 minutes, and that Tylenol didn't bring your fever down at all. I think you need to go see a doctor."

Emily looked up at John as she continued, "I'm gonna take you to a doctor. Have you looked at yourself in a mirror lately? You look pale as a ghost."

"I know I do, John. You know how I am. I don't get sick very often but when I do it's bad. I just don't want to go to some backwoods quack up here, and I don't want to ruin our trip and make us go home." As Emily said this, tears were building up in her eyes.

John had seen Emily get sick before so he knew she was

getting ready to cry.   Well, at least it was raining out so, John wouldn't be missing out on any fishing. He was discouraged at the thought of just getting to the cabin and already having to leave, but he remained calm and said, "Well, Emily, don't be sad. We'll just go back home, get you to the doctor in the morning, and then maybe we'll come back up all next week, OK?"

Emily's tears were now overflowing and rolling down her smooth cheek.

John kneeled down beside the couch, kissed her on the forehead, and said, "It's all right, Em, I'll pack everything up and maybe we can get you to the doctor today."

"OK," Emily responded as she wiped off her cheeks with the sleeve of the gray sweatshirt she was wearing.

Well, that sucked, but John knew that if Emily went and saw their doctor they would be back here in only a few days. The alternative would be John having to deal with Emily being sick and bitchy for a week in close quarters. So the decision for John was easy. Nathan on the other hand would be very disappointed.

John would explain to him that they were coming back in a couple of days once Mom felt better, and he would understand.

Emily lay on the couch shivering. She could see Nathan's disappointment when John told them they were going home, but what could Emily do? She would make it up to him when they came back up. Even though Nathan was disappointed, Emily was proud of the way he still helped John get everything packed back up into the Suburban.

Emily sat watching as John came back into the cabin for her he said, "All right, Em, we got everything loaded up. You're the last thing I need to get from inside."

Emily slowly got up from the couch. She walked toward John with the blanket still wrapped around her. John held the door open for her and as she passed, he said, "I have a pillow and a blanket for you in the Suburban."

"OK. Thanks, John," Emily replied as she walked out the cabin door around the front of the Suburban and stepped into the passenger side. Emily closed her eyes.

John locked the cabin up and got into the vehicle. Both Emily and Nathan were lying with their eyes closed, sleeping. This made for an easy drive for John who made good time heading south for home. Before long John found himself driving down the flat farm-lined roads of lower Michigan again.

It was around six, and John figured they had about 45 minutes until they got home. Well, Emily wasn't going to be able to make it to the doctor today. John had phoned, and they said she could come in anytime, but they were only open until four. He would take her first thing in the morning though. As John got closer to his home, the roads became more and more familiar. Finally, the familiar feeling changed into the great feeling of when you're arriving home as John eased the blue Suburban into their driveway.

THE
CONFRONTATION

John swerved slightly as he made his way down the dark road. He was still half asleep as he drove toward the lit up sky of Croswell. There wouldn't be much open there at this hour. John was heading for the 24-hour Shell gas station to get Emily some type of stomach medicine. She had specifically told him to get Imodium AD, but John knew he wasn't going to a pharmacy.

The gas station might have the Imodium, but if not he hoped they would have something that could settle Emily's stomach better than the Pepto she took when they got home. They had gotten back around seven in the evening, and Emily had gone straight upstairs to bed. He had let Nathan go spend the night at Billy's house. It was better for John, too. With Nathan gone, it was one less thing he had to worry about.

Emily had been sleeping for a while so John thought she was better. Now it was one in the morning, and Emily had kept him up for the last hour. Even though it was this late, John didn't mind taking care of Emily while she was sick. All had been well the last couple of days. He would have liked to stay longer at the cabin, but what could he do? Emily hadn't planned on being sick. It was refreshing to John having to deal with normal problems.

Nathan had quit having nightmares. He had quit seeing the dark man, and now Emily had a little stomach flu. The stomach flu was something John would be more than happy to deal with. He thought back over the whole burglar incident and what a crazy

169

emotional roller coaster ride it had been. John was relieved to be moving on with his life, even though moving on meant dealing with the stomach flu at some ungodly hour of the night.

The road was empty so John pushed the speed limit well over what he normally would go. Even though he didn't mind dealing with what he considered everyday problems, he did want to get back to sleep some time tonight, so he sped up even faster.

The last time he had been speeding down this road was the night he had been attacked. That seemed like such an eternity ago now.

Now that John's life had been normal for a while, he realized how stressed out he had been because of work. He knew that the first night he had been attacked but wouldn't admit it to himself. At first after the attack, John had problems getting little things about it out of his head. These little things all added up. Put on top of being so stressed out by work, it had caused John to create the whole dark man thing. John found that amusing now looking back on it all.

John had always felt so bad for crazy people, pitying them because they could not control their mind. He kept thinking the whole thing had gotten started because he was getting older now. His mind may have lost a little bit of its ability to handle stress. John figured that was all right though because he wasn't going to stress his mind out with crazy sixty-hour work weeks again. It was just too much for him anymore.

With sixty hours at the office piled on top of twenty hours of commute time, John was putting in eighty hours a week at the office. He had been doing this for almost six months, and maybe it had finally just taken its toll. John couldn't help but to feel weak both physically and mentally. He shouldn't though. When he was younger, he had done years and years of stressful times at work and made it through. From now on, he was going to be a forty-hour-a-week guy. John tried to convince himself that he had already done his hard time, so it was time to let some of the young guys shine now.

John had always done well at work, but he knew his body had given him a warning to slow down. It was easier to convince himself that he was just kind of stepping down for the young guys rather than admitting he was just getting too darn old.

But he was. Hell, when he was in his twenties, he would have worked eighty hours a week plus party til the wee hours every night. Actually, even in his thirties. Since the big 40, John could definitely feel Father Time catching up.

He was never going to let himself get as stressed out as he had gotten this last year. There was no way he was going to let himself turn into one of those high-blood-pressure workaholics who had ulcers and gave themselves a heart attack at fifty. Shit, fifty was less than ten years away for John, so he needed to start taking care of himself. The first thing he was going to do was quit working so much. He remembered back to that serene, glassy morning on the lake. This was when it had struck him that the whole incident had been made up by his body in order to scare himself into resting.

Well, it worked. From now on he was taking it easy. What the heck, he had put away quite a nest egg over the years. John could actually afford to go into full retirement if he wanted to. But that would drive him crazier than he had been driven by overworking. What he had to find was a happy medium between working and not working. He would start out at forty hours a week. The big thing he was also going to cut back on was taking so many business trips.

Coming closer to his destination, John could make out the Shell symbol shining brightly on the gas station. He slowed down as the entrance approached and eased the Buick under the bright canopy of neon light.

Nathan was standing in the dark, staring out the window into the night. His face was pushed up against the glass. The steam that his breathing was creating combined with the glare coming from the small night light behind him made it impossible to see anything at all.

As he stared out into the darkness, a light came on across the road. Nathan now recognized the light, which was increasing in size, as the garage door of a house. As he looked in the garage, he saw a blue Suburban and a brown Buick. It finally came to Nathan: that was his house he was staring at. But why? What was he doing staring out the window at his own house? He was confused as he saw his dad's car pull from the garage and drive down the driveway. The car turned onto the main road and passed in front of the house.

Nathan was even more confused now. Something wasn't right. His body felt slow and groggy as he turned to look at his surroundings. The room was softly lit by the green nightlight glowing at the foot of the bed. Nathan saw Billy sleeping on his side on the top trundle bed but as his eyes moved down, he was shocked to see himself sleeping on the lower bed. This seemed weird to Nathan as his eyes were drawn back to the window. He could barely make out his blue house across the road.

His house was lit up as if a moon beam was shining down directly upon it. It was bright enough to see the colors of the house but dim sort of, too. Almost like a huge nightlight was above it. All the windows were dark in the house except Nathan's parents' room. He could only see the white of the curtains shining from the light behind it. For some reason Nathan knew his dad had left and gone somewhere. He saw a silhouette in his parents' window and recognized it immediately as his mom.

As his mother's silhouette disappeared out of the window, Nathan could hear a strange noise coming from the distance. He looked back across the fields behind his house and could see a dark storm on the horizon coming toward them. The storm had tall dark clouds with lightening flashing around them. The thunder was getting louder as the storm approached.

The floor beneath Nathan began to shake, and the windowpane he was looking through was now vibrating noticeably. The noise from the storm was intensified by a large dark ocean which was surging and rushing toward Nathan's direction.

Nathan got that creepy feeling through his body again like something else was there with him. It was now rushing all around Nathan trying to get into his head. He put down his mental guard and let it in.

The same voice of the dark man came alive in his head saying, "It is coming. You must stop it."

Nathan didn't know what the dark man was talking about so he said, "Who?"

The dark man's voice echoed, "Look at it coming!"

Nathan looked at the raging sea and storm coming in his direction and asked, "But what do I . . . ?"

In the middle of asking what he should do, his thoughts were frozen from the sight of his mother's silhouette through his parents' window. Nathan could tell it was his mother not only by the shape of her silhouette but also by the sense of love that he felt being emitted from her direction.

The feeling of love he had felt from his mom was pushed away by the hair standing up on the back of his neck and an intense tingling sensation throughout his upper body. His eyes moved to the second window of his parents' bedroom where the large silhouette of the dark man was.

Nathan was even more confused now as the dark man's voice popped into his head again, "You must tell her. It is going to get her."

Confused, Nathan yelled over the increasing roar of the oncoming sea, "How?"

"Wake up," the voice came again louder in Nathan's head. "Wake up and go to her. Only you can stop it."

Nathan looked away from the window and back to the bed where he could see himself sleeping. Crouched next to him was the dark man. The dark man was shaking him, and its voice came alive inside his head again. "Wake up!"

The noise of the oncoming sea was intensifying, and the house was beginning to shake all around Nathan. The voice echoed through his head again. "Wake up! Wake up, Nathan!"

Then, like the snap of a light switch, his eyes came open, and he lay there awake staring at the dimly lit ceiling of Billy's room.

He was breathing rapidly, and his heart was pounding fast in his chest. Nathan thought, that was a weird dream. Nathan looked over at Billy who was on his side, facing away from him, sleeping. He then looked over at the window facing his house across the street. For some reason, Nathan was being drawn toward that window to look out just like in his dream. He felt as though his mother could be in some type of danger. He wanted to get up and look out the window but was frozen in place right now. Nathan wasn't sure if he was still dreaming or if this was real now. He reached his right hand up and pinched himself. "Ow, that hurt." Well, that was that. Nathan realized he wasn't dreaming any more.

He glanced back up toward the window he had been looking out in his dream and then realized he could look out. What's the worst that could happen? If the dark man came out, then he would just wake up Billy.

Nathan pulled the blanket off him and eased his feet off the bed careful to not make any sound. He set his feet on the soft carpet, then took a couple of steps to the window and looked outside. It was hard to see anything because of the glare of the night light behind him. But as Nathan moved his face closer to the glass, he could make out his house across the street. What made Nathan's curiosity run wild was the garage door being opened just as in his dream. The light was on in the garage and his dad's car was gone.

Nathan was instantly alarmed because as he glanced over at the red digital clock by Billy's head, it was 1:10 in the morning. So why had his dad left so late? Nathan had been having a dream of a dark man in his house behind his mother. As Nathan remembered his dream from earlier, his eyes made their way up to the only two lighted windows of the house; his parents.

Nathan didn't see the silhouette of his mom or any dark man figure. He did have a weird feeling coming over him just like he had in his dreams when the dark man was by him, though. It seemed to be coming to him from the second window in his parents' room. What if the dark man in his dreams was trying to help him and tried to tell him he needed to go protect his mom. Nathan felt an overwhelming need to go to his home and protect his mother.

As Nathan stared at the window of his parents' room, he could feel the sense of both his mom and the dark man coming from that direction. Even though, he was scared Nathan decided he would go to his house and help his mother. Nathan didn't know where his dad had gone but knew that he had left.

Nathan crept across the room and over to the door. He turned the knob slowly and slipped through the door while only opening it slightly. Nathan knew from sneaking around Billy's house before that the door would squeak if opened past about one quarter of the way.

Nathan made his way through the dark hallway leading to

the stairway. The hall and stairway were carpeted so he easily walked down the stairs without making a noise. A light from the kitchen shined from the bottom of the staircase. As Nathan crossed the living room toward the front door, he glanced into the kitchen to see where it was coming from. The light shined brightly from above the stove. Nathan didn't ever remember that being on before, but it looked like there wasn't anybody up. He quietly walked to the doorway and found his Nikes in the pile of shoes by the front door and crouched down to slip them on. He kept nervously glancing back at the kitchen expecting to see one of Billy's parents there as he quickly tied his shoes.

Nathan stood up and undid the dead bolt on the front door and then slipped outside pulling it shut behind him. Nathan had to walk extra slow to keep the motion lights on Billy's front porch from coming on. Nathan eased his way off the porch and out of their range. He glanced over at his house and got a creepy feeling so he paused. As he stood, a car's headlights came from his right so Nathan ducked behind a bush. It looked as if a vehicle was nearing quickly. Hiding behind the tree, he flipped the hood of his sweatshirt over his head.

Emily awoke suddenly as her body jumped. She opened her eyes and looked up at the familiar outline of her own room. She felt clammy and sweaty. She realized where she was and then rolled over to look for John.

Everything came back to her at once. She had sent John to the store to get her some Imodium for her upset stomach. She had been confused like this all day. Emily's stomach gurgled as she rubbed it. A bad cramp came through her side, and she leaned up on her elbow thinking she might have to get up to go to the bathroom again. It passed quickly though as she lay back down and looked up at the ceiling.

The room was pretty well lit by the bathroom light which she must have forgotten to turn off. As she rolled over to get off the bed, she froze in place as a strange tingling sensation ran through her upper body. All the hair stood up on the back of her neck, and Emily was instantly creeped out. Her eyes slowly moved across the room to the darkness that led into the hallway and stopped.

Just as she had felt earlier today at the cabin, she could feel something staring at her from inside the darkness that filled the doorway. She looked harder trying to make it out but was unable to. She was absolutely frozen in terror.

She couldn't see anything in the hallway but she could tell there was something there, and it was evil. Emily was terrified at the feeling of staring some evil creature eye to eye. She wanted to get up and run, but her body and eyes were locked in fear as the darkness began to move.

John had been driving fast as he left Croswell. The bright lights from town were now mere specks in his rearview mirror. He was going faster than normal as he cut through the darkness toward home. He was pushing 90 miles an hour as he thought of what a hero he would be when he got home with not only the Imodium but also Popsicles and ginger ale.

As John's house approached on the right, he could see the garage door open and light coming from it. John's eyes moved from the garage up toward the windows of their bedroom which were also lighted. Maybe Emily was up sick still, or she had fallen asleep with them on.

As John stared up at the windows, he began to get a tingling sensation throughout his upper body, and the hair on the back of his neck stood up. He realized that he was getting the same feeling he had before when he saw the dark man. Only there was no dark man this time right? John felt confused. His confusion turned to anger as he saw a large silhouette in the second window of his room. It paused for a moment, and then flashed in the direction of where their bed was located in the room.

John raced his car into the driveway then sped into the garage. He wasn't sure if what he just saw was real, but it gave him that same sensation he had received the last few times John had seen the dark man. As John opened the door, he remembered Jenny's voice saying, "You don't understand, John. You won't have a chance to protect whomever it is coming for. It will simply come and get them when you are gone." Well, this Gatherer must not have planned on John coming home.

As John quietly but quickly pushed the car door shut, he reached over and grabbed a putter from his golf bag. Everything was all so clear to him now. He must sneak up on the Gatherer and get it, but he must be fast because it could be getting her right now.

John walked over to the garage door and then slipped his shoes off. He was going to need to be fast and quiet if he was going to get this thing. John carried the putter in his right hand and opened the door to the kitchen with his left.

He tiptoed quickly across the kitchen then through the living room to the oak staircase leading up to their room. John took a few quiet steps on the staircase then on his third, a loud creak came out. John froze for a second. When he stopped, he heard Emily's quiet muffled cries as if something was covering her mouth as she was trying to scream.

A surge of terror then rage rushed through John. John immediately bounded up the rest of the stairs, turned, and ran down the hall toward their room. The door was wide open, and as John neared, he could hear sounds of a muffled struggle. John burst into the doorway and saw the dark man crouched down over Emily. It had its elbows pinned on Emily's shoulders and was holding her wrists just above her head. Emily was squirming trying to get away. John could see the terror in her now-bulging eyes as a large hissing noise came from the dark man. It was mouth-to-mouth with Emily as it sucked the air from her lungs. As John rushed toward the dark man, he raised the golf club above his head. John took one large last step and swung the club down violently at the dark man.

As the club neared the back of the dark man, it seemed to sense the club. In a flash the dark man looked back, saw the club, and jumped off Emily. Emily gasped for a split second as the dark man got off her. The club struck her in the forehead and her gasp turned into a small squeak as her head was pushed deep into the pillow from the blow. Emily's eyes rolled back in her head and her mouth lay gaping open. John stood in shock for a second. A trickle of blood was coming out of Emily's mouth as he let go of the golf club in horror. His horror intensified, and he said loudly, "Oh, my God," realizing that once he let go of the club it stayed in the same

177

position due to being deeply embedded in Emily's skull.

John looked at Emily's forehead closer and was terrified seeing that the club had disappeared out of sight into her broken skull. Where the shiny club stuck out of her skull, it was sunken in, as if a baseball had been smashed into her forehead.

John knew he had to get Emily to the hospital immediately if she were to have a chance of survival. He bent over and picked Emily up, then turned to go to his car so he could get her help. As John turned, he froze as the dark man was standing in the doorway staring at him. John got the same feeling he had before when he saw the dark man.

With large tears beginning to come from John's eyes, he hysterically yelled, "Look at this! Look at what you've done!" But the dark man stood motionless.

John took off running toward the dark figure. As he ran, John yelled, "Get out of my way, you bastard!" As John neared, it dashed down the hall, turned, and disappeared down the steps. The golf club, which was still lodged firmly in Emily's forehead, caught on the wall as the room turned into the hallway leading out. This spun John back around as the club was ripped out and fell on the floor. John looked down at the head of the putter which was dark red. He knelt down closer to the club and then said, "Holy shit!" Realizing there were large chunks of fleshy gobs on the tip of the club head.

John's cheeks were streaked from the tears that were pouring down them. He laid Emily gently on the soft white carpet next to the golf club which laid in a pool of blood.

John leaned over Emily and said softly, "I'm sorry, baby." He sobbed a second and then continued, "I didn't mean to, I was just trying to protect you from it." He then kissed her on her cheek.

As he did, John saw Emily was still breathing and thought head wounds always look bad. John realized he must pull himself together if he wanted to save Emily. He picked her up and then turned and quickly went down the wood staircase. As he went down the steps, John glanced around for the dark man but didn't see anything so he proceeded to the kitchen heading for his car.

Nathan had been confused when the car he had been hiding from had ended up being his dad. Nathan had watched his dad from the distance get out of the car very quickly. Then his dad grabbed something big and hurried inside leaving the garage door open behind him.

Nathan had been horrified at seeing his dad acting so strange. Why had he rushed into the driveway so quickly and what did he grab? Nathan had crept up to the road's edge wanting to know what was going on. He wondered if he had been too late and maybe the burglar had come back. Nathan had a chance to be a hero, but instead it looked like his dad would get the badge from the police department.

Nathan froze at the edge of the road as he heard a commotion coming from the direction of his parents' room. He was alarmed at the loud fighting sounds he heard. Even more terrifying was watching what he thought to be his father's silhouette as it smashed something down right in the spot where he knew his parents' bed was.

There had been a little chaos after that and Nathan thought he heard his dad yell something, but his father's voice sounded hysterical and was hard to make out.

Nathan had been standing frozen for several seconds when he thought he heard a sound coming from the garage. Nathan's knees were shaking as he focused harder on his surroundings. As he stared, he was absolutely motionless as he saw the dark man come running out of the garage and speed down the road towards him. Nathan was scared and getting ready to run as the dark man stopped and stood across from him staring. Nathan only sensed one thing coming from the dark man now, and it was evil. He knew it wasn't trying to help him.

Just before he turned to run, Nathan paused, seeing his father come frantically out the doorway. Nathan couldn't quite make out what was going on because the dark man blocked his view but his dad seemed to be hunched over, carrying something. Whatever it was, he quickly put it in the passenger's side then ran around to the driver's side of the car. Nathan, trying to scream for his dad, stepped onto the road and held his hand up to his mouth to yell. Before he could shout, his dad got into the car and shut the door. Well, that was it, Nathan thought if he was going to get away

179

from the dark man now, he was going to have to get his dad's attention.

His dad backed out of the garage, spinning the car around quickly, and headed down the driveway toward the road. It was probably a hundred yards to his driveway, Nathan thought. He started sprinting as fast as he could toward his father. As he ran, the dark man ran up next to him and then seemed to go all around Nathan like he had a black force field all around him. Nathan felt as if he had put on a pair of dark sunglasses but still kept running toward his dad.

As John sped to the end of the driveway, he was up to about 20 miles per hour when he rounded the corner and put the accelerator to the floor. Emily's head clunked loudly off the glass, so John reached over with his right hand and straightened her limp body while he guided the Buick with his left. His eyes moved up in the distance where he was surprised to see the dark man running straight at him. John pushed hard on the already bottomed out accelerator trying to pick up more speed to smash the dark man. The dark man was running at him with his hand out as if to say stop.

As John really got close, it stopped and tried to leap out of the way, but the Buick hit the dark man dead center as it rolled up on the hood and then over the windshield. John looked in his rearview mirror and saw the dark image land on the road behind him. John thought he saw it move, so he locked up the brakes. As the Buick came to a screeching halt, John put his arm out instinctively and held Emily in place.

He glanced back over his shoulder and saw the dark image moving as if it were trying to get away. John thought he knew what to do now. Everything was clear to him as he threw the car into reverse and accelerated backward toward the huddled figure. The dark image was on its knees trying to get up as John's vehicle neared. Once again, it held up its hand before impact as if it were trying to get John to stop.

John laughed in his head at the thought of it holding its hand up as if he would take any type of mercy on the dark man for all the torment it had caused in his life; he was glad to be smashing it with his car. John knew that this time he had gotten the dark man good as the car lifted up over top of it upon impact. He could hear its body noisely thunking underneath the floorboard as the vehicle passed over top.

As the front of the car passed over it, a tire caught the body and flipped it over to the shoulder of the road. John took his foot off the accelerator and locked up the brakes. He stared at the huddled mass in front of them and then looking over at Emily's bloody face he realized he had to get to the hospital, so he threw the car in drive and took off.

Brad had first awakened from the sound of tires squealing in front of his house. He got up and looked out the window and was surprised to see a car backing up over what looked to be a small person. Just before the car hit, the person put up his hand trying to get the driver to stop.

Brad stood paralyzed in disbelief, as the car then backed all the way over the person and stopped to make sure it didn't move. Once the driver had been satisfied, the vehicle sped off toward town. He stared into the darkness for a moment wondering if what he saw was real. He then looked further across the road and could make out John's house. It was easy to see into the well-lit garage area and notice John's car was gone.

Brad blinked in disbelief and then said, "Oh, my God! What is going on?" He quickly walked up to Billy's room and peeked inside. Billy was asleep on the top trundle bed but Nathan's bunk was empty. The image of the tiny person flashed into Brad's head as he realized it very well could have been Nathan out in the street. Brad said in a gasping whisper, "Holy shit!" as he turned and bounded down the hallway and down the stairs.

Brad was very nervous now. He had a bad feeling running through him as he ran across the living room to the front door. He quickly threw on a pair of shoes, then opened the door and raced across the porch. As Brad came down the stairs and across his driveway, the motion detectors picked him up and the front yard was lit by the large floodlights mounted high on the garage.

Jen must have heard all of the commotion because as Brad

ran down the driveway, he heard her voice yelling out behind him, "Brad, what is it? What's wrong?"

Brad yelled back, "I think something got hit on the road." Then as he neared the huddled up mass on the edge of the road, he yelled back franticly, "Jen, go inside and call 911. Hurry!"

As Jen turned to get the phone, she was yelling, "What is it?"

Jen disappeared in the house, and the air was silent as Brad kneeled down over the red shirted, small body. He was almost certain it was Nathan but could not identify the person yet because it was laying face down and had the hood of a sweatshirt pulled over its head.

Brad slowly rolled the body over. He reached up and pushed the red hood off the face to reveal Nathan. The light from Brad's house only shined on one side of Nathan's face, and Brad was surprised at how bad he looked.

As Brad's eyes moved from Nathan's face down, he could see he had very serious injuries. Both of his legs were twisted around awkwardly, and his back had felt odd as Brad had rolled Nathan over. Brad figured he was probably killed on impact from what he witnessed.

Brad glanced up from the body and over at John's house. He wondered if it was John's car that hit Nathan. From the dark it kind of looked like a Buick. He wondered who would have hit Nathan in John's car, then realized as he looked closer, the inside door heading into John and Emily's house was wide open.

Brad was confused now. Maybe the intruder had come back and attacked Emily and John. Billy's room had a clear view of John and Emily's room across the road. Yes, it was all making sense to Brad now. Brad figured Nathan had somehow heard some commotion across the street and went over to investigate; then, the intruder had hit him in John's car.

Brad stopped, horrified, realizing that if the intruder had stolen John's car and the door of the house was open, John and Emily could very well be dead inside their home. His eyes moved from the garage up to where the bedroom was located.

With all the chaos that had been going on, Brad knew that John would have been out in the road by now, but as his eyes focused on their bedroom windows, he could sense that something was not right. The windows were dimly lit through the sheer white curtains. His stare was broken by Jen's yelling voice.

"The ambulance is coming, Brad!" As she came across the porch, he noticed she had the phone in one hand and a blanket in the other. She hit the bottom of the stairs and continued, "What has happened?"

Brad turned looking back up to John and Emily's window. Through the sheer curtain on the second window, he thought he saw a silhouette pass by quickly. Oh my God, he thought. What if that was John or Emily and they were hurt? Seeing the shadow had given Brad the creeps and a tingling sensation ran through his upper body. The hair on the back of Brad's neck stood up as he stared up at the window. Brad stood and yelled back to Jen who was now approaching, "Cover him up with a blanket. I'm gonna go get Emily and John!"

As Jen approached Nathan and saw his twisted body, she let out a small scream then ran up to his side and crouched down. Brad looked over at Emily and John's open door to the garage and began to run down the road to their driveway. Jen's crying was beginning to fade as Brad approached the driveway. He turned up the driveway thinking it was so clear now. Brad knew exactly what he must do. He must go and help his friends.

Brad got up to the open garage door, took a few steps inside the garage, then stopped, looking at a trail of blood that came out of the door to the kitchen and led to the garage where John's car usually parked. Brad gasped as he stood staring at the blood.

Brad's mind now raced through possible scenarios that could have happened to lead up to this incident. He wanted to go inside to help John or Emily but was frozen in place by shock at the sight of blood. Brad's knees trembled a bit as he crept over to the half opened door. He wondered who had been driving the car. He thought back to earlier when the car had backed over Nathan.

Brad thought neither John nor Emily would have done this, so maybe there were two attackers, and one had been wounded. Yes, maybe that was it. Well, if that was the case, then maybe Brad didn't have to be scared of what was in the house. An image of John and Emily lying inside the home dead flashed through Brad's head as he stopped and looked inside the house through the open door.

The lights inside the house were off. Brad stared inside for a moment, debating whether or not he should go in or if he should just holler. He listened for any sign of life, but there was only silence. Brad thought about how he had thought he'd seen something move upstairs. He decided that if it was Emily or John then he should yell inside. They would yell back, and it would also tell them he was friendly so they wouldn't shoot him if they were barricaded in a room or something.

That seemed to be the best thing to do, so Brad put his hand up around his mouth then yelled into the dark house, "Hello, anybody home?"

Brad stood there staring in the darkness, listening for any response, then took his right hand and knocked on the door loudly.

His knocks were accompanied by him putting his hand up to his mouth making a bullhorn shape around his mouth and yelling a little louder this time. "Hello? Emily, John? Hey, is anybody home?"

He listened intently for a moment. There was still no response, so he yelled as loud as he could, "Hello? Anybody home? Emily, John. Hello?"

Brad was confused now. If he had seen movement in the house and whoever moved wouldn't respond to him, it could be the intruder now. Maybe there were multiple attackers or maybe they had taken John and Emily. Brad wasn't sure which one of these scenarios could be true if any. He was scared looking down at the blood thinking that whoever had made the blood on the floor could still be in the house. If he was going to go in, he needed some protection so the same thing wouldn't happen to him.

Brad noticed John's golf bag sitting a few feet away from the door so he quickly walked over to it. Brad scanned the bag looking for the shortest, strongest club. Unable to locate the putter, he grabbed the pitching wedge and walked back over to the dark doorway.

If he was going to do this, he'd better get going. If one of his friends was hurt, he had to help them even though he was scared. Brad stepped into the kitchen. He felt around on the wall, and finding the light switch, he flicked the lights on. Brad stood in the kitchen a moment, gaining his courage and than slowly followed the blood trail, to the living room.

He peeked around the corner into the living room, reached around the wall, and turned on the lights. After scanning the room for several seconds and listening for any noise in the house, Brad cautiously stepped into the room.

The blood trail stained the light carpet in the living room. The blood was thick enough to leave a very noticeable trail. Brad's eyes followed it across the living room to the bottom of the oak staircase.

The blood looked shiny against the dark wood background. As his eyes continued to the top of the stairs, Brad stopped. His eyes moved to the chandelier hanging high above the stairs. It was dark as was the entire upstairs. Now that Brad was getting deeper inside the house, he wondered to himself what he was doing. Seeing the chandelier hanging unlit high above the staircase gave Brad a creepy sensation.

He knew by the amount of blood in the trail he had been following through the house that whoever had left this house was hurt very seriously. The left side of the top of the staircase was dimly lit by a light coming from down the hall. Brad having been in this house countless amounts of times knew that the only room at that end of the hall was Emily and John's. He was partially paralyzed by fear as he stared up the staircase. At the same time he was trying to listen for any movement in the house.

Brad was carrying the golf club up on his right shoulder as if he was going to bat a ball. The grip felt a little slippery due to the intense sweat coming from his palms. He took his left hand and dried it on his shirt and did the same to his right. By all this blood, Brad knew he was going to have to mean business if an intruder was still in the house.

Brad tried to control his hurried breathing as he began to walk across the living room to the bottom of the staircase. Once at the bottom, he had to try to walk quieter as the carpet turned to hard wood. It had taken him a couple of moments to build the courage to climb up the stairs and to face whatever was at the top. So now that he was going, there was no turning back.

Brad was trying to make his way up the staircase quietly, but as he got to about the third step, a loud creak sounded out. His heart pounded rapidly in his chest. He felt as if the creak had echoed through the entire house. He stopped and wondered for a moment if he should just turn around and wait for help. He stood for a moment then decided he must go on. His friends might be up there wounded, and he must help them out. In the distance outside he could hear the sounds of sirens getting louder. Well, that was that, Brad thought. What kind of best friend wouldn't go upstairs and check things out? If the roles were reversed, he knew that John would have gone right into his house trying to help him and Jen.

If there was somebody still in the house, Brad could easily run outside ahead of them. He was pretty fast and figured if he was scared enough, he could make it out to the police faster than anybody. Realizing there was help outside gave Brad a sense of courage as he made his way to the top of the staircase.

He turned left toward John and Emily's room. The door was open and the room was lit by what looked like a light shining from maybe the bathroom inside the bedroom. His eyes moved to the floor where a golf club lay.

There was a large dark puddle of blood in the floor that Brad stood staring at. He glanced back over his shoulder towards Nathan's room making sure nobody was hiding behind him. Brad quickly made his way around the mess in the hallway, then peeked his head around the doorway, looking in the master bedroom.

Brad couldn't see anybody so he slipped inside. His eyes darted all over the room. He held the golf club in the air above his shoulder and turned looking all directions. He moved over to the bathroom door and pushed it fully open with his foot. The bedroom lit up a bit more from the light in the bathroom. Brad sighed, exhaling deeply. He lowered the golf club down to this shoulder and switched the light on in the bedroom.

With the light now on, Brad's eyes were instantly drawn to the large red bloodstain on the pillow of the bed. Then realizing what this meant, he said out loud, "Holy shit!"

Somebody had, by the looks of the blood on the pillow, killed somebody in John's bed. Brad was creeped out by the room now. He wanted to get out of this house and back over to Jen and the police or ambulance. Whatever that siren had been he heard earlier.

Brad felt as if he had seen everything in the house he needed to see. His mind couldn't handle all this, so he rushed across the bedroom to the doorway leading out. As he came to the doorway, Brad paused at the large pool of blood.

He slowly looked at the putter, then held out the golf club he had. It was from John's set. Whoever had attacked Emily and John had used John's own golf club against him. Brad looked at the blood spot on the floor, then over on the bed and said out loud, "Oh, my God."

Brad, seeing both blood stains, realized whoever had run over Nathan in the road had probably killed both Emily and John. This made sense to Brad due to the two large puddles of blood. He crouched down looking closer at the golf head. Brad squinted at some large chunks of flesh stuck to the putter head. Realizing it was chunks of brain he said out loud, "Oh, shit."

Brad stood up and quickly made his way over to the staircase and headed down. As he passed through the living room, he glanced back over his shoulder up at the hallway. His fast walk turned into a run as he dashed into the garage.

Coming out of the house into the garage, Brad could see the flashing light of the police car by where Jen was. He was now in a panic.

Neither Emily nor John was in the house. At least they weren't anywhere he had looked. He had seen the two large blood-stains. This meant maybe they were both dead. Maybe the killer had taken their bodies away in the Buick as evidence.

Brad wasn't sure what was going on as he ran down the driveway. He was sure whoever was driving John's car wasn't Emily or John though. As he got ready to turn on the road, Brad saw flashing lights now coming from in town. It was a large vehicle moving quickly.

As Brad came running up into the light of the police officer's vehicle. The officer and Jen were crouched around Nathan who was covered in a blue blanket which Jen had brought out earlier.

Brad approached, stopped, and said in a frenzied, half out of breath voice, "It doesn't look good over there."

Jen and the officer looked up. The officer asked; "What do you mean? Your wife said you went across the street to get his parents?"

"That's what I'm saying. Something has happened. It looks

like there was some kind of attack over there. There is a lot of blood and stuff. But I didn't see either Emily or John. It looks like somebody came into their house and hurt them."

"What, John! What has happened?" Jen screamed looking up from Nathan.

The officer stood up and asked, "You're saying his parents are hurt?"

"Brad, what has happened?" Jen blurted out again.

Brad wasn't able to focus, so he said, "Jen, I don't know what happened. I didn't see anybody hurt. Just take care of Nathan, the ambulance is almost here." John pointed in the direction of town at the ambulance which was only few hundred yards away. He then switched the direction of the conversation to the policeman and continued, "I don't know where his parents are. All I know is I saw Nathan's dad car back over him in the road and take off over that way. I didn't see any bodies in the house but there is a lot of blood. You need to get some help out here officer. Brad squinted at the small name tag above the officer's right breast pocket and continued, "Lampton."

"I was just out here last week and did a report . I remember this boy and his dad John Watley right?"

"Yep," Brad responded.

Officer Lampton looked down at Nathan and shook his head in disbelief. "I showed him my police car and everything. "I can't even recognize him."

The headlights from the ambulance which pulled up behind the police car made the area more lit up. Brad could see the officer getting caught up in the moment so he said, "Hey, yeah it sucks, but you need to radio to all units to stop his brown Buick. Whoever is driving it ran over Nathan. I saw it all."

THE MADNESS

John awoke in his sweaty delirious state. What was going on? Where was he? He kept having the same dream over and over again. In it he had smashed Emily's head in with a golf club. He then had run Nathan over in his car. What? No, that couldn't be right, he thought as he rolled his head around with his eyes still closed.

John softly moaned, "No."

What was going on? Why couldn't he quit dreaming about this? No, that wasn't right. John groggily thought he had run over the dark man on the way to the hospital. He hadn't hit Nathan. That was impossible because Nathan had been over . . . Where had Nathan been?

John opened his eyes then shook his head back and forth in disbelief. He slowed down the shaking into the quiet turning of his head back and forth. John squinted as his eyes moved from the bright neon light which flickered from high above him in the ceiling down to the shiny, padded white wall.

He was sitting in the corner of the room with his knees up to his chest and his back pushed tightly in the corner. John sat staring at the small, square window located in the top of the door leading out of the room.

John couldn't focus. His mind was cloudy and slow. They must have drugged me, John thought as he looked down at his arms. He had been sitting here looking around now for a couple of minutes, and he hadn't even noticed that his arms were tightly held in front of his chest by same strange shirt he was wearing. As he stared at the shirt, he thought, "Oh, my God. Is this a straight jacket I'm wearing?"

John didn't know what was going on, but he was going to get to the bottom of it. He went to stand up but found it very hard. He was in an awkward position and unable to use his hands. Oh, well, he thought as he calmed down. His eyes moved back up to the small, square window. John's mind was too groggy to focus on standing anyway.

He closed his eyes for a moment, and the image of his father's face popped into it. John's father was pointing at him, yelling at him. For what? John opened his eyes, and his father disappeared. Was his dad saying that he was in trouble for killing Emily and Nathan? What?

No, no, this wasn't true, John thought. In thinking for a second about the accident, his thoughts went to Emily. He remembered trying to stop the dark man from killing her. When he had swung at it, the dark man had moved, and John had accidentally hit Emily. Then what had happened?

John's head bobbed down and slowly lowered until his chin bumped into his chest. His head quickly snapped back erect again. Oh, yeah, John thought. He had then driven Emily to Sandusky to the hospital. It was usually a 45-minute drive, but John laughed a second thinking of how he had made it there in only 20 minutes. But John remembered when he got there something wasn't right.

The police. What? John's thoughts faded out again, and his head slowly lowered. Once his chin hit his chest, his head snapped back up erect again. This time though John's thoughts returned back to the small square window as he thought he saw a shadow pass by.

John scrunched down in the corner and quietly mumbled to himself, "Get away from me, you mother fucker!" The shadow passed by quickly and John realized it wasn't the dark man. What? John thought. The dark man. Where? He needed to stop the dark man before it . . . John's eyes closed again, and his head slowly lowered back down to his chest. John pulled his knees up tightly and began to cry. What was going on? Why was he in this room? The image of Jenny saying "Lifetime of torment" kept playing in his mind. The drugs finally overcame his confused mind and a quiet black was all he felt.

A few moments went by, and the shadow John had seen outside the small window became the face of a young, blonde male orderly as he peeked inside at John. He turned around to the police officer who was watching the room and said, "Yeah, it looks like its working. I think he is sleeping now. Let's go tell the doctor. God, we gave him enough tranquilizers to put out an elephant. I wonder what got him so worked up?"

The state policeman who had been posted outside the holding cell of the third floor of the hospital responded, "You seriously don't know?"

"No, I just came in from the back parking lot. My shift started 15 minutes ago," the orderly responded.

"Oh, well, I helped escort this nut in from outside the emergency room. He has been in the cell, yelling and freaking out for an hour now".

"Oh, yeah?" the orderly responded and asked, "What was he doing outside the hospital?"

"Well, he pulled up to the emergency room with the police chasing him. Since I'm a rookie, I'm doing my first year at the hospital a lot, so I heard all the chaos and went running out.

"The state police and the county cops pulled up behind him and got out with their guns drawn. Apparently they thought it was a stolen car that a burglar had. I'm not sure why they thought this."

"Anyway, this nut here," the policeman motioned toward John's cell then continued, "he got out of the car hollering and screaming about his wife needing help. Then they ran up and handcuffed him. Apparently, he smashed his wife's head in with a golf club then ran his son over in the road. When they told him about his son, that was when he had to be put into a straight jacket."

The young orderly's brow crinkled, "He did what? Are you kidding me?"

"Well, that's what it looks like. We have units out at their house right now. It's over by Croswell."

"No shit!" The orderly shook his head in disbelief then continued, "God, you always think things like this happen down in the city, but not here. I never heard of anything so crazy."

John's head snapped back as he was awoke by a noise. He squinted because of the bright light. His eyes moved over to the small window. He seemed to summon up all the strength he had and yelled, "Fuck you, dark man!! You mother fucker!!" He tried to stand but managed only to fall over on his side.

The policeman took a couple of steps back, pulling the orderly with him away from the door. As he did, he said, "Shhhh." Then whispered, "Stand over here so he doesn't see you. When he first got locked in there, I noticed he kept seeing my shadow in this window and flipping out like that."

The orderly walked back over to the window and peeked inside. Seeing John curled up in the fetal position, he said to the state trooper, "Well, I think he's out again. I'll go let the doctor know."

"All right," the police officer said.

As the orderly walked away he said, "Well, the great thing about the state of Michigan is there's no death penalty. That bastard will have his whole life to sit in a little box and think about what he did."

Mary was rushing around the house trying to get it ready. It had been almost six months since that terrible night, when she had been called in the middle of the night by Jen. Mary had rushed right up to the hospital. It had been so traumatic for her to hear about Emily's death upon her arrival.

Mary thought how she had to pull herself together in order to go see Nathan who had been severely injured. Then she had spent almost the entire six months in the University of Michigan Medical Center, almost four hours from her home. She had flown to the center accompanying Nathan and had stayed by his bedside for almost his entire recovery. If a recovery was what you would call it, she thought as she opened the front door of her house and threw salt onto the newly built wheelchair ramp on the front of her house. Brad had gotten somebody to build the ramp at her house

192

and prepare a special bedroom and bathroom for Nathan, too.

God, Mary didn't know what she would do without his and Jen's help. They had gotten her entire house ready for Nathan's return. All of them had grown so close through Emily's funeral and the long trial. It was a miracle that Nathan had lived, so she was thankful. She just couldn't help but feel sorry for him since he was almost completely paralyzed now. Nathan's back had been broken so far up his body that the only thing he could control was his right hand. It was still a bit shaky though, but he managed to drive his wheelchair around with it.

Mary had actually been talked into coming back home early by Jen and Brad who were now with Nathan. They had come often to visit, and Billy was beginning to feel more comfortable around Nathan in his new state. Brad was driving Nathan back in the new van Mary had purchased for transporting Nathan.

She knew Nathan had it pretty bad, but caring for him had given Mary a new spring in her step. She no longer took naps all day or just laid around being depressed, because she knew what she needed to do for Emily. Mary was doing the best that she could to try and make Nathan happy again, the way a kid should be. She remembered that she could actually feel her life slipping away from her before the accident. Now though, it was strange, she felt young again, full of life. It was as if she had been given a purpose again in this world. She closed the front door and walked back to her kitchen. A timer went off, and Mary put on an oven mitt and slowly opened the door. She removed three small cake pans and set them on the stove to cool.

Mary was going to make Nathan his favorite type of dessert. She knew he loved German Chocolate cake, and Mary had made this one from scratch. She looked at the clock and figured they should be arriving pretty soon.

God, the last six months had been a blur, Mary thought. She had never talked to John or gone to any of the trials. She was too busy with Nathan. Brad had to be a witness, and Mary could tell that it hurt him to have to go on trial against John.

After his testimony the Detroit Free Press headline was "Best Friend Sinks Accountant." The article went on to say Brad had tearfully relived that night on the stand. Mary kept thinking of how Brad said Nathan lifted his hand as if to say, "No, don't run over me." The thought of this sent shivers up her spine. When she had been first told about it, she cried every single time she thought of it. Sometimes when Nathan was in physical therapy and she watched him move his right hand around trying to get strength and coordination, Mary wondered if it was the same hand that had been raised to try to stop his own father from running over him.

God, she still couldn't believe that John could have ever done such a terrible thing. As Mary walked over to the window hearing some commotion in her driveway, she couldn't help but to think about how sad it made her to see Nathan trapped inside his useless body.

She had a hard time accepting the fact that he would never get better. She even had a harder time thinking about how Nathan's doctor told her Nathan would probably live a long life. He told her this as if Mary should be happy. At least the doctor had said Nathan still had full mental capacity.

Mary wiped a tear that had built up in her eye, moving the curtain to the side she looked out the window. Seeing the van pull in, put a smile on her face as she walked to the front door and welcomed Nathan to a new home...and his new life.

Printed in the United States
132685LV00003B/269/A

9 780977 852581